"You might be onto something, Striker."

"You think RBN operations overseas are short of cash?" she asked.

"Why not?" Bolan said. "It makes complete sense based on the intel."

"Given the state of the world economy, it's likely they're starting to see a rapid depletion of funds. They need to get more money from their investors or find new ones. But I'm thinking the latter would take too long."

"Which means they'd need to get all the financial data they could on those financiers," Brognola concluded.

"Striker, do you think Godunov's looking to crack that list?" Price asked.

"I think he plans to have Lutrova crack the New York financial network and suck it dry."

Don Pendleton's Mack Bolan®

Infiltration

A GOLD EAGLE BOOK FROM

WORLDWIDE®

TORONTO • NEW YORK • LONDON
AMSTERDAM • PARIS • SYDNEY • HAMBURG
STOCKHOLM • ATHENS • TOKYO • MILAN
MADRID • WARSAW • BUDAPEST • AUCKLAND

Recycling programs
for this product may
not exist in your area.

First edition March 2011

ISBN-13: 978-0-373-61543-8

Special thanks and acknowledgment to
Jon Guenther for his contribution to this work.

INFILTRATION

Printed in U.S.A.

To be prepared for war is one of the most effective means of preserving peace.

—George Washington
1732–1799

My battle plan remains a constant: that I be prepared to wage war until a threat is neutralized. I don't see peace breaking out anytime soon.

—Mack Bolan

CHAPTER ONE

A tail could make any number of mistakes, and Mack Bolan, aka the Executioner, knew most of them.

This time his followers had been in a hurry not to lose him in Boston's morning rush hour, and they got too close in the sudden logjam of traffic caused by road construction. Bolan had spotted the vehicle with two men in the front seat as he left the rental agency at Logan International. But what made him suspicious was when a second vehicle identical to the first, occupied by two different men, came up behind him. With their suits and sunglasses, all four were either government types or trouble.

Bolan bet the latter.

Fortunately, it didn't come as much of a surprise to him. A request from Hal Brognola at Stony Man Farm had brought the soldier to Boston. The President of the United States deemed it of some importance, a fact Brognola had pointed out when briefing Bolan less than eight hours earlier.

"The man we're interested in is Bogdan Lutrova," Brognola had said.

"Who's he?"

"He's a Russian citizen who was caught by Customs agents attempting to enter the country under a false identity," Barbara Price, Stony Man mission controller, had answered.

"And what we know about him," Brognola continued, "is much less than what we don't."

"Meaning?" Bolan asked.

Brognola pulled an unlit cigar from his mouth, an old habit that wouldn't seem to die, and sighed. "We suspect that Lutrova is a member of the Russian Business Network. You're familiar with this organization, I presume."

Bolan nodded. Yeah, he was more than familiar. The RBN was a multifaceted enterprise with its hands into just about every form of cybercrime imaginable. They ran child porn sites, botnets, spam scams and virtually any other internet fraud money could buy. The RBN had been elusive, nearly impossible to destroy, given their size and wealth. A large number of intelligence sources were keeping tabs on the RBN's operations, but none ever seemed solid enough to get close to its heart. For some time now, Bolan had considered launching a full-scale blitz again the RBN, but he knew it would have required the full resources of Stony Man, not to mention weeks or even months of surgical strikes against key sites. When Brognola called and hinted at the possibility he might have an alternate way to get at the group, Bolan jumped at the chance.

"We don't have any proof Lutrova was here on a mission for the RBN," Brognola stated.

"What else might have brought him here?" Bolan asked.

"Well, it's possible he's on the run and he came here looking for sanctuary," Price said.

"At least that's the song and dance he gave Customs officials," Brognola added. "Lutrova fed them some story about business associates who were unhappy with him. He demanded legal representation and asylum. In return for information, of course."

"But since he's not an American citizen," Price said, "Customs agents were only required to assign him a liaison from INS."

"Which really just means an interpreter," Bolan said. "So why not deport him and make it a public show? If the RBN is after him, as he claims, you'll know soon enough whether it's true."

"We considered that. Unfortunately, some analyst in the CIA picked up on the fact that Lutrova had been caught trying to enter the country illegally, and immediately filed a special report that wound up in the President's daily brief. That, in turn, filtered down to a request by the Man that we investigate Lutrova's claims."

Bolan shrugged. "So you want me to go to Boston to question him? That sounds more like a job for Justice Department types. I'm not sure how I can help in this."

Brognola sighed. "Striker, you've been telling us for a while now that the RBN is becoming bigger and more dangerous by the day. After this latest incident, I'm inclined to agree with you. And I've told the President as much on more than one occasion. Now, it could be that Lutrova's just jerking our chain, and if that's the case then there'll be hell to pay. But there could be more hell to pay if we don't give this a closer look. In either case, I can't think of anyone who can get to the bottom of it faster or better than you."

"Not to mention you've been studying this group," Price said. "You're the closest thing we have to a subject matter expert. Not even our contacts at the NSA could give us any definitive answers."

"All right," the Executioner replied. "I'll check it out."

So Bolan had made his way to Boston via an early commercial flight. His forged credentials identified him as an intelligence analyst with Homeland Security. Bolan knew how to play the role, just as he did so many others. He had practically invented the technique beginning as far back as his war against the Mafia. He called it role camouflage, a method by which he could "appear" to be who he was by acting as people would expect him to act. He'd used these methods many times before, with considerable success.

So it came as a surprise when Bolan picked up on the fact that someone was following him, leaving him to wonder if the RBN's eyes and ears might actually have extended inside the federal government. Bolan figured staying in role and not letting on he knew these unknowns were tailing him was the best tactic. Besides, he couldn't take the offensive without risking innocent bystanders, and it wouldn't avail him anything. Better to pick a time of his own place and choosing.

Yeah, he'd deal with them if and when they proved hostile.

BOLAN MADE the downtown offices of the FBI at One Center Plaza in less than thirty minutes.

The soldier parked his vehicle in a parking garage so he could observe the entrance through the rear-view mirror. He waited long enough to spot the sedan as it cruised past. Bolan smiled and removed his Beretta 93-R from its shoulder leather. He expertly checked the action, then holstered it and made his way toward the elevators. The parking garage was one area that lent itself as a suitable place to take them if he had to. For now, he'd let them stew.

Bolan rode the elevator to the sixth floor and eventually pushed through the heavy glass door marked with the U.S. Customs logo. A receptionist at the desk smiled at him, but she had a no-nonsense glint in her eye. Bolan passed her his forged credentials and announced his business with Lutrova. The woman nodded before returning his badge and ID, along with a visitor pass. She suggested he take a seat, then picked up the phone.

The Executioner declined the seat, instead opting for a quick session with a water cooler in one corner of the reception area. As he crossed the room and helped himself to one of the paper cups, he looked over his shoulder to scope the hallway visible through the all-glass entryway. This was only one of two large federal office buildings at One Center Plaza. City Hall, City Hall Plaza and some county courthouses—as well as a major interchange station overseen by the Massachusetts Bay Transit Authority—occupied remaining areas in the government center.

Any criminal organization, even one as vast and bold as the Russian Business Network, would have been insane to try anything in here. Apparently, the RBN

fell into that category, because as Bolan tossed back
the cold water and dropped the paper cup into a waste
can, the four men in suits stepped off an elevator, each
of them toting a machine pistol.

"Down!" Bolan yelled.

CHAPTER TWO

The receptionist seemed dazed, but got the message as Bolan cleared his Beretta 93-R from its shoulder leather and went prone. The gunmen opened up simultaneously with their machine pistols. The glass entrance shattered under the assault, and dangerous shards flew in every direction, while others rained onto Bolan and the secretary, who was now under the cover of her desk. Hot lead burned the air above the soldier's head before it shattered more glass or punched through the plasterboard walls to leave heavy, choking dust in its wake.

Bolan sighted on the surest target and loosed a double-tap. The weapon bucked in his grip as two 185-grain 9-mm hollowpoint rounds traversed a path to one gunner's chest. The impact drove him into a large potted plant and carried him over the other side. The heavy ceramic pot teetered and landed on top of him, spilling soil everywhere.

The first man going down distracted the one next to him, and Bolan seized the advantage. He triggered another pair of shots. The first one went low and to the left, but the second struck the man's hip. The guy screamed and his weapon flew from his fingers. His hands went to his shattered bone and he dropped to his knee on his uninjured side. Bolan sent a third round downrange, which struck the target in the forehead. The top of the enemy's skull came away with devastating effect, and he toppled prone to the carpet.

The remaining pair got wise to the fact that their numbers were halved, and quit firing to find cover from the Executioner's bullets. As one guy dived for a chair in the hallway, Bolan caught him with a slug to the left side. The bullet went clean through, narrowly missing the heart and instead ripping through shoulder muscle. The clip brought a cry of pain from the gunner, but it wasn't lethal.

The injured man's partner managed to get behind a support beam jutting from the wall, but the thin plasterboard proved hardly adequate to stop Bolan. The warrior flicked the fire selector switch to 3-round burst mode and triggered two volleys. The first trio of rounds punched through the flimsy wall. One of them grazed the gunner, and he twisted away, straight into the line of the second 3-round burst. The bullets drilled through the man's ribs and shoulder, one of them puncturing both lungs before the man sprawled into the hallway on his back.

The surviving gunman broke cover and swept the area with his muzzle, trying to keep his head down as he reverse-stepped toward the elevator bank. Bolan switched out magazines in a heartbeat and leveled his pistol. He triggered another 3-round burst, and then a second, and all six rounds hammered his opponent. The impacts drove him backward, causing his arms to windmill, and making him stagger like a drunken puppet until he crashed into the far wall. He slid to the ground and left a gory streak in his wake.

The echoes of gunfire hadn't even died when a

half-dozen Customs and Homeland Security officials, accompanied by a near equal number of FBI agents, fanned into the room with their weapons drawn. They spotted Bolan and began to yell at him to drop his weapon. The Executioner knew that, in the heat of the moment, anything other than compliance would be suicide, so he laid the weapon on the ground and kept his hands where he could see them.

One of the agents stepped forward and retrieved the pistol quickly, while a second bent to put handcuffs on him. Too far.

Bolan grabbed the man's wrist. "That's not going to happen."

"Stop resisting!" the man said.

The Executioner whirled onto his back so fast the agent didn't have time to react. Next thing he knew, Bolan had a forearm around his neck and his legs wrapped against the man's hips, effectively pinning him in place.

"I said, that's not going to happen," Bolan repeated. He looked at the other agents, all of whom had guns pointed at him, and added, "you have my weapon and that means I'm no longer a threat. But I'm on your side and there's no way you're going to handcuff me like a criminal."

"Okay, okay!" one of them replied. He holstered his pistol and gestured at the others to back off. "Put them down for now, boys. Everybody just take it easy."

When they had complied, Bolan released the agent who had tried to cuff him, and got up, before hauling the dazed man to his feet. The agent stepped a respectful distance away as he rubbed his neck and eyed the soldier with venom. Bolan didn't let it affect him, instead turning to the balding man who seemed to possess the air of command among the others in the group.

Bolan indicated that he was going to reach for his credentials, and once he got a nod from the head agent, he flipped them out and held them high. The agent stepped closer, quickly inspected them and then nodded with a satisfied expression.

Bolan stuck out his hand. "Name's Cooper. I'm with the intelligence sector of Homeland Security."

The man nodded again and took his hand. "Scott Hampton, deputy chief of U.S. Customs, New York. You're here about Lutrova?"

"Yeah," Bolan said with a nod.

Hampton looked in the direction of the four deceased. "You always bring this kind of entertainment to the party?"

Bolan couldn't help but crack a smile, wondering if he might get along with Hampton, after all. "I like to keep things lively."

"I don't suppose you could tell me…" Hampton's voice dropped off suggestively.

"Not a clue," Bolan said. "But if I had to guess, I'm betting they're Russian."

"You think they were after Lutrova?"

"Right."

"Any idea how they might have known about you? Maybe how they managed to follow you?"

Bolan shook his head. "I spotted them tailing me the moment I left Logan."

"And you came here anyway?"

"Look," Bolan said, putting a little edge in his voice, "I didn't think they'd actually storm this place with guns blazing."

"Okay, okay, don't get your panties in a wad."

"Let's just focus on finding out who they are and who sent them, Hampton," Bolan said. "We can worry about blame later."

"And how do you propose we do that?"

"If they were here to punch Lutrova's ticket, it's logical we start with him. Especially since that's why I'm here to begin with, and they latched on to me instead of one of your people."

"Christ," Hampton replied under his breath, rubbing his temples.

"You okay?"

"Yeah," he told Bolan. "It's just I feel a migraine coming on. Along with a whole hell of a lot of paperwork."

BOGDAN LUTROVA didn't come off as particularly special. He didn't seem all that bright, either, but Bolan knew appearances weren't trustworthy. Lutrova's long, blond hair hung in unkempt and dirty strands. Brown eyes, deeply set and lined with circles, peered with a mixture of suspicion and curiosity at Bolan's imposing form entering the room.

Bolan met the look with frosty indifference as he stood opposite Lutrova, who was seated at a gray metal table in one of the U.S. Customs holding rooms.

"Who are you?" Lutrova asked in a heavy Georgian accent.

"Shut your yap," Bolan said, jabbing a finger at him

for emphasis. "Four of your friends out there just attempted to kill me."

Lutrova scoffed mockingly. "What friends? I have no—"

The Executioner reached across the table and one-armed Lutrova out of the chair. He dragged the Russian computer hacker across the table and pushed his head down so that the edge buried itself in a painful nerve just under Lutrova's chin. The man squealed something in Russian, but Bolan doubted the outrage would have been intelligible even in English.

"Let's start again," Bolan said with a steady increase of downward pressure. "We're not going to play games right now because I'm not in the mood for them. You're also not going to play the victim, since we both know better than that. You know where I'm coming from now?"

The man made some additional sounds the Executioner couldn't understand, but the furious movement of Lutrova's head made it apparent he understood the new terms of their relationship. Bolan nodded in satisfaction and released his hold, propelling Lutrova into his chair with a shove. The door opened and Hampton entered—followed by a short, swarthy man Bolan recognized as the guy that had earlier attempted to cuff him—in time to see Lutrova's scrawny form land hard in the seat.

"I see you're getting along," Hampton said with a smirk.

"I was just explaining the rules to Mr. Lutrova," Bolan said.

Hampton nodded, gestured for the other agent to close the door behind them, and then sat on the edge of the table to one side of Lutrova, dropping a thick manila folder in front of him. It hit with enough force that Lutrova jumped in spite of himself. A red divot had formed on his chin, a lasting reminder of Bolan's "explanation."

"You're in deep shit, Lutrova," Hampton said. "You know what's in that folder? It's a list of names, the names of the hit team sent to kill you and anybody else who got in their way. It seems your friends in the Russian Business Network don't like you too well."

Lutrova didn't say anything at first, but a slight movement of Bolan in his direction made him quickly change his tune and throw up his hands. "Wait! Wait! Don't touch me. I'll tell you what I know. But you must protect me."

"No way," Hampton said. "Your associates out there just tried to kill a bunch of my people. And the fact that they're foreigners here on American soil, attacking American federal buildings, makes that an act of terrorism. Which means you're not entitled to any protection."

Lutrova looked at Bolan, who was staring at him, his arms folded. When he looked back at Hampton, who raised his eyebrows to indicate he was serious, Lutrova's defiant expression transformed into defeat. They had him dead to rights and he knew it; worse yet, Lutrova knew he couldn't do a damn thing about it. And that's exactly where the Executioner wanted him.

"You can see, Lutrova, you don't have many options," Bolan said. "You can take a risk with us, spill everything—"

"And we mean *everything,*" Hampton interjected.

Bolan continued without missing a beat, "Or you can take your chances with your friends in the RBN. But you should know, if you don't already, that whoever you're working for has the means and connections to make you dead very quickly."

"We put you in protective custody, you might have a chance," Hampton said, taking Bolan's lead. "But you're definitely a dead man if you go inside the system."

"And what do you wish in return?" Lutrova asked.

"Everything," Bolan replied.

"Which is?"

"All information you have about your comrades in the Russian Business Network, including why you entered the country illegally and why they want to kill you."

"I keep telling you, I don't know—"

"Don't play games, Lutrova," Bolan said, putting an implicit edge in his voice. "You've already spilled the fact you're in bed with the RBN, and I know all of your qualifications."

Lutrova sneered. "Like?"

"You were formally trained at the Moscow Power Engineering Institute, top of your class. After that, you dropped off the face of the earth for ten years. For the past three years, the RBN cybercrime network activities have increased a hundredfold or more. And then you suddenly show up here and now."

Hampton folded his arms. "So once more, what's you doing here?"

Lutrova took a deep breath and a hint of resignation appeared in his expression. "I was sent here by Yuri Godunov. You know this man?"

Bolan scanned his mental files but couldn't recall the name.

"What about Godunov?" he prompted.

"He is perhaps one of the greatest leaders we have ever known. He is connected to people in nearly every country, and extremely elusive. There is nothing you can do to stop him now."

"What's the angle?" Hampton asked.

"What do you mean by this angle you speak of?" Lutrova asked in turn.

Bolan put both palms on the table. "He means what's Godunov's plan?"

"Mr. Godunov does not reveal his plans to me. I only know that he sent me to break into the New York banking sector. I was ordered to fly in through Boston, and once here I was to then take a rental car to New York. I was to meet him there. But now that you have taken me, I am a liability to him. He will come after me and kill me, and there is nothing you can do to stop him."

Bolan couldn't be sure they were getting the truth. He'd have to run Yuri Godunov's name through Stony Man Farm's data banks to get more intelligence. If anyone could come up with something on Godunov, it would be Aaron Kurtzman and his team. Meanwhile, he would be forced to sit on Lutrova—keep the Russian computer hacker on ice—while he waited to find a way inside Godunov's organization.

"Let's take a break," Bolan suggested to Hampton.

When they were outside the interrogation room, he stated, "I don't like it."

"You think he's lying."

"On the contrary. I think he's completely legit.

Lutrova might be a cybercriminal, but I know the type. He's scared and with good reason, and he's looking to make a deal."

Hampton sighed and leaned against the wall, the resignation obvious in his tone. "I don't have any deal to offer him, Cooper. I'm a government hack, just like you, and the policy on terrorism is strict. It looks like we're going to have to turn him over to the boys from Homeland Security."

"You let me worry about that."

"You're not really from its Intelligence, are you?" Hampton inquired with a smile.

Telling Hampton anything more than absolutely necessary might compromise Stony Man's security. It wasn't that he didn't trust the Customs official, but the plain fact of the matter was that this kind of red tape was what made Bolan's job harder. He'd have to get clearance to take Lutrova with him. They would go straight to New York so Bolan could find out exactly what was going on through other means best left unexamined. If the Executioner tried to get chummy with Hampton, or left Lutrova under the protection of U.S. Customs, Godunov's people would try again and that would only leave Hampton in a predicament. No, he'd have to keep tabs on Lutrova and take him to New York.

"Who I am or work for isn't important," Bolan said. "I'm with intelligence and that has to be good enough. I need to make a phone call. That call is going to generate another call, and I'm betting within the hour you're going to be able to get this completely off your hands."

"What are you saying?"

"Lutrova has to come with me."

"Where? To New York?"

Bolan nodded.

"No offense, Cooper," Hampton replied, coming off the wall now, "but I'd have to say that's going to be pretty dangerous. If you *are* nothing more than an intelligence analyst, which I highly doubt based on the handiwork I just saw out there, you'd be committing suicide."

"Again, that's my worry. Not yours."

Hampton shrugged. "Well, I can't say as I like it, but I have the sneaking suspicion it isn't going to make much difference what I think. I'd bet somebody in a much higher pay grade is going to make the decision for me."

"That would be a safe bet."

Bolan turned to leave and Hampton said, "Hey, Cooper? Just watch your ass out there. If these guys tried once, no doubt they'll try again."

"That's what I'm counting on," Bolan replied.

CHAPTER THREE

After Yuri Godunov finished listening to the report from the head of his internal security team, he slammed a fist on his desk.

Their operation, *his* operation, had taken an ugly turn, and Godunov wasn't certain how to get it back on track. Thus far, his plans to slip Bogdan Lutrova into the country right under the noses of U.S. Customs had gone off without a hitch. What he hadn't expected was the destruction of the four men he'd dispatched to liberate his premier hacker.

"This is what I pay you good money for, Volkov," Godunov had told the mercenary leader known at large as the Wolf. "You were responsible for taking care of this for me. What went wrong?"

The Wolf cleared his throat. "I'm not sure. We weren't expecting to meet that kind of resistance. I've been informed that our team was put down by one man."

"One man?" Godunov's expression turned apoplectic. "You mean four of your best men, trained by some of the finest methods I could buy, weren't able to take out one man? You must be misinformed!"

"I'm not, sir, I can assure you. I verified the information as soon as it came to me."

That was probably true. The Wolf had spies inside

every major U.S. law-enforcement agency, not to mention plenty of civilian workers on the payroll. That kind of network took vast resources, and those resources were quickly diminishing. That was one of the main reasons for Godunov's plan to crack one of New York's largest financial institutions, Chase Manhattan, and pilfer everything he could before they got wise to his plan. Along the way, he expected to pick up quite a bit of information on those individuals who were financing the RBN's activities.

Godunov's organization spread far and wide. He didn't head up the RBN—such a position could only be held by one who could walk the *real* halls of power back in the mother country—but Godunov occupied a prime position. He took his orders straight from the head of their worldwide society of profit and mayhem. Godunov then filtered that down to the hundreds working for him. Of course, he knew that a lot of them marched to their own drummer. Most he'd even caught skimming profits. But there was plenty of wealth to go around. As long as his superior didn't miss it, Godunov was willing to look the other way now and again. It wasn't as if he had a big choice, however. The RBN employed thieves, and that meant he had to expect his workers to steal here and there.

The RBN operations remained large only because Godunov had learned to be extremely cautious. The network survived through an infrastructure comprised of thousands of small front companies, many only on paper. A growing list of financiers actually invested in these companies, and as long as their "stock options" were showing steady returns—with the occasional bonus—they didn't ask a lot of questions. But times were tough, with the world economy being what it was. That had forced Godunov to find more creative ways of getting money, and so they needed to get information on the funds of those anonymous financiers, so they could access those funds without attracting undue attention.

That was the plan Godunov had assigned Bogdan Lutrova to put into action. Now, though, it seemed that four of the Wolf's team members were dead, and Bogdan had appeared to drop off the map.

"What's your recommendation?" Godunov finally asked the Wolf.

"I could not make one until I have more information. Certainly, we need to find our…asset."

"Indeed. I will leave that in your hands. But don't screw this up again, *comrade,* or I will hold you personally responsible. Do you understand my meaning?"

There was a pause before the Wolf answered, "I do."

Godunov bid him farewell by dropping the receiver into the cradle and muttering, "Incompetence. Sheer incompetence."

He sat back, rubbed his eyes and sighed. Now he would have to play a waiting game. What he couldn't understand was why they had moved Lutrova and, moreover, done so in secret. Such a move typically involved a considerable amount of time and bureaucracy, but the Customs officials had somehow managed to make it happen quickly. The bungled attempt of his men to liberate Lutrova meant they had shown their hand early. While faithful, and capable of following his script to the letter, Lutrova might see the cause as lost, and roll on their organization, figuring he could cut a better deal for himself by cooperating with the U.S. authorities.

What bothered Godunov most was the talk of this mysterious stranger the Wolf had spoken about. Godunov thought he'd worked every angle, but such a development could signal that the Americans had been onto their plans from the beginning. Either way, it didn't matter, since Godunov hadn't pinned all their hopes on Lutrova. He could implement a fail-safe if absolutely necessary, although he hesitated to do so unless the circumstances became dire. Such a fail-safe would involve ordering the Wolf to do whatever was necessary to find Bogdan Lutrova and terminate his life. There could be no loose ends—everything would need to be tied up neatly so as not to risk exposing the RBN leadership to scrutiny.

For now, all Godunov could hope was that it wouldn't come to that.

"THIS ISN'T going to work," Bogdan Lutrova said.

"You've already said that," Mack Bolan replied. "Repeating yourself isn't going to change my mind, so why not just shut it down for a while."

"Because they're going to figure it out." Lutrova sighed. "Yuri is a smart man. He'll see through the deception and he'll kill you on the spot. And me, too."

"He won't if you play your part right," Bolan said. "Besides, Godunov needs you. He wouldn't have gone to such lengths to let everybody else know how important you are, otherwise. Or risked exposing his plans."

Lutrova had no reply for that, and Bolan knew he'd struck a nerve. The soldier had never really bought the idea that Customs catching someone like Lutrova red-handed was merely a stroke of good fortune and nothing else. He'd suspected from the beginning the RBN had concocted this entire charade to throw them off the track, and Bolan's plan to insert himself into the organization as a freelancer searching for employment was little more than a way to capitalize on their deception. The fact that he'd more or less blundered into the situation didn't matter—Bolan would use every advantage to get at the heart of the organization.

He had contacted Stony Man, and Brognola promised to put Kurtzman and Price to work on identifying this Yuri Godunov. It surprised Bolan that he hadn't heard of the guy when Lutrova first mentioned his name, and part of him wondered if he even existed; it seemed possible, however unlikely, that Lutrova was just lying to them to stall for time. Bolan didn't think so. Lutrova was bright, sure, but he didn't come close to being a criminal mastermind and this Yuri Godunov sounded like the type who would never hire an underling smarter than him, anyway.

As if on cue, Bolan's cell phone buzzed inside his jacket pocket. He answered midway through the second ring. "Go, Bear."

"We've got some updated info on your boy Godunov, Striker," Kurtzman replied. "You're not going to like it."

"That's usually a given," Bolan said with a frown. "Talk to me."

"Yuri Godunov's been long suspected of ties to the Russian Business Network, but nobody's ever been able to pin anything on him. In fact, he went as far as getting permission to operate business concerns within the United States quite some years ago, and is protected just one level beneath diplomatic immunity."

"Meaning?"

"Meaning that he enjoys some sort of special consideration because his business concerns—which, by the way, are nothing more than probably shell and paper companies—are directly involved in dealings with Russian heads of state."

"In other words, there's a profit to be made by one or more of our politicians in Wonderland."

"Right."

"What else do we know?"

"Well, Godunov's never made his presence in the country a secret," Kurtzman replied. "He owns an estate in the West Hamptons and he regularly makes business trips to New York City. I'm sending the actual GPS coordinates to your phone as we speak. I also hacked into his computer network at his office. Can you believe this guy actually rents space at the Chase One Plaza in Manhattan?"

"I believe it."

"According to his records, he's in town all week on business. One entry we found was very cryptic at best, and we think it's probably the meeting he had scheduled with Lutrova."

"That would make sense," Bolan said. "He'd be expecting that situation long resolved by now. What about the hit team in Boston?"

"None of them were Americans, and three of the four were here illegally. We think they're part of a free-lance team of mercenaries, but I can't pin down which one."

"So we're not much further than we were before," Bolan replied.

"Sorry, Striker. I wish I had more solid info for you, since I know going cold into a situation is tough, but there's just not much there. If this Yuri Godunov is as crooked as the folks in the CIA's counterintelligence unit say he is, well, you can bet he's gone to good effort to cover his tracks and hide any goings-on that would even hint at impropriety."

"Understood. Looks like I'll have to work this one by ear."

"If I get anything else, I'll contact you."

"Just hold on to the info and wait for me to reconnect," Bolan said. "I don't know what I'm up against yet and I wouldn't want to put your end in jeopardy."

"So don't call you, you'll call us?" Kurtzman replied with a chuckle.

"Just like that."

"Okay. Be careful, Striker."

"Out here."

Bolan disconnected the call and spared a glance at Lutrova. The young hacker returned the look but didn't say anything. "Seems like your pal Godunov is legit," Bolan said.

"You doubted this?"

"I doubt everything," he stated. "Call it a character flaw."

"You are still convinced your plan to infiltrate Yuri's organization will succeed."

"I've already told you it'll be fine if you just play along like you're supposed to."

"I'm not convinced."

"You don't have to be convinced," Bolan said with an edge in his voice. "You just have to be convincing."

"And how do you know that I will not simply betray you when we finally meet with Yuri?"

"I don't. But I do know that if it goes hard, you'll be the first person I take with me. You see, if Godunov doesn't have you, then he really has no ability to move forward with whatever scheme he's cooking up. And if you go along and he finds out later that you've rolled over to our side, he's still going to kill you. At least you have a chance going the distance with me."

"Some would call this blackmail, which is nothing less than a criminal activity in itself. That would make you no better than the rest of it."

"I call it strategy," Bolan said, savvy to the fact Lutrova was simply trying to bait him. "Now let's get down to business. I have information that Godunov was supposed to meet you here. Is that accurate?"

"I am not sure where I was supposed to meet him. I had instructions only to wait once I'd been caught, and that he would send someone to collect me. That is the extent of my knowledge."

Bolan considered his options. He knew the location of Godunov's West Hampton estate, but taking Lutrova straight there concerned him. If he did, Godunov would be immediately suspicious about where Bolan had gotten his information, particularly since it seemed Lutrova didn't know anything about it. That left the downtown offices at Chase One Plaza as his best bet. It would have been the logical decision if he hadn't known anything about Godunov's private residence.

The plan was designed to be simple and straight-forward.

Godunov needed something desperately in order to execute whatever designs he had on the New York financial system. Bolan had that something in his grasp. It wouldn't be much of a stretch to get Godunov bartering for the goods. Bolan had opted to use an old cover that Kurtzman was able to resurrect whenever needed. The alias Frankie Lambretta had served him well during his war against the Mafia, and later he'd used it on occasion when penetrating organized crime. On a couple of occasions, Kurtzman had killed him off or put the identity into the prison system. Once more, Bolan would be out on the streets with credentials as a former Mob hit man that just about any criminal organization would be proud to have on its rolls.

Bolan checked his watch and noted it was just past 1600 hours.

The Executioner had traded his government-issue suit and tie for slacks, a black polo shirt and a brown leather jacket to protect against the biting winter winds of New York City. He'd purchased baggy jeans and a sweatshirt for Lutrova, along with an overnight bag that contained a change of clothes and a toothbrush. The hacker's hands were free, but Bolan had bound his feet with thick plastic riot cuffs to lessen the risk that the guy would try to take off. The Beretta 93-R rode in shoulder leather, and Bolan had stashed the remainder of his arsenal on the backseat of the rental.

His bag of tricks included twin satchel charges of C-4 plastic explosives configured with blasting caps and a remote detonator. It also contained a .44 Magnum Desert Eagle with spare magzines and ammo, a carbine version of the Fabrique National Herstal SA FNC with plenty of spare 5.56 mm NATO ammunition. Bolan didn't expect too much in the way of serious trouble at this point, but better prepped than dead.

He made a right off Chambers Street onto Broadway, and could see the Chase Manhattan Plaza building towering in the distance, one of the tallest structures in New York City. Construction on the sixty-floor building had been completed in 1961, and it was still one of the fifty tallest buildings in the world. The only other tenant beside J.P. Morgan Chase & Co. was Milbank, and the recent addition of Godunov's puppet firm Vastok & Karamakov, Ltd.

Bolan had to admit that Godunov's attempt to operate like an open and legitimate enterprise was a gutsy move. It also spoke of the man's great arrogance that he thought he could actually get away with it and not fall under the scrutiny of the federal government. Still, he'd proved adept at avoiding trouble so far. Bolan planned to change all that. He wondered exactly how Godunov would react when he walked straight into the man's offices with the RBN's prize puppet under his arm.

They arrived at One Chase Manhattan Plaza, and Bolan circled the block twice before choosing a belowground parking structure two streets over. After he parked and killed the engine, the soldier flipped out a knife and cut the riot cuffs from Lutrova's ankles. Some mixture of surprise and relief spread across Lutrova's features, but Bolan ignored that. Instead, he favored the hacker with a warning smile.

"You're liberated only for the time being," Bolan said. "Don't forget you're still on a very short leash. You double-cross me, and I'll kill you in the blink of an eye. Understood?"

The relief in Lutrova's expression melted. "Yes."

"Good. Now let's go met Yuri."

CHAPTER FOUR

The walk to One Chase Manhattan Plaza took under five minutes, but another ten elapsed before Bolan located Godunov's office suites on the twenty-eighth floor.

He'd managed to get through the security with his firearm, thanks to the forged credentials provided by Stony Man. It never ceased to amaze him how easy it was to get past a uniformed security detachment with an itty-bitty gold badge. The officer in charge had barely scrutinized his identification, taking more of an interest in Bolan's companion. And with good reason. Despite the new threads, Bogdan Lutrova hardly carried the demeanor or attitude of a model citizen. Fortunately, Bolan had been able to explain it all away by letting them know that Godunov was expecting him, and they were eventually waved through.

When they stepped off the elevators, Bolan heard Lutrova take a sharp breath. He scanned the hacker's face and then followed his gaze until his eyes came to rest on a tall, bald man with a beak-like nose and pursed lips.

"Godunov?" Bolan asked.

Lutrova nodded.

The soldier grabbed Lutrova's arm and guided him steadily in Godunov's direction. The Russian crime lord was standing at the reception desk, flirting with the secretary. Bolan would have paid a nickel to have a picture of Godunov at the moment the man's attention focused on the pair. For a long time—or so it seemed—Godunov didn't say a word. At first, Bolan thought the guy might try to act as if he didn't know Lutrova, but a glance at Bolan told him attempting any such charade would be pointless.

"Mr. Godunov?" Bolan said in greeting.

The Russian nodded, taking up the act, and offered his hand. Bolan decided to shake it so the secretary didn't get nervous and start punching buttons. Godunov immediately released Bolan's hand and then turned to look Lutrova in the eyes. A patina of disgust washed over Godunov's expression and then dissipated just as quickly into one of cordiality.

"Bogdan, it is very nice to see you."

"And you, sir," Lutrova muttered.

Godunov didn't miss a beat. "I trust your trip was… uneventful, gentlemen?"

"It was," Bolan replied. "Our apologies for being late."

"Not at all." Godunov swept his arm in the direction of the hallway behind the massive main reception desk manned by four young women. "Why don't we adjourn to my office, where you can get off your feet? I'm sure you're both exhausted."

"Thank you," Bolan said.

With the show of pleasantries dispensed, Bolan and Lutrova followed Godunov down the hallway to a pair of double doors at the end. As the Russian opened them, Bolan reached into his jacket and rested his hand on the butt of the Beretta 93-R as he shoved Lutrova between Godunov and himself. If any trouble waited on the other side of the door, he figured Lutrova would buy it first and give him time to react.

The office was devoid of combatants, and while Bolan relaxed somewhat, he didn't completely let down his guard. Being a paranoid and suspicious type was just part of the role camouflage. It would take quite a bit of convincing to make Godunov buy the story he was about to spin, and prove even more difficult to earn Godunov's trust enough to hire him. He was hoping that Lutrova would be the trump card in his hand, and it was one Bolan planned to play very early.

Once they were inside, Godunov's demeanor became venomous. "Who the fuck are you?"

Bolan remained calm, with an expression that implied Godunov didn't intimidate him. "Not important. What's important is that I have something here I think you want."

Godunov exchanged glances with Lutrova, and then asked Bolan, "What makes you think that?"

"I have my sources."

"Maybe your sources are wrong," Godunov said, moving to a position behind his desk.

Bolan reached into his jacket.

Godunov raised a palm. "Easy."

"As long as you keep your hands where I can see them. Try anything and you'll be dead before help can arrive."

"You seem a bit jumpy, Mr.…"

"Just never mind that right now. What I want to know from you is if pretty boy—" Bolan jerked his head in

Lutrova's direction "—is worth anything to you. If not, I've got some buyers who could put him to work on some pet projects they got going."

Godunov laughed. "You're not actually here to sell him to me. Are you?"

"So you're saying he's not worth anything to you."

"That's not what I said," Godunov replied.

"Look, don't make a jerk out of me, pal." Bolan bristled in true mobster fashion to help sell the act, then continued, "You want to pull someone else's rod, then you go ahead and do that. Me, I'm just a man who looks for business opportunities wherever I can find them."

"Well, you must understand my position," Godunov said, switching tact to appeal to Bolan's sense of reason. "You're asking me to basically turn over my own hard-earned cash for this young man. What makes you think he's of any value to me?"

"Because I know where I took him from," Bolan said. "How do you think I knew you'd be here?"

Godunov appeared to seriously consider this, and then gave Lutrova a look that was murderous, at best. It seemed Lutrova had given away information he shouldn't have—or Bolan had given away something *he* shouldn't have, slipped up in some way, and that had made Godunov very suspicious. In any case, it didn't appear the Russian crime lord planned to show his own hand, since his original demeanor returned in a moment.

"You're saying that it was you who snatched him from U.S. Customs?"

"That's right," Bolan replied. "That so hard to believe, pal?"

"Put yourself in my shoes," Godunov replied, spreading his arms. "You show up here, armed, with something that doesn't really belong to you. You tell a crazy story about how you wrested this man, whom you do not know, away from a group of armed U.S. Customs agents—"

"Not a group," Bolan interrupted.

"Excuse me?"

"You said I took him from a group of agents. Not true. He was with just one man when I found him."

"And who was this man?"

"Don't know and don't care," Bolan said. Inside, though, the statement confirmed his suspicions that Godunov—or someone in his employ—had a mole inside the U.S. Customs offices.

"And how did you even know where to look?"

"I got my sources," Bolan said. "Listen, let's cut out all the BS and get right to the chase. I have some inkling of who you are, and you can, and most likely will, find out who I am before too much longer. Hell, I wouldn't doubt you got cameras all around this room right now, and you're running that high-tech face recognizing stuff. Well, fine with me, then we don't have to waste a lot of time. Now I've got something here you want, and I went to a lot of risk to get it. The question is, are you willing to pay for it, and if so, how much? That leads to another question, and that is whether or not you're impressed enough with my work that you might want to offer me a job."

"You're looking for work?"

"No," Bolan said flatly, "I'm looking for an opportunity. You can provide something solid, then we talk.

Otherwise, I'm walking out of here now and taking your prize with me."

"Then I guess there's nothing more to discuss," Godunov said.

That's when Bolan's senses went into high gear.

The pair of goons who emerged from two separate panels hidden in the walls came bearing sound-suppressed .22-caliber pistols. Bolan half expected a bit more firepower, but Godunov would have had trouble getting anything more past building security. Bolan had counted on that, and it looked like he'd proved his theory.

They came hard and fast, but the Executioner was ready. Bolan brought the sound-suppressed Beretta 93-R smoothly into play and took the first hood with a 9 mm Parabellum slug to the chest. The impact spun the gunner into the thick plate-glass window of the big corner office, and he bounced off, leaving a bloody splotch as the only evidence of his presence. The goon from the panel about sixty degrees to Bolan's left tried to flank his position, but the Executioner found cover behind a leather couch that provided him with a good defensive posture.

Bolan got the second target with a double-tap to the head. The first round punched through the gunman's face even as he was taking aim: his finger curled reflexively against the trigger and a bullet discharged into the carpeted floor. Bolan's second round creased the top of the guy's skull as his body started to topple, and deposited a patch of blood and flesh on the wall behind him.

The subsonic cartridges from the Beretta 93-R had

suppressed any significant reports. Coupled with their distance from the front desk and the fact that the heavy door was closed, Bolan figured the fight hadn't been heard. He doubted that anyone even occupied the adjoining offices, but if they had it still might not have made enough noise to cause alarm. Either way, Bolan now had another hurdle to overcome with Godunov.

"This isn't what I came here for," Bolan said as he leveled the pistol at the Russian. "I'm not looking for a fight."

Godunov's voice was icy. "Then you shouldn't have come here with your deals."

"I guess I shouldn't have," Bolan said.

He looked at Lutrova and said, "Let's go, pal."

They were nearly at the door when Godunov said, "Wait!"

Bolan turned and eyed him.

"I didn't say I couldn't be reasonable," the man continued with a mock smile. "After all, only a fool wouldn't explore all his options. Such relationships are built on an equal measure of trust."

"Trust and loyalty aren't my problem," Bolan said. He grabbed Lutrova's arm and thrust him into a nearby seat. Lutrova hit it with surprise on his face, and glanced at Bolan, who pretended as if he wasn't there. "I'm a freelancer. I've built a reputation on getting a job done. You want what I have, then you have to pay for it. Keeps things simple."

"Then you won't mind giving me your name," Godunov replied.

Bolan made a show of considering it, and then shrugged. "Guess I've got nothing to lose. Name's

Frankie Lambretta. I used to work for the Righetti Family until this last stint in Otisville."

Godunov nodded knowingly. "The upstate New York prison facility. I'm familiar with it. But surely you have a parole officer you answer to."

"Not anymore," Bolan said with a cool smile. "He met with an unfortunate accident."

"You are a man of style then."

"I'm a man of profit, plain and simple. Now are you interested in doing business with me or not?"

Godunov sighed and took a seat. "What's your price?"

"I'll take twenty-five g's for the genius there," Bolan said. "And a job."

"I'm not sure I have a place for you directly in my organization," Godunov replied.

"Don't be sly, pal."

"Not at all." Godunov reached carefully for a card on his desk and extended it to Bolan. "But I believe I know someone who would be interested in your work."

Bolan cast a cautionary glance at Lutrova before walking to Godunov's desk and snatching the card. He studied it a moment, a plain white card with only a phone number. "What's this supposed to do for me?"

"Call that number and ask for the Wolf."

Bolan cocked his head with skepticism. "You pull anything on me and I'll kill you, friend. You can bank on it."

"Again, we agreed that any relationship should be built on trust."

Bolan gestured toward the two corpses on the carpet. "Like that? That's your idea of trust?"

"Surely a man of your talents must understand my position. I have gotten this far by being cautious. The people I work for absolutely demand this. If I weren't, neither my life nor that of our friend here—" he waved at Lutrova "—would be worth anything."

Bolan nodded and pocketed the card. "Fine. I'll just hold on to my catch until you have the money."

"No need." Godunov reached into a drawer, again careful not to make any sudden moves, and withdrew three one-hundred-dollar-bill bundles. He tossed them on the desk and said, "There's thirty thousand in cash. Let's call the added five a measure of my good faith."

Bolan didn't hesitate before scooping them off the desk and pocketing them. "Fine. Consider us square."

He wheeled around and headed for the exit.

"One more thing," Godunov said as Bolan reached the office door. "I will be looking into your background. If you are not who you say you are, I *will* find out. And when I do, you would be better to take the money and disappear rather than attempt to deceive me."

Bolan flashed a cocksure grin and replied, "Yeah. You do that."

ONCE BOLAN LEFT the building, he walked several blocks past the parking garage to check for marks. Nobody appeared to be tailing him, so he circled back to the garage and retrieved his rental. He contacted Stony Man after putting some distance between him and Godunov's offices.

Barbara Price answered. "How did it go?"

"I think I'm in," Bolan said. "I need another favor.

Do some looking into any mercenary groups operating in the U.S."

"Sure. Are we looking for anything in particular?"

"Not certain yet, but I have a moniker called 'the Wolf.' I don't know if it means anything, but I if you cross-reference it with known freelancers, you may come up with something solid."

"Will do. Hal's here now, too. Anything else you can tell us?"

"Godunov's definitely careful," Bolan replied, "but I don't think he's calling all the shots with the RBN. He specifically mentioned that the people he works for expect him to be careful, which tells me someone sits above him in the ranks. Still, I get the impression he's close to the top."

"Any idea what he's up to, Striker?" Brognola asked.

"Hard to tell this early on," Bolan said. "He's going to check into my background, and I gave him the Lambretta cover just as we discussed. Bear's got that tightened up?"

"Definitely."

"So what do you have in mind for your next move?" Price asked.

"I'm going to get in touch with this contact he called the Wolf," Bolan said. "See where that leads me."

"You could be walking into a trap."

"Probably. But I'm banking on the fact that whoever this contact is, he'll be chomping at the bit to recruit some new talent, particularly since those I took out in Boston were likely part of his team. One thing's for sure—Godunov doles out all the wet work to specialists.

I don't think he's got any internal people other than for
personal security. So the sooner you can get me some
intel on this contact I'm supposed to make, the easier
it will be to gain a picture."

"We'll get on it right away," Brognola promised.
"Give us two hours?"

"Fine," Bolan said. "I can lie low for that long."

"What about Lutrova?"

"I left him there for a price," Bolan said. "That
should firm up my cover some as being in this strictly
for profit. I just hope our timing's good."

"Well," Price said, "we've done some other snooping
into Godunov's background. He's operated here in the
U.S. for about the past five years. That's left significant
paper trails, even if they only lead back to shell or paper
companies."

"I imagine he's attempted to deal in smaller transactions?" Bolan inquired.

"You're absolutely correct," Price replied. "After
9/11, the federal government instituted new policies
relative to financial transactions. Any single transaction
of ten thousand dollars or more requires the receiv-
ing institution to generate what's known as a currency
transaction report. The CTRs are typically routed to
the compliance departments for those banks, who then
file them with a central database. These CTRs are then
analyzed and flagged against a list of known financiers
for terrorist or other national and international criminal
organizations."

"So Godunov's managed to slip through the cracks
by keeping the amounts of his transactions low?"

"Exactly. And since he's never directly involved, his name has never been on the list," she explained.

"We've taken care of that, though," Brognola interjected. "We had him added as soon as you contacted us with Lutrova's story. Speaking of which, do you think he'll roll on you?"

"It's always a possibility, but I'm confident he's scared enough to keep his mouth shut. He knows if he tells Godunov that he was coerced into cooperating with us, it will likely cost him his life. I think he'll pull through it."

"Agreed," Brognola said. "It's not like he has a choice."

"Well, we still don't know what Godunov plans to use him for," Price said.

"We know Lutrova's an expert hacker and a technology genius. I think Godunov plans to exploit his talents in some way, and I'm guessing it has something to do with the funds they're channeling through all the bogus investment accounts."

"You think it's money being used to fund RBN operations overseas?"

"Why not?" Bolan said. "It makes complete sense in light of what you've uncovered."

"You could be on to something, Striker," Price replied. "Given the state of the world economy, it's likely they're starting to see a rapid depletion of funds. The only way for them to continue their efforts would be if they get more money from their investors, or find new ones. The latter would take too long, so for the sake of expedience they may be attempting to tap the current list."

"Which means they'd need to get all the financial data they could on those financiers," Brognola concluded.

"Right," Bolan said. "And I think that's what Godunov may have brought Lutrova in to do."

"You think Godunov's looking to crack that list?" Price asked.

"I think he's going to do a lot more than that," Bolan replied. "I think he plans to make Lutrova crack the New York financial network."

"Okay, but to what ends?"

"To suck it dry in one fell swoop," the Executioner replied.

CHAPTER FIVE

Yan "the Wolf" Volkov rubbed his temples in an attempt to abate the splitting headache.

His conversation with Yuri Godunov hadn't gone well, although it had gone about as he expected. What Volkov couldn't understand was how four of his people had been put down so quickly and efficiently by one man. The bigger problem came from the fact that none of his contacts in the U.S. Customs had seen this man or gotten their hands on the security tapes in One Federal Plaza. Volkov didn't even have a rough description, and that would make it next to impossible to identify him.

The other thing that bothered the Russian mercenary was the why of it. What reason had this man had for killing the team sent to retrieve Bogdan Lutrova? Had he been expecting them? And if so, did that mean Volkov had some sort of leak inside his own operations? His people had always been loyal in the past, never a one turning against him. That had to do partly with his training methods and partly from the fact that he paid them very well.

Soldiers-for-hire were a superstitious and close-mouthed lot. They generally didn't talk to anybody about what they did, for any reason. Loose lips could get those in the business killed very quickly, or lead to ostracizing on a global scale. This most recent event had not only put Volkov's head on the chopping block, but his reputation, as well—his employer wasn't known for being the forgiving type.

Volkov sat back in his chair and thought about his options. While he took his instructions from Godunov, he knew the money came from someone higher. That someone—Volkov didn't know exactly who, but he had his suspicions—expected positive results every time and wouldn't hear excuses if things went sour. Volkov had to admit he'd never been in a situation quite like this one before. He'd almost declined the job when he heard how Godunov wanted to do it, but saying no wasn't really an option. He was on retainer, a contract of sorts, and that meant whenever they told him to jump he simply did it. Everything else got put aside and there wasn't even any asking "how high"; he was expected to get it done quickly and efficiently.

The plan hadn't been very good to start with. It would have been much simpler to get Bogdan Lutrova into America in secret. There were many ways to smuggle such persons into the country without much trouble at all—the Wolf had plenty of mechanisms in place for such an operation. In fact, human trafficking remained a financial mainstay of his operations, and as long as he didn't do anything to expose the RBN, they were content to look the other way. Of course, he was mandated to remit a certain amount of his profits to them—kickbacks for certain of them to look the other way—but that was simply the cost of doing business. And Volkov didn't mind paying off those individuals, since it didn't cut that deeply into his profit margin.

This present problem, however, had become another

issue, with a magnitude of complications. If Volkov had any hope of setting this right, he would have to locate the mysterious stranger who'd killed his men, *and* find Bogdan Lutrova. It didn't really matter if—

A rap at his office door broke his concentration, and he barked, "Yes?"

The door opened enough to reveal the heavily made up face of his secretary. She was a short, blond, petite woman—midtwenties, Volkov recalled—who hailed from the same area of the Ukraine as he. On occasion she performed more than just secretarial duties for him, although she expected to be compensated for such things. Nothing in life was free.

"Mr. Volkov? It is Mr. Godunov for you. He's on your personal line."

"Put it through, Mira," Volkov said, leaning forward to put his hand on the extension, and muttering curses as to what the man could possibly want *now.*

When Volkov answered, Godunov said, "I have our asset here with me."

"What?" Volkov could feel his stomach knot. "You mean—"

"Yes, I mean *that* asset."

"But how?"

"It seems we have a new benefactor," Godunov said. "I'm almost sure that this man is working for one of our competitors, but there is a remote possibility he's legit. He was looking for work, and so naturally, I sent him to you."

Volkov wanted to laugh out loud. The one enjoyment he got from dealing with Godunov was the man's penchant for being extremely careful in his telephone conversations. Volkov had assured him time and again that this particular connection was scrambled, and only the very best electronic communications thieves in the world could perhaps decrypt the complex algorithms utilized to mask their conversations, but Godunov insisted on keeping the talk all business.

"What are you looking for me to do with him?" Volkov asked.

"That would be entirely up to you. Although I believe you will probably need to subsidize your staff, given your recent turnover, yes?"

So the bastard wasn't planning to let it go. Stick the knife in and turn it a few times just to make sure he kept Volkov in what was "his place." Well, the Wolf knew how to play that game as well, and he wasn't planning to fall into Godunov's trap so easily. This situation would require deft handling, at best.

"Yes, I believe I could find a place for him here. Do you have the details?"

"He goes by the name Lambretta. I'm having him checked out as we speak."

"He has other connections?"

"He indicated as much," Godunov said. "Although I don't believe he's friendly with those particular contacts anymore. He was away on an extended business trip for some time and is now back in the area looking to establish a new territory with new clients. Based on what I've seen of his résumé, he might prove useful to you. Assuming his references check out, of course."

Of course, Volkov thought, but he said, "I will await his call then."

"Yes, do."

"I assume that your other assets are intact?"

"It would seem so. I'm still inspecting them."

"You'll let me know, then, if something is damaged or missing."

"Of course," Godunov replied, but not without some acid in his voice.

"I shall wait to hear from you."

Volkov hung up and rubbed once more at his temples. So, another riddle had presented itself for him to decipher. Volkov had to wonder if this mysterious stranger that showed up with Lutrova was the same one who'd killed his men. It didn't seem improbable, but Volkov couldn't risk killing the man out of hand, either. If he checked out and Godunov thought he could be of some use, Volkov wouldn't turn it down; at this point, he'd already taken significant losses among his ranks.

The Wolf always kept his operations relatively small. At no time did he employ more than twelve individuals, and that number had just been cut by one-third. He had other resources upon which he could call at a moment's notice, but as he only employed freelancers, none of them were bound to take any assignment he offered. It seemed almost too convenient that this new opportunity would have dropped so easily into their laps, but Volkov was willing to take a chance if Godunov vouched for it.

This way, he couldn't be held responsible if something went wrong. It would all fall onto Godunov's shoulders, and Volkov could walk away clean.

The regular extension, the one used for public business, buzzed, and Volkov picked it up immediately.

"I'm looking for the Wolf," the caller said.

"You've got him."

"I was referred by a mutual business acquaintance."

Good! This one was careful, didn't assume it was wise to use any names; at least that spoke to his experience. If he'd been sloppy right off, Volkov would have dismissed him as an amateur and hung up immediately.

"Yes, I was just told to expect your call."

"I assume we need to meet." It wasn't a question.

"That would be best," Volkov said. "I have a particular place in mind."

"I'd prefer we do this on some neutral ground," the man replied. "You'll understand that I can't be too careful. I'm a stranger to the area, and it wouldn't be proper or respectful to impose some sort of intimacies until we get to know each other better."

"You sound very savvy," Volkov said. "I've been informed your résumé is impressive. I've also noted that you have quite a bit of experience, although it seems you've been seeking work for some time. I take it the prospects have not been good?"

"They've been scarce with this economy," the man replied. "So are you willing to interview on my terms?"

"I think that can be arranged," Volkov said.

The man immediately gave him an address for a quiet, out-of-the-way spot down on the waterfront. It was a café of some sort; though Volkov had never been there, he did know of it. The environment catered to a yuppie clientele, business class types, so meeting in that place wouldn't seem out of the ordinary. They agreed to rendezvous in one hour.

"Come alone," the man said, and hung up before Volkov could reply.

Oh, I most definitely will not *come alone,* Volkov thought.

BOLAN DIDN'T TRUST the Wolf, but his mission required he make the connection. This guy was obviously the muscle for Godunov, who was the apparent brains of the operation. Not that Bolan would make the mistake of thinking the Wolf was stupid; a soldier didn't live long if he had a habit of underestimating his enemy. The name of the game was cunning and a healthy respect for the abilities of somebody with the Wolf's background.

Ten minutes before the meet, Bolan reconnected with Stony Man. The information Price could offer him was scant, at best.

"I'm afraid we can't tell you a lot about this guy," she said. "He covers his tracks pretty well."

"Surely he's left some sort of trail."

"Most of this came from an old friend I have in the NSA's Signals Intelligence unit, and there's not much to go on," Price told him.

"I'll take whatever I can get."

"We think his real surname is Volkov, first name unknown. Possibly raised in the Ukraine, but that's also unconfirmed. There are about three dozen men with that last name, all of whom hail from northern Russia, and about half that many the right age and type suitable for the Wolf's kind of work. We're pretty certain he's operated in about a half-dozen countries and under a variety of aliases."

Bolan sighed. "Sounds like a lot of ifs and maybes, Barb."

"I know, Striker, and I wish I could give you more, but that's what we've got. I'm not keen on the idea of you going into this situation on such weak information."

"I've done a lot worse recently," Bolan said.

Price laughed, because she heard the grin in his voice. "Yes, that you have."

"What about this moniker, the Wolf. That jingle any bells with your sources?"

"Yes, we did get that much. Volkov is actually Russian for wolf."

Bolan chewed on that a moment before replying. "Okay, sounds like I'll just have to go for broke on this one and hope fate deals me one more decent hand."

"Don't take any risks, Striker," Price replied. "If it gets too hot you can always pull out and regroup, give us time to hit this from another angle."

"I don't think we have that much time, Barb, but I'll keep it in mind."

"Be careful."

"Out here," the Executioner said.

He sat in his rental and studied the harborside café and surroundings, watchful for anyone out of the ordinary. Chances were slim to none that Volkov would follow his instructions to come alone, and if he did have additional men, Bolan knew they'd be professional enough to make themselves conspicuous. The soldier figured if he played his cards right he'd walk away from the meet. He'd picked the place at random out of a phone book, after checking with a local shop owner for a decent public venue to conduct an impromptu business meeting. The shop owner had taken one look at Bolan with an expression that implied he wasn't buying the whole business meeting story. Obviously, this area was used more to conduct meetings between unsavory characters than Bolan had first surmised. Still, the shop owner's recommendation had seemed acceptable.

Bolan kept one eye on the storefront and checked his watch. Ten minutes until the meet was supposed to go down, and so far he hadn't seen anything to alert him that trouble brewed in the near future. But again, he couldn't rely on that alone. The Wolf hadn't survived this long without being careful, and he would most certainly bring backup, even if he bought Bolan's cover and story as a down-on-his-luck enforcer looking for work.

The entire thing was thin at best, but Bolan knew he didn't have any other options. Without this charade he stood almost no chance of getting inside Godunov's operations. Even this move wouldn't necessarily put him in the center of things unless he could convince Godunov that some "outside force" threatened the operation. That would be the crux of his story to the Wolf, and maybe, just maybe, Bolan could pull it off.

He scanned the crowd in front of the café again, and this time he spotted the mark. The man was tall and muscular, his conditioning visible through the tan slacks and black T-shirt he wore. It wasn't so much how he looked as how he moved that allowed the Executioner to pick him out of a crowd. Trained and experienced combatants carried themselves in very specific ways, and while those telltale signs weren't obvious to the untrained observer, they spoke volumes to a professional like Bolan. This was definitely the Wolf.

The soldier got out of his sedan, locked it and proceeded straight toward him. He reached the café just as the mercenary stepped inside and began to scan the crowded tables.

Bolan came up behind him and quietly said, "Looking for me?"

The Wolf, aka Volkov, turned and glanced at him in surprise. They were about the same height, although the Russian might have had an inch or two on Bolan. His blond hair and cool blue eyes reminded Bolan of Carl "Ironman" Lyons, Able Team's fearless leader, but that's where the similarities ended. Where Lyons possessed a humoring demeanor just beneath the cynical surface he wore, there was nothing even remotely gregarious about Volkov. Bolan guessed there was only hard, cold granite in the muscular chest of this guy, and a psychopathic nature born from a love for killing—and it was obvious Volkov had done a lot of it.

"Not a good start, sneaking up on a potential employer," Volkov said with a sneer.

"Funny, I didn't think I was 'sneaking' up on you," Bolan replied with an equal amount of acid in his voice. He had to be conciliatory, but he also needed to maintain the aura of a hardened Mob enforcer. It was important in his role that he show Volkov he wouldn't just flip over and show his belly to anybody; such a move would cause him to lose any and all credibility in the Russian's eyes, and more than likely lead to trouble.

Bolan glanced outside, and although he didn't spot

anybody, he said, "I see you didn't come alone like I told you."

"You seem to have forgotten your place here, Frankie," Volkov replied. "You're here asking *me* for something, not the other way around. I do whatever the fuck I want to do. You get me?"

Bolan made a show of looking uncertain, letting Volkov think he'd taken him off his guard, and then he smiled. "Yeah, sure… I get you, pal. No need to get your shorts in a bunch. I was just feeling you out, is all. I'm pretty careful when it comes to choosing the people I work for. I don't want to end up getting my throat cut because the crew I'm with or its leader has no jewels. Know what I'm saying?"

Volkov nodded. "So what is it you want?"

"Well, since you know my name, then I assume our, uh, mutual friend contacted you and told you I was looking for a new crew."

"I saw some tables out there," Volkov said. "Let's sit outside."

Bolan nodded and the two men made their way to a table on the fringes of the patio. The rest of the harbor-side dock was busy, as lunchtime had finally arrived. Longshoremen and suits from nearby businesses had started to flood the area, cramming like sardines into every coffee shop, deli and grill they could find along the harbor. The sun streamed down onto the dock and took much from the bite of the slight breezes off the water. It actually turned out to be a pretty nice day for mid-February in New York.

When they were seated, Bolan got straight to business. "So I understand you may be looking for some additional hands."

Volkov nodded and waited for him to continue.

"Hey," Bolan said, "those guys that your boss sent after me in his office… I hope they weren't *your* guys. Because I was just defending myself. Guy's got a right to do that, huh?"

"I don't provide private security for Mr. Godunov," Volkov said. "I operate, shall we say…independently. And yes, I'm in the market for new talents. But I'm not sure you're going to work out."

"Why not?" Bolan splayed his hands in true Italian fashion and said, "What's the beef you got with me? We barely know each other and you're already backing down."

"I'm not backing down," Volkov said, his gaze roving among the crowd. "I'm just saying that I don't know if your type of skills and training would fit into the outfit I run. You're used to doing things a certain way, and anybody I bring on board would have to adjust to doing things *my* way. Your résumé says you're a little on the wild side, taken to doing things your own way, and I cannot afford that kind of risk. It's a liability to me and to the people I work for."

"Hey, listen, pal, I get results."

"That may be," Volkov replied, now meeting Bolan's gaze directly for the first time. "But I don't want results at the cost of compromising my position. I want *loyalty*. I want *obedience*. I expect you to do things my way and only my way. Do you think you can do that?"

Bolan appeared to think about it for a while, and then said, "Yeah, I suppose I could give it a try."

Volkov stood. "Oh, you'll have to give it more than a try, Frankie." He slid a card across the table. "Be at that address tomorrow morning, 0600 sharp."

"Oh-six what?"

"That's six o'clock in the morning."

"Uh, kind of early."

Volkov raised a finger. "Remember our agreement. My way."

"Yeah, yeah… Your way."

So just like that, Bolan was in. Although there was one small problem: it had been a little too easy.

And the Executioner knew he was about to find out why.

CHAPTER SIX

Eduardo Capistrano had made his fortunes on the philosophy there was a sucker born every minute.

He didn't see how this made him any different than the hundreds of other traders and foreign investors. After all, dealing with companies in other countries— particularly those in the E.U.—had always been more lucrative. There weren't the regulations to deal with that he faced in the U.S., and he didn't have the IRS crawling up his ass every tax season. No 1099 interest statements or foreign income investment slips; nobody from the Securities Exchange Commission sniffing around, crapping on his lawn and the like.

No, all Capistrano had to do was sit back and watch the cash roll in.

Sure, every once in a while he'd have to field a complaint from some yuppie calling from his mansion up in the Cape, take the occasional panicked call from a rich bitch sunbathing her sculpted body courtesy of modern medical science. But a kickback here or a few grand in interest dividends usually kept them at bay.

After all, they didn't need to know Capistrano was pulling down over a mil-and-a-quarter a month. He'd given up his personal integrity and kept his mouth shut, and it had definitely paid off.

And it wasn't just the cash. There were the other

perks to think of, like the young, dark-haired Hispanic woman squirming her head deeper into his lap as she stretched her sensuous, athletic body on the sofa. His sixty-inch plasma televisions with the wireless internet and the high definition picture-in-picture. The vacations to exotic locales like Cancun, Rio de Janeiro and Greece, or the "business trips" twice a year to Paris. Ah yes, and how he could he forget Italy? Eduardo Capistrano had never thought such a lifestyle could be his, but it was there for the taking if one was willing to take a few risks.

Despite the fact the activities weren't exactly on the legit side, Capistrano had never worried about repercussions. The people with whom he did business—rumors flew around circles that it was the Russian mob, but nobody really had any proof—weren't willing to show their faces in public. They couldn't afford that kind of scrutiny, so it didn't much matter what he said or did. He could go where he wanted and when he wanted, and the people who took his money had nothing to say about it.

Capistrano enjoyed the very best life had to offer. He worked from home, kept his nose clean and attended all the latest social events. He had two kids in a posh Catholic school. He went to the best parties, wore the best clothes and rubbed elbows with others as rich as him—although they were typically a bit more famous. And he *never* allowed himself to be in the limelight.

There were two men he paid who were responsible for making sure he stayed that way. They accompanied him just about everywhere he went, made sure his path was clear and that nobody was putting his nose in Capistrano's business. His men were more than just bodyguards; they ran his errands, maintained round-the-clock security on his home and prevented anyone from getting too close when he was in public.

Capistrano never allowed anyone to photograph him and he didn't do interviews. Hell, even the half-dozen companies he owned were managed by boot-lickers who got their jollies from driving their BMWs to work and throwing wild poolside parties with others of their species. As long as they did what they were told and signed the papers they were ordered to sign, Capistrano didn't give a shit what they did.

But all of that lent to his surprise when a tall, distinguished looking type showed up at his front door asking to speak to him. Capistrano's security chief told the man to go away, but that didn't seem to make any difference. He wasn't an overly big man, tall but lean, and not very dangerous looking, so Capistrano thought about telling his man to throw the guy out on his ear. Still, discretion was the better part of valor, and so he let Nick show the guy into the parlor, Capistrano still lived in a part of the world where houses had parlors, near the Hudson River.

"What can I do for you, Mr...."

"My name's Godunov, Yuri Godunov," the man said.

Capistrano could feel his blood run cold at his extremities, and he had the sensation of a marble being lodged in his throat. He had only a moment to decide how to react, and he decided not to react at all. But the very name alone told Capistrano just about everything he needed to know. He hadn't really believed the rumors about the Russian Mob, but this guy, his accent and his name and just every damn thing about him, screamed of Russian until it practically dripped from his pores.

"And what can I do for you, Mr. Godunov?"

"You know what you can do for me," Godunov replied, his smile chilling Capistrano more.

"I'm afraid I don't understand."

"I think that you do," Godunov said. Capistrano started to reach for his panic button beneath the desk, but the sudden appearance of a small pistol in Godunov's hand stayed him.

"I wouldn't do that, Mr. Capistrano," Godunov said. "I am not a man taken to violence, but I can assure you that I know very well how to use this. So instead of doing something you will regret, albeit only for a very short time, perhaps you should listen to me very carefully."

Capistrano merely nodded as he pressed his lips together. "You have my attention."

"There are a number of things that have occurred recently, things that greatly disturb me."

"What are you talking about?"

Godunov waved the muzzle ever so slightly and said, "Remember that I said you should listen carefully. That is best done with your mouth shut. Now as I was saying, the people to whom I answer are very disturbed by your recent indiscretions. You're being downright greedy, in fact. You see, we've allowed you to continue for about as long as can be reasonably tolerated. But in these very tough economic times we must protect our assets…which means protecting *you*, Mr. Capistrano.

You enjoy the freedom you do because you're a producer, a man who knows how to get money out of even the most destitute. The difficulty that is presented to us, however, is that you have not been quite as generous as we'd hoped. That is about to change."

"Look, I don't know who you are or who you work for but—"

Godunov's laugh dripped with derision. "Come now, Mr. Capistrano, do you think me a fool? Look at this place. Look at it! You live like a king, but you give like a peasant. And I'm here to deliver a message, one that would be in your best interests to heed."

"I don't respond to threats, Mr. Godunov. I make them."

"You make *nothing* apart from us, Eduardo. We have been patient and allowed you to keep the majority of the funds from your investors. Now it is time to return what you have borrowed."

"Borrowed?" Capistrano laughed so loudly he thought he might fall out of his chair. "Everything that I have I earned."

"No." Godunov shook his head like a petulant child. "Everything you have *we* earned. You are not an independent operator. You never were, in fact. We just let you think you were. All the paperwork for those companies you allegedly own is utterly worthless. None of it is legal or binding. You were so busy scooping up the pot that you forgot you had put others in to play the game for you. Those individuals were very cleverly placed through our own machinations, and they have done a marvelous job of keeping our operations afloat while making money. Now it's time to return what you've borrowed, and with interest."

"I don't have any of this money that you're yapping about, pal," Capistrano lied.

Godunov shook his head in disbelief. "You just don't seem to understand what I'm telling you. Yes, that must be it....You are stupid, perhaps? Let me explain this in a way that will assuredly make things clear for you. Your monies and holdings, all of them, will be transferred to the control of my people within the next twenty-four hours. If you attempt to interfere with us, we will take everything you own and exploit it for our gain. That includes those lovely children of yours. How are they enjoying that special school they attend? Are they getting good grades? I would hope that their father would want to cooperate with me, because I can tell you that they would fetch a very nice price in some areas of the world."

Capistrano could hardly believe his ears, but he didn't doubt a single word of it. Godunov hadn't come here to kill him, despite waving the gun. He'd come to explain that everything Eduardo thought was his didn't, in fact, belong to him at all, and probably never had. He'd made the crucial mistake of not looking too closely at his business associates, and in the end it had come back to bite him. He was left with no choice now but to cooperate. Just as the people he thought had been working for him, but had actually been working for Godunov, were doing.

Capistrano sighed and leaned back in his chair, suddenly feeling much older than his thirty-eight years. "What do you want me to do?"

BOGDAN LUTROVA STARED absently at the computer monitors as rows of data whizzed by.

The program he had written to penetrate the New York banking system had involved much more than simply hacking the data. No, this system had taken months to build, putting the pieces in place a little at a time so as not to alert the security sniffers and lock-out programs meant to deter individuals from doing the very things he had done. When it came down to it, breaking down those barriers involved a give and take; it was the equivalent of an electronic dance, really.

Getting into the system required Lutrova to insert specially designed scripts to test various areas of the New York Central Financial Data Exchange, allowing some scripts to be discovered while he deftly diverted others. There was an unspoken rule in the information security field that the more American security specialists were able to stop attempted hacks, the more confident they became in the integrity of those systems. Such attacks were intended to make them put more faith in their systems than they had a right to expect. It was an old trick, but one that worked frequently.

Once Lutrova had discovered the weaknesses in the system security, it had just been a matter of sending bits of his program into the system. When it came right down to it, computers knew only one language—the binary language of ones and zeroes—and it was a language Bogdan Lutrova had become extremely fluent in over the years. He wasn't about to let this slip out of his hands.

Godunov's plan had been simple enough, ingenious really—using the embezzled funds from the RBN's biggest financiers against them. The monies and securities they had buried weren't difficult to find; in fact, the money was right under everyone's noses. It just wasn't easily accessible. The RBN could have attempted blackmail or extraction by more conventional methods, but by doing it in this fashion they wouldn't draw any attention to themselves.

It would still take some footwork on the part of Yuri and his mercenary team, but Lutrova had decided not to bother himself which such trivialities. His only concern, as his masters in Russia had instructed, was to get the information they needed so the funds could be moved. How the "contributors" dealt with their sudden change in fortune wasn't anything he needed to concern himself with. His only task was to make sure the transfers took place when Yuri Godunov wanted them to.

In a way, Lutrova wondered why he was so worried. There wasn't anything they could do to him without ruining their own plans. At this point in the game, the leaders of the RBN had invested a tremendous amount of resources into this operation. The payoff for Lutrova alone would be half a half-million dollars and a place of his own for the rest of his life. He'd picked an estate outside of Geneva for his retirement, a strange choice to many, but one he knew would suit him perfectly. Who would think to look for the RBN's premier hacker there?

In spite of it all, Lutrova knew he was expendable. *Everyone* was expendable in the RBN; the organization thrived on self-reliance and survival. When they had something, they took it. When they needed to generate money, they beefed up their pornography sites and sexual slave trading. If they wanted to bring down some high-tech corporation, they would turn to their vast pool of talents, which comprised many like Lutrova, to destroy that company's information systems infrastructure.

The slam of a door caused Lutrova to jump, breaking his concentration. Or had he been daydreaming? he wondered. His vision was blurry and his eyes itched. He turned in his seat to see Yuri Godunov enter, a newspaper under his arm and a briefcase in his hand. He would look like any other businessman on the crowded streets of New York City's financial district, but beneath that facade was a heartless killer and taskmaster. Lutrova didn't really like Godunov and never had; he always acted superior to anyone else. And in a way, Lutrova felt glad that he'd managed to keep his new relationship with the Americans from the man's scrutiny.

Godunov stepped into the spacious quarters he'd set up. The place certainly was roomy, and Lutrova had to admit he couldn't complain about his accommodations. He was well fed, and there were plenty of changes of clothes—all in his size and to his discerning tastes—with just about anything he wanted being little more than a request away. Godunov had set him up with an intercom where he could call on the house staff to fulfill every wish.

Of course, heavily armed guards patrolled the grounds day and night. A large wall of thick mortar ten feet high and topped with wrought-iron spires surrounded the estate. The grounds were fully wired, according to Godunov, with electronic motion and sonic monitoring by day and infrared by night. The place was a veritable fortress, and despite his elegant surroundings, Lutrova could not help but feel he was in more of a prison than an estate.

His mind screamed at him to open his mouth and confess his indiscretions, to beg for his life and promise never to be weak again. But his flesh could not bring himself to do it, and he simply looked at Godunov, with a masked expression he hoped would be unreadable.

"How are the operations coming?" Godunov asked as he set his props on a leather couch.

That was just like the bastard—only concerned with business. "The information is being downloaded as we speak. It shouldn't be more than a few hours before we have everything we need."

Godunov sat on the sofa, crossed his legs and withdrew a silver cigarette case and matching lighter from his suit coat pocket. He sighed as he chose a slender brown cigarette and lit it. Through a cloud of smoke he said, "You are certain we cannot do this remotely. We *must* be on-site?"

"There is no way to actually transfer the funds unless we are on-site and able to physically plug into a terminal. The program can only retrieve the information we need, such as the account numbers and balances. We must still be on-site to plug into a terminal, so that the actual transfers can take place. The bank computers will not permit movement of funds of this size without that confirmation. It's part of the security features."

"And the time we will have to be inside," Godunov said. "It will not take more than five minutes?"

"I've already explained that three times to you, Yuri. Why do you keep asking me?"

"Because we are running a tremendous risk here," Godunov said. "We have planned this down to the last detail, and we are relying on you to make good on the numbers you give us. Not to mention that we cannot be expected to hold our position any longer than that. As soon as the transfers start, federal authorities will be alerted and agents will be sent to the New York First Financial Bank immediately. If they catch us while we're still inside, we will be required to fight our way out."

"If you already have the money by then, what difference will it make?"

Godunov chuckled, inhaled smoke from his cigarette and shook his head. "Oh, my dear Bogdan, you really have no idea. It is not merely about having the money. Having it does our people little good if we aren't there to make sure the wealth is distributed. Only *you* know the locations where the money is going and only *you* have access to them. If we are forced to do battle with the police, there is little chance that you will survive, since nobody will be able to protect you."

"I will do my part, Yuri," Lutrova said, "just as I've promised."

"But of course you will. I never doubted that. Why are you acting so furtive, my friend? You have been as nervous as a cat since you arrived."

"It is nothing," Lutrova replied, his mind racing furiously. "My time with that American gangster shook me up a bit more than I thought."

"You have been around such men before."

"Yes, men on *our* side. But there was something about him I did not trust."

"Well, his references checked out, and he does appear to have some unique talents that I feel we can exploit. However, if it turns out he is not who he says he is, then I can assure you that he will be dealt with accordingly. You no longer have to worry about him."

"Good."

"I am a bit curious, though, what transpired while you were in custody of the U.S. Customs."

"What do you mean?"

"You did not talk to them?"

Lutrova cocked his head. "Talk to them about what? What exactly are you trying to imply, Yuri? Do you think that I would betray you?"

"Did you?"

"Absolutely not!"

Godunov's eyes flashed as he stared at Lutrova, although he smoked calmly. After a time, he said, "Okay, my friend, okay. I believe you."

But something in Lutrova's gut told him that Yuri Godunov knew.

CHAPTER SEVEN

The morning sun was peeking over the horizon by the time Mack Bolan arrived at the address Volkov had given him.

The rallying point turned out to be a dumpy house in the heart of the Bronx. The soldier had hoped the placed was isolated enough that he could do recon, but his luck didn't hold out on that count. The houses were close together. What frustrated him most was that he knew what Lutrova planned to do and he had some idea of when; he just didn't know how Godunov would put it together. He also had to keep one eye on the Wolf through this; the guy wasn't trustworthy and Bolan didn't think he'd yet bought into the Frankie Lambretta cover.

One thing Bolan had become convinced of: neither Volkov nor Godunov ultimately called the shots here. The entire operation was being led by someone much higher up—someone with both financial and political clout that far surpassed the wildest imagination. That was the head Bolan would have to chop off the Hydra before he could make a dent in the RBN, and it was an operation he surmised would take him straight into the flames of perdition before it was over.

Bolan swung the nose of his vehicle into the drive and eased to a stop behind a silver SUV. The soldier quickly withdrew his Beretta, checked the action and then holstered the weapon. Volkov had instructed him to dress in business attire, so Bolan had opted for a conservative gray suit with silver pinstripes, light blue shirt and light gray silk tie. He had no idea what awaited him beyond the doors of this shack of a house with peeling paint and weathered shingles. For all he knew, he could be walking straight into an ambush, one for which he had physically and mentally prepared himself during his drive.

Bolan climbed out of the sedan, walked to the door and pressed the buzzer. He stood there a minute and realized he hadn't heard the buzzer from inside, so after waiting a minute he knocked. Soon he heard footsteps and then the door opened to reveal an unfamiliar face. Bolan searched his mental files, but didn't recognize the guy. Probably another freelancer who had managed to stay under the radar of law enforcement; it appeared Volkov remained consistent in his hiring practices.

The guy had sandy-brown hair and blue eyes a few shades darker than Bolan's. He looked at him through the ratty screen a moment—sizing him up, as most professional guns-for-hire would—before opening the door and gesturing for him to enter. As Bolan crossed the threshold, the guy stuck out his hand.

Bolan noted the Southern accent as he said, "You Frankie?"

"Yeah," he replied with a nod as he shook the man's hand.

"Come on in, the boss is waiting."

The man led him through a cramped hallway with a worn hardwood floor that appeared dusty with disuse.

They continued to a back room that opened onto an equally cramped kitchen. Two other men dressed in business suits sat there. They looked up as the two entered, and Bolan's escort gestured at them.

"That's Igor, that's Keck."

Bolan appraised each man in a moment. Igor had a short and wiry build; he wore his blond hair in a high-and-tight cut, and his hazel eyes flashed with intensity in the light of the bare bulb dangling from the ceiling. Keck looked almost East Indian or Pakistani. A thin, faint scar ran down the left side of his face near to his ear, and Bolan gauged it as a knife wound of some kind, perhaps from straight razor. He also wore his dark hair short, and his expression seemed unreadable.

Each offered his hand in turn, and Bolan shook them briefly. The speaker then said, "I'm Billy, but everybody just calls me Southpaw. We go by first names only here. Guys, this is Frankie."

Bolan nodded at them and then asked, "Where's the Wolf?"

"Right here."

All eyes turned to the kitchen entrance, and Bolan felt a chill crawl up his neck. He hadn't even heard Volkov come in, and that was no mean feat. Bolan always maintained a keen awareness in his surroundings, yet Volkov had somehow managed to approach his rear flank without a sound. The Executioner filed that fact away, intent on making sure it didn't happen ever again.

"And I don't go by that whenever we're in public. You call me Yan or boss, don't much care which. Got it?"

Bolan nodded. "Suits me."

"Fine." Volkov made a show of looking at his watch. "You're right on time. That's good news, because it means you listen and pay attention to detail. Let it become a habit and you just might have a future with this crew."

"Wilco…boss."

Volkov nodded and his expression seemed to soften slightly. "We only have a few minutes, so I'm not going to spend a lot of time explaining this to you. Our first job is we got to head upstate to Saint Bartholomew's. I can explain more on the way up there. This is initiation for you, so I'll keep the details simple. You'll follow instructions given by me or Southpaw, there. He's in charge when I'm not present. Understood?"

"Fine. But I'm just wondering why we're going to a church."

"Not a church, a school."

"Catholic prep school," Southpaw added, but he quickly shut his mouth when Volkov threw him a look.

Bolan filed the information for later while pretending not to notice the exchange between him and Southpaw. If Volkov had just used his real first name, Bolan knew it would be easier to pick him out of the list of potentials compiled by the Stony Man team. The mention of the school was of a bit more interest to the Executioner, but it also left him with a sense of trepidation. A group of grown men dressed in business suits were going to a Catholic school in upstate New York? Bolan didn't get it—there *had* to be some connection to Godunov's activities, but he couldn't see it.

Without another word, the men prepared to leave as

per Volkov's instructions. They decided to go in two separate vehicles, with Bolan, the Wolf and Southpaw in one—probably they wanted to keep an eye on the newcomer—while Igor and Keck took the other. Fortunately, Bolan's rental had the most room, so they opted to let him take the wheel. Bolan counted this decision a fortunate stroke of luck; at least he'd have access to his entire arsenal.

It took them less than two hours to reach the up-state location. On the surface, St. Bartholomew's wasn't much different from any other Catholic school. Bolan could only surmise there had to be something of value inside the school. He'd already activated the GPS homing signal on his cell phone so that Stony Man had a track on him. Not that he was worried; the Executioner could most assuredly take care of himself in such a situation. What bothered him more was that they were headed into a potential fire zone filled with innocent teachers, school staff and children.

And Bolan wondered how he would keep the blood-shed confined to the enemy.

IT WASN'T LONG after they arrived at Saint Bartholomew's Catholic Preparatory School that Bolan could pretty much deduce the enemy's plan.

Volkov ordered him to pull the sedan to the curb on the far side of the grounds, the entire length of which was bordered by a brick wall, with wrought-iron spires on top covered by the gray-white fingers of dormant ivy. He then instructed Southpaw to stay with Bolan while he went to confer with the other two, who had followed them in an older blue van. The thing was just nondescript enough not to draw attention, but Bolan didn't doubt it had quite a number of special modifications. Not as practical as the virtual war wagon he drove, which was, unbeknownst to his new "colleagues", filled with an arsenal of unspeakable firepower.

It would prove to be just what Bolan needed as he engaged Southpaw, aka Billy, in casual conversation.

"So what's the deal here?" Bolan asked in his best Italian tough guy manner. "We just s'posed to sit out here and freeze our butts off while the other guys get all the action?"

"The boss knows what he's doing."

"Yeah, well, so far I'm not that impressed. How long you known him?"

Southpaw took a deep breath and let it out noisily as Bolan watched him do some quick mental figuring. He finally said, "About two years, I guess."

"You guess?" Bolan made a show of chuckling. "You don't know how long you been working for the guy?"

"I just said about two years. You deaf or something?"

"What sort of missions have you done? See a lot of heat?"

"I've seen my share." Then Billy added, "You know what, Frankie, I think you ask too many questions."

Bolan raised his hands in a show of defense. "Hey, I don't mean nothing by it. Just making conversation."

"Well, just stop talking so—"

Volkov rapped on the passenger window and gestured for Bolan to roll it down. He did and Volkov stuck his head inside, his breath visible in the biting morning air. A quick look at the clock told Bolan it was almost 0820 hours, probably just before the first period began inside the school.

"Okay, here's the deal. You come with us Southpaw. We're going to need your very unique talents in providing a distraction while we do this. Igor and Keck will stay with the van while Southpaw's doing his thing."

"What about me, boss?" Bolan asked.

"You're going to be our wheels." He gestured toward a low, squat building that sat to one side. Bolan could see the reflections of sunlight on metal and the occasional movement of vehicles. "See that? That's the front gate entrance. We're going to send the van through, and the van's going to pick up a very specific package for us. You're going to provide a way for me and Southpaw to get out once that's done. We're hoping this will throw off the cops in case we run into trouble. You'll wait right outside that front entrance. There end up being any problems, you take out the guard and then you wait for us. Everything goes off right, you still wait for us. Got it?"

"Simple," Bolan said with a nod.

"You better learn something quick, Frankie," Volkov replied. "There's a big difference between simple and easy. The two aren't the same. Got it?"

"Yeah, sure. I got it."

"Keep in touch," Volkov said as he tossed a high frequency radio on the seat next to Bolan. He and Southpaw then walked to the van and jumped in.

"All right, you reading me?" Volkov's voice said a moment later.

"Reading you four-by-four," Bolan replied.

"Let's do this," he said. "You lead us in and then

park *outside* the gate, where you can make a break for it, if necessary. But you don't move until we're on board. 'Cause I promise that if you double-cross us, I'll find you and kill you. You can be sure of that."

Bolan decided not to reply, instead waving his hand so that Volkov understood he got the message. Fate had dealt him a decent hand on this one, making it possible for him to operate on his own. Now all he had to do was figure out what they had planned, then determine how to stop that plan and still keep anyone from getting in the line of fire. A full-blown fight on the grounds of a Catholic school would be completely unacceptable. He'd have to play this one very close to the vest.

Keeping his pace slow but steady, he approached the main entrance to the school. He'd obviously been right about the start time, because the place was absolutely packed with vehicles, some of them double-parked to drop off kids, while others rolled through the gate. The Executioner kept his eyes open for any running room, counting vehicles and spaces between them as the numbers ticked off in his head. A group of children traveled along the sidewalks, pressed Catholic uniforms gleaming in the morning sunlight as they proceeded toward their school. Others rode with their parents, a good number of vehicles ranging from BMWs to Mercedes to Bentleys, not to mention a gaggle of imports.

Whatever these guns-for-hire had planned, Bolan was almost positive this would amount to a grab. But of whom? Out of the few hundred, perhaps many hundred children that attended Saint Bartholomew's, why would Godunov have ordered his mercenary team to target just one? Or perhaps two? Bolan's best guess was that they needed these kids for leverage. Volkov had mentioned that Southpaw would be providing some sort of deception, that he would use his "very unique talents" to do that.

Bolan began to consider just what those talents might be, and the best he could figure was that Billy would distract school officials and security while Volkov and his cronies grabbed their prize, stashed it in the van and then made their escape. The police would probably get a description of the sedan and maybe latch on to that, while the others made their escape in the van with their prisoner.

But what could they want? A teacher or other school official? Not likely. He couldn't see any connection between them and the banking industry in New York City, at least not a legit one. That left the most valuable of all. A child! Bolan considered any other viable alternatives, and didn't see any. Volkov's target *had* to be one of the students. They probably planned to smuggle the kid away in the van while they made their escape in the sedan, with all eyes on them.

At first, Bolan wondered if they might be planning to drive the van into the school area and blow it up—the "distraction" that Volkov had originally talked about. On further consideration, he realized that didn't make any sense. These were professional mercenaries operating under Godunov, not terrorists, and he didn't see these types going around committing senseless acts of violence. It wouldn't buy them anything but unwanted attention. No, the Executioner saw a more diabolical plot; one that likely involved one of the schoolkids.

Whatever the plan, Bolan knew he had no choice—he'd have to take down the Wolf and his team.

Hard. Fast. Soon.

BOLAN WAITED until he was within a few feet of the gate and then skirted the line of vehicles by moving into the oncoming lane when he saw an opening. He reached the opposite side of the main entrance and pulled to the curb, as Volkov had directed. The only difference would be that he had formulated his own strategy, one that didn't include waiting in the sedan for the rest of his "team" with the engine running.

It took almost ten minutes for the van to finally make its turn into the parking lot. As soon as they were out of view, Bolan scooped the radio off the seat, got out of the car and walked down the sidewalk to the main gate. A small shelter stood at the entrance, occupied by a lone figure in a plain blue uniform with white shirt and tie. The only thing that marked this guy as staff was the name tag above his breast pocket.

Bolan opened the door and flashed his Homeland Security credentials. The man made a cursory inspection and then his eyebrows rose, his face registering the fact that he was clearly impressed. Obviously, Saint Bartholomew's Catholic Prep School didn't get a lot of federal agents showing up willy-nilly.

"You got a phone in here?" Bolan asked.

The old man nodded. "Yes, sir. Just a house phone, though. Goes to the main building."

"Pick it up, contact the office and tell whoever answers to call the police. Right now."

"Is there a prob—"

Bolan shook his head. "Right now."

Something in the Executioner's look, or maybe just his indomitable presence, prompted the older man to reach for the phone. As he punched in the number, Bolan's eyes flicked to the Plexiglas window of the shelter and watched as the van rolled to a halt to deposit Volkov and Southpaw in front of the doors to the main campus building. Staff mingled with parents outside, herding the children to their classes. Bolan made a quick check of his watch and realized the first bell would sound in less than fifteen minutes.

Whatever Volkov and friends planned to do would have to go down almost immediately, to be successful.

Bolan nodded to the man once he hung up to confirm he'd done well. Then the Executioner returned to his sedan, disengaged the automatic lock on the trunk and withdrew his weapons bag. He took out one of the two satchel charges, made sure the remote detonation receiver was active, then tossed it on the floor of the backseat. He turned and jogged down the sidewalk to the end of the block. Bolan rounded the corner and looked for a place where he could have some privacy. He located a portable toilet—weird place for such a structure, but fortunate—and quickly entered and locked it.

It was cramped but workable.

Bolan stripped off the business attire in favor of his skintight blacksuit and combat boots; he decided to forgo the load-bearing equipment harness this time around. While a number of handy accessories were attached to the LBE—several M-69 fragmentation grenades and a Ka-bar fighting knife included—the Executioner figured he wouldn't have any use for them. This mission called for split-second timing and the crack marksmanship skills that had earned him his reputation.

The soldier crammed the suit and shoes into the bag, shrugged into the shoulder harness holding his Beretta 93-R, and withdrew the FNC. While the carbine-style assault rifle wasn't the most practical tool for this activity, he knew it would do in a pinch due to the plain versatility of the weapon. The FNC had been manufactured with the same care as its 7.62 mm grand-father, the FN-FAL. Chambered for 5.56 mm NATO rounds, the weapon had become a mainstay of Bolan's arsenal primarily due to its accuracy and durability.

And at that distance, even without a scope, he fig-ured the effective range of the rounds he chambered would provide a high first-hit capability.

Bolan returned the weapon to the bag before exiting the portable toilet and heading toward the high wall that bordered the school campus. In the distance, he heard the first wail of sirens as they approached the school. With any luck, he hoped to have the job done and be gone before he attracted any attention whatsoever. The soldier threw the bag over the wall and followed after it, vaulting himself up until he could get a handhold on the wrought-iron spires emerging from the top. He landed on the other side within a few seconds, retrieved the bag, then began to maneuver his way through a nearby copse.

When Bolan had reached the tree line and found a suitable point of cover—behind a tree that branched out in such a way as to provide a V-shaped notch—he knelt and withdrew the FNC. He extended the folding stock and locked it into place with a click, then set the forward hand rest in the notch to steady the weapon, and located the van through the sights. The wall behind him blocked most of the wind, he estimated a distance to target just short of 120 meters.

The Executioner settled the stock against his shoulder and sighted on the driver's side window of the van. He recalled it had been Igor behind the wheel, which meant Keck was in back, since only Southpaw and Volkov had exited. That accounted for only fifty percent of the team, and Bolan didn't take much comfort in those odds. The chance that one or more of them might escape seemed probable. All he could do at this stage of the op was to wait it out and hope for opportunities.

The waiting game had begun.

CHAPTER EIGHT

The Executioner didn't have to wait long.

Maybe two minutes elapsed before he picked up the faint buzz coming from somewhere inside the main building. If he had to venture a guess, it sounded a lot like a fire alarm—that was the distraction Volkov had mentioned. Those fire alarms were known for spraying dye, so Southpaw probably had some sort of electronics background, and had managed to engage the alarm system in some other fashion than pulling it. In either case, such an alarm at this particular time would cause quite a bit of confusion, and in that confusion they would be able to do just about anything.

Bolan made sure the van was clear of bystanders, then squeezed the trigger.

The first 5.56 mm NATO round left the barrel of the FNC at a muzzle velocity of 965 mps. It crossed the expanse in the blink of an eye and shattered the van window. Even from that distance, Bolan saw a spray of blood emanate from the interior, and knew he'd hit his mark. He lifted his eye from the sight only a moment and attempted to locate Volkov or Southpaw. He didn't see either of them, so he returned to the sight and waited for some other sign of movement.

The noise had grown considerably, and Bolan sincerely doubted anyone on-site had even heard the report from the FNC. The sudden movement inside the van at the front confirmed that fact—probably Keck trying to figure out what had happened. Bolan waited a moment to ensure bystanders were still clear of his immediate fire zone, and squeezed off a second shot. He couldn't see any blood this time, but the movement he'd spotted a moment earlier ceased. With any luck, this had also been a kill shot.

The sirens were close now, a clear signal it was time to go.

Bolan stashed the FNC in the weapons bag, shouldered it and returned to the wall. As soon as he reached the opposite side and cleared the side street for police vehicles, he dashed down the sidewalk to the corner. Bolan stopped in the shade of a tree that grew just outside the wall, its spreading canopy showering him in shadows. He waited one minute, watching with interest as the first police vehicles began to arrive.

Another wailing siren, this one a little deeper, started up in the near distance, and Bolan figured it was probably the fire-rescue units. If he stood any chance of taking all of Volkov's team, he would have to do so soon. It didn't take long for his full plan to come to fruition as he saw Volkov and Southpaw emerge from the gate entrance and rush toward the sedan. They didn't have anybody with them. *Good*. Bolan had managed to prevent them from accomplishing their mission. The pair stood just beside the sedan a moment, clearly uncertain what to do, but then Southpaw opened the driver side door and made some gesture to Volkov.

The two men jumped into the car.

Bolan smiled. He'd left the keys in the vehicle on

purpose, knowing full well their survival instinct would be strong. They weren't fanatics or terrorists; they were mercenaries, and as such lived purely for fortune and glory. The engine roared to life and the sedan edged away from the havoc, heading on a direct course for Bolan's position. As soon as they were clear of the area, Bolan withdrew the remote detonator, keyed the transmitter switch and pressed the button. He turned away and made the cover of the thick tree trunk just a moment before the blast whip-cracked through the clear morning air. A red-orange fireball consumed the sedan interior a millisecond after, with enough superheated gas to force the windshield to implode before it came away completely from the frame.

The sedan kept rolling another ten feet before it bounced onto the sidewalk and the friction on the undercarriage caused it to grind to a halt. Bolan didn't give the sedan another glance as he trotted back to the portable toilet and changed into his business attire. By the time the police and fire department sorted it out, he would be aboard a transit commuter headed back to the city.

Just another businessman headed for the office.

BARBARA PRICE'S footsteps echoed back at her as she entered the annex on a mission to find Harold Brognola.

She could barely keep the sheaf of reports under her arm, the financial information of more than one hundred possible RBN supporters. In most cases, the intelligence they'd pulled had proved anything but useful—most of the people on the list were heads of major corporations, or other executive officers who seemed clean enough. They paid their taxes on time, maintained good reputations and were involved in their communities.

Of course, many corporate bigwigs were infamous for keeping up appearances while they did drugs, engaged prostitutes and gambled away small fortunes in backroom poker games at the seediest establishments society had to offer. Somehow they managed to keep squeaky clean in their personal and professional finances.

Price found Brognola in the briefing room of the operations center. The Stony Man chief sat at the table, working an unlit cigar in one corner of his mouth. An LCD terminal-style monitor—one of many that folded out of the long table—cast a blue-white glow against his skin.

"Good morning," Price said.

Brognola only grunted in acknowledgment, obviously fixated on calling up data on his computer.

Price sat in a chair across from him and set down the thick folder of papers with a sigh of relief. She placed her palm on top of the pile with emphasis. "I've just finished pulling that candidacy list, based on the holdings in Godunov's bogus investment firm. We have nearly one hundred names here, and they're all strong possibilities."

That caused Brognola to stop what he was doing and look at her intently as he pulled the cigar from his mouth. "Did you say *all* of them?"

"I did."

"We couldn't narrow it down more than that?"

Price smiled. "That's down from a list of over two thousand Aaron and I started with early this morning. Striker's hit against Yan Volkov and his team turned up a number of surprising connections. Most of these companies that have been funneling dollars through the RBN are run by notables in the high-society circuit. They're multimillion-dollar CEOs and investors in foreign exchanges."

"Well, if Godunov and the RBN have a decent game going for them, why the need to bring in Lutrova?"

"I think the well is starting to run dry. With the high level of security-backed debts and financial derivatives that are completely valueless in the American economy, the real money now has to come back. They plan to suck the financial system dry of whatever's left of the cash, and plan to get it through whatever means are available."

"So what's the significance of the people on this list?"

"Well, these are all major players in companies that do business with Godunov's firm, either directly or through a string of overseas shell and paper companies. You see, while the idea of bank cartels is considered a theory of extremists or anarchists, they actually exist. And they serve at the pleasure of the criminal element on a global scale."

"I don't doubt that," Brognola said with a halfhearted chuckle. "They pick my pocket every April 15."

Price smiled. "That's often where it starts, to be sure. But the reason they choose to hide their monies in derivatives is because of the way it spreads it out. They extend into interest rates, foreign exchange, commodities and equities, and so forth. This gives them a way to hide the money until it's needed. But because the derivatives have no value, they can't be converted to hard cash quickly. And the RBN is always in need of that, because it's virtually untraceable in the exchange-based world economy today."

"And these individuals who've amassed the wealth are now being told they're going to have to part with it," Hal mused. "Which means they're not going to be too happy when the message gets delivered."

"Right," Price said. "That's where this list comes in. Combined, these people possess twenty-three percent of the liquid cash assets within the New York financial system."

Brognola whistled.

"Striker said that Volkov and his team tried to pull off something at a Saint Bartholomew's Catholic Prep School in upstate New York." Price turned to a nearby terminal and typed rapidly on the keyboard. A minute later, the large screen at the end of the table lit up with the face of a young, handsome man of Hispanic descent. "We cross-referenced the names of staff and children at the school, looking for any sort of connection. We found one. This man is Eduardo Capistrano, founder and CEO of Lansing Underwater Technologies."

"Whoa, that's big time," Brognola interjected. "Even I know that name."

"Most anyone who keeps up on weekly business news does," Price replied. "His organization, just one of the several he owns, has private and government contracts in a volume that's unprecedented for any manufacturing firm in the American industrial base today, let alone the rest of the world. Capistrano had a self-made fortune by the age of twenty-four. He's socially reclusive and this picture is quite old, since he despises being photographed."

"So we think Capistrano's being squeezed in some way?"

"Absolutely. He has a son and daughter that attend Saint Bartholomew's, and that's where Volkov said they had a mission. Striker thinks Volkov's team planned to kidnap the children as insurance for Capistrano's assistance."

"Assistance in what?"

"Well, we're not positive, but it's entirely probable that Godunov's using him in some way with their plan to bilk the industry dry."

"Let's think about this a second," Brognola said. "Suppose that you want to get your hands on all the financial holdings of the wealthiest individuals in a given financial sector. In this case, we've obviously narrowed the target to New York City. Now, the only way to do that is crack the banking security network, which we know Bogdan Lutrova claims to have done."

"And which we're ready to shut down once Lutrova makes the program active," Price interjected.

"The only problem is you can't move this kind of money in cash without generating a whole lot of paperwork. One currency transaction report filing to the government by a foreign operation inside the country, such as Godunov's firm, in this case, and the FBI will have agents crawling all over the place."

"So they plan to move the holdings into offshore accounts electronically?"

"Right," Brognola replied. "And the only way to do that is to get inside the physical plant."

"Well, Capistrano *is* a member of the risk assessment team at the Chase Manhattan Company, given his vast financial experience."

"Which is also where Godunov happens to have his front company."

"That must be the target, Hal," Price said. "It makes absolutely perfect sense."

"We need to let Striker know as soon as possible."

EDUARDO CAPISTRANO checked his watch as he entered the Chase One Plaza.

He couldn't believe he'd made it here so soon after getting his kids off to school, then climbing into his Mercedes and having Nick chauffeur him into the city. The man who called himself Yuri Godunov had been quite clear regarding his expectations. Eduardo believed every word the Russian said when he threatened to take his kids and sell them into the human trafficking sector. He was a very dangerous man, much more dangerous than anyone Capistrano had ever had to deal with before. Until now, Capistrano had a sweet deal, but that time had come to an end.

His palms were sweaty as he handed his identification badge to the guard and dropped his briefcase onto the conveyor that would pass it through X-ray. His skin felt clammy and his face flushed, and he hoped it didn't show too much. Capistrano had followed Godunov's instructions completely, including having no cell phone devices on him and providing no way for anyone to get in touch with him. He'd also arrived a little earlier than usual so as not to draw much attention from people.

Capistrano's hopes that his nervousness wouldn't show were empty. One of the guards, a guy who Capistrano faintly recalled having seen on a number of occasions before, seemed to recognize him immediately.

"Hey, there, Mr. Capistrano." The guy cheerily greeted him with a heavy Bronx accent. "How you doing today?"

"Fine, fine," Capistrano replied, his voice a little hoarse.

"Hey, Mr. Capistrano, you feeling okay?" the guard asked. "You don't look so hot, sir."

He tried to smile. Wilkins…Eddie Wilkins! That was the guard's name. "Yeah, Eddie, just fine."

"You remembered my name."

"Of course," Capistrano said, in a quick recovery. "I try to remember everybody's name, Eddie."

"Well, thanks a lot, Mr. Capistrano," Wilkins said as he handed over his briefcase. "Most people aren't so generous."

"My pleasure."

Capistrano took the briefcase, turned on his heel and continued to the bank of elevators. He checked his watch again as he stabbed the call button, then waited for what seemed an insufferable amount of time. He'd been forced to tell Nick to wait in the car, that he wouldn't be long. There were a dozen preparations he needed to make before Godunov's man could actually slip inside to get the job done.

Once they had the information, and had moved whatever money they could, Capistrano knew that the list of those who were tapped out would have to be eliminated. He wondered how he could have ever allowed himself to become so soft. When he'd first started out in this business, Capistrano had earned a reputation for being utterly ruthless and cunning as a businessman. He'd also been known to operate in much the same way on his less than legitimate dealings. Sure, the occasional kickback or shady deal came with some risk; he'd always known that, really.

But this was something else entirely. This Godunov had threatened not only Capistrano's life, but those of his kids. And Capistrano knew that Godunov would make good on the threat, when it came right down to it. He could only hope that Godunov would view his cooperation as a sign that he wouldn't cause trouble, and maybe, just maybe, Godunov would keep his word to get out of Capistrano's hair.

If nothing else, Capistrano knew he had plausible deniability. If the authorities questioned him, he could claim complete ignorance, citing that whatever improprieties had been committed were done behind his back and in his name. Sure, he'd signed many of the documents, but not really understanding all of the legalese. Yes, that was it! He could claim he'd been the victim of fraud and corporate abuse. He could swear to set things right and no longer allow such activities to go on within *any* of his companies. And of course he would be happy to let federal agents come to his operations in the future and inspect the books anytime they liked.

Yeah, Capistrano was already forming the heart-wrenching speech he'd give the jury, telling them how he'd been duped by people he thought he could trust. In an age of progressive concepts like social and economic equality, the redistribution of wealth, he could claim that he was just trying to look out for the little guy while his executive officers committed all this heinous fraud.

Capistrano felt better as he boarded the elevator, his stomach a little less queasy as the doors closed and he felt the shift of gravity as the car started to move. He had only about an hour to prepare for the arrival of Godunov and whoever else might show up, and he didn't want anything to go wrong in the process. He couldn't allow anything to happen to himself or his children.

He would do whatever it took to keep all of them alive.

CHAPTER NINE

As soon as Mack Bolan arrived in New York City, he made contact with Stony Man Farm to give them an update on recent developments, as well as the demise of Volkov and his mercenary team. He'd opted not to use his cell phone so he wouldn't be overheard, so a pay phone in an abandoned subway station did the trick nicely.

Though he'd eliminated Volkov's team, he knew the mission was far from over. It would take some time before Godunov even became aware the situation had gone south for Volkov, and that his chief gun-for-hire was no longer in the picture. Bolan couldn't be sure how Volkov fit into the RBN crime czar's plans, but he figured there would be a time and place to concern himself with that, and this wasn't it.

When Bolan arrived as his hotel, he changed out of the suit and donned the more casual attire he'd worn before—black polo shirt, tan slacks and a brown leather jacket. A pair of deck shoes completed the ensemble, but with special, nonslip neoprene soles. He stripped and cleaned the Beretta, returned it to its shoulder holster, then proceeded to clean the FNC. Before he was through, Bolan knew, he'd need some additional firepower. The remaining satchel of C-4 plastic explosives wouldn't provide the kind of show he intended to unleash against Godunov's estate.

The plan was that once he got a foothold inside the organization, posing as Lambretta, and managed to eliminate the front-line opposition, he would then turn to the task of hitting the RBN where it hurt most. That meant going after the organization's business interests—a meth lab near the river, a staging house for human trafficking operations and a business front for money laundering. All of the information had come firsthand from Kurtzman and team, who had used their high-tech wizardry to identify the obviously bogus real-estate investments of Vastok & Karamakov, Ltd.

But first Bolan needed wheels and fresh armament.

Plenty of 5.56 mm ammunition remained for the FNC, so in order to avoid carrying additional munitions he figured it was best to get something compatible. Stony Man had connections in nearly every city for this kind of thing, but the Executioner didn't really have time to run that down. He was in complete blitz mode now; the numbers were running down, and it was important he take out the appetizers before hitting the main course. It would be the only way to keep Godunov on the run, ultimately boxing him into a corner exactly where Bolan wanted him.

A phone call to a nearby contact bought him a meet in thirty minutes.

Bolan slung his bag over his back and took the elevator to the first floor. With the rental he'd picked up in Boston now just a scorched shell, he figured it was time to reach out to friends. He left his key card at the front desk, as was his custom before heading out for an op, then grabbed a cab into a not-so-nice area of Brooklyn. The cabbie obviously thought him a nut when Bolan asked to be let out on a filthy, quiet street in one of the worst sections of town, but he didn't argue when Bolan passed him a fifty.

Once the cab was out of sight, Bolan walked a half block to a house he hadn't seen in some time. Oddly, the place didn't look all that different than the last time Bolan had paid a visit to this part of New York. It was a typical multifamily dwelling: narrow and stories tall, with a white clapboard exterior. A large casement window took up half the front, and a crumbling brick-and-mortar stairwell led up to a dirty door with cheap, metal house numbers nailed to it.

Bolan climbed the steps and rapped twice.

The rest of the street remained eerily quiet, the echo of a dog barking the only sound in the overcast morning. The winds had died, but the sun that had appeared earlier that morning during Bolan's rendezvous with Volkov had given way to a heavy cloud cover. At least it had gotten a bit warmer; it would be a perfect time for an assault against the purveyors of death.

The door whipped open and a short, skinny man covered in a layer of grime stood there. He wore torn jeans and an old long-underwear top that hadn't been white since the latter part of the Reagan years. A plaid flannel shirt of indistinguishable color covered most of the latter, except for where it hung open in front. He wore his dingy hair in a ponytail and sported a matching salt-and-pepper beard. The only striking thing about the man was his light green eyes.

Bolan immediately noted the hint of a pistol butt peeking from the waistband of the guy's jeans.

For a moment, the man didn't say a word, then his eyes grew wide. "I'll be dog shit on the sidewalk. Striker!"

Bolan looked around to make sure nobody had overheard, and then held out his hand. The guy immediately took it and then pulled him forward in an awkward embrace. Bolan didn't reciprocate, but just let the guy have his moment. Once it had passed, he was invited inside.

To have called Tom Remick anything but a patriot would have been an understatement. A veteran of the Vietnam War and a dozen other skirmishes in the aftermath, Remick was a soldier's soldier. It was too bad that after twenty-four years of service he lost it all when taking a bullet that shattered his kneecap and effectively ended his career. He left the service on a medical, at the rank of first sergeant, with full pension and benefits. But the scars he carried weren't something Remick could live with, and he quickly fell to drugs and poverty, the natural order for disturbed vets that don't get the proper care.

Remick had been anything but disillusioned, however. He decided to take up the one profession in which he could earn a decent living: gunsmith. Remick soon realized that customizing and repairing guns was only the tip of the iceberg, and before long he'd become involved in arms dealing. But Remick was no ordinary gunrunner. He was a master at arms, providing weapons only to the most law-abiding citizens, on the basis they had a constitutional right and obligation to protect themselves.

While most purchases were under the table, cash-only deals with no registration or paperwork required, Remick didn't sell to just anyone. And every purchase typically meant the individual would have to take Remick's course—part of the fee they paid for one of his untraceable guns—along with a solemn oath they would only use the weapon he provided for defense. Most would have thought the man crazy, but Mack Bolan knew better. Remick was a force for good who believed that if America was to stay great, its citizens would have to be responsible with the tools that were provided to defend life and liberty.

Remick waved Bolan toward a seat, a ratty sofa covered with a layer of fine dust. "Take a load off, pal."

"I'd like to," Bolan said. "But I'm here on very official business."

Remick chuckled and bared a row of tobacco-stained, crooked teeth. The ones that were real, anyway. "All business and no fun. You're going to turn dull, Striker."

Bolan had never told Remick his real name—hadn't even given him his cover name—although the man hadn't seemed to mind. When they first encountered each other it had nearly been the death of Remick. He liked to tell the story different, and Bolan afforded him that much.

"What the hell's wrong with you?" Remick asked. "You don't call, you don't write…."

"I've been busy," Bolan replied with a knowing smile.

The vet waved at him. "Aw, the hell with ya. No sense of humor."

Bolan gave him the ghost of a smile. "About my business…"

"Yeah, yeah." Remick reached into the refrigerator, probably one of the most modern fixtures in the entire house, and retrieved a beer. He offered one to Bolan, who shook his head, then popped the top and gulped half the contents. Smacking his lips with a smile of pure satisfaction, foam from the beer still playing across his upper lip, he said, "What have you got on your mind?"

"I'm in need of some hardware."

"Light or heavy?"

"Heavy."

"Well, then, my friend," Remick replied with a belch, "come on this-a-way."

Bolan followed him through the kitchen to the back of the house. They went outside and negotiated a path of chipped, deteriorating flagstone mixed with sand that led to a one-car garage barely big enough for an Italian sports car, let alone a midsize vehicle. Remick unlocked the door, then reached through it and flipped a switch on the wall before entering. Bolan didn't see any lights come on, so he figured Remick had either alarmed or booby-trapped the garage against unwanted visitors.

Once they were inside, Remick closed the door, enshrouding them both in darkness. Only a moment elapsed before Bolan saw movement, and the floor gave way, revealing a steeply inclined stairwell leading into a cellarlike space. The soldier had to duck to avoid hitting his head on the low ceiling, but he was no less impressed. Racks of firearms lined the walls, nearly every kind of variant imaginable. The choices ranged from machine pistols to military-grade machine guns. Yes, the Executioner had definitely made the right choice, coming here.

Remick downed the last of his beer, crushed the can and tossed it into a garbage can filled to the rim with them. He watched as it tumbled onto the floor, looked as if he planned to pick it up, then waved the incident away. He then made a grand, sweeping gesture to the library of destruction surrounding them.

"What's your pleasure?"

"I'll need something in 5.56 mm," Bolan said as he walked the narrow aisles. The weapons were in locked racks, with a giant table in the center. He knew that beneath that table would be plenty of additional arms, probably enough to fight a small war, but he didn't think he'd have to encourage Remick to break into that stash.

The perfect choice caught Bolan's practiced eye. He turned and pointed to the weapon like a bird dog on a quail in the bush. Remick smiled and walked over to liberate Bolan's choice from behind the lock bar. Bolan hefted the M-16 A-3/M-203 combo. Like its predecessors, the M-16 A-3 variant was a highly accurate and reliable weapon, but the special appeal of this one was that Remick had removed the carrying rail to reduce the weapon profile. He'd also equipped it with a highly advanced electro-optical, multipurpose reflex sight. Designed by a company in Or Akiva against the exacting standards of the Israeli Special Forces, the sight provided both passive and active reflex, along with red or IR laser designators. The M-203 just sweetened the sale.

Bolan reached into his pocket and withdrew a fifty-note bundle of hundred-dollar bills. He handed it to Remick, who didn't even bother to count it, but instead stuffed the cash in the breast pocket of his flannel shirt.

Remick clapped Bolan on the shoulder. "Need any ammo?"

Bolan shook his head. "All set on that side. Could use another box or two of 9 mm, though."

"Hard ball or SJHPs?"

"Box of each should do."

Remick went to a metal safe beneath a case that sported machine pistols, and punched in a five-digit combination on the electronic keypad. The safe opened immediately and he withdrew the requested munitions. He started to close it, snapped his fingers, then withdrew an OD green satchel. He set it on the massive table and opened it for Bolan's inspection. The Executioner spotted the half-dozen 40 mm HE grenades inside, and nodded. Remick dropped the two boxes of 9 mm into the bag and cinched it up.

He glanced at the weapons bag on Bolan's shoulder. "Doesn't look like that's going to hold the Colt. You got any other options?"

"I was hoping you knew somebody who could hook me up with wheels," Bolan said. "I need something midsize, probably a small SUV."

"Toyota 4-Runner do you?"

"Perfect."

"I'll make a call."

As they climbed the stairs and Remick sealed up the armory, he said, "Wish I was a little younger, Striker. I'd volunteer to join up with you on this one."

"You wouldn't want to follow me where I'm going."

Remick clasped the lock with a snap, then his eyes flicked to Bolan. Even if the very dim light streaming through the edges of the construction paper covered by plastic garbage bags, Bolan could see that what he'd said disturbed Remick. The Executioner hadn't meant it to come as an insult.

"You know goddamn good and well I'd follow you into any hellfire you could drum up, my friend," Remick said. "You must understand by now. I owe you my life... and then some. There ain't a place on this godforsaken blue marble where I wouldn't mix it up with you. Not a one, even if it meant the time had come to meet my maker."

"I got that," Bolan replied. "But this has to be my fight. You know that."

"I know," Remick said. "I don't always understand why you feel you have to walk it alone, but I know. We'll always be brothers in blood, though. Eh, Striker?"

"That we will, Tom," Bolan replied.

THE EXECUTIONER'S ride showed less than a half hour after Remick made his call. True to his word, someone delivered the SUV out back.

Bolan loaded it up, said his goodbyes and soon was headed for a warehouse in the waterfront district not too far from where he'd first met Volkov. Bolan considered his options on this first run and realized there weren't many. He'd be hitting the facility in broad daylight, and there wouldn't be much running room. A recon was in order first. He parked his SUV in an empty lot that provided coin-operated telescopes bordering a walking path, and then scrambled down a rocky crag until he reached the gritty, crushed-rock shore of the river.

Bolan had removed the viewfinder from the M-16 A-3/M-203 combo and now used it to observe the warehouse.

Fortunately, it occupied a fairly large space void of bystanders, a natural choice, since they were ostensibly manufacturing methamphetamines inside. The warrior panned the entire grounds. A few trucks and a couple of pallet loaders were parked outside, but there wasn't any activity. Bolan lowered the sight, took a deep breath and forcibly let it out through puffed cheeks. It was *too* quiet. Seemed overly easy, in fact. He had learned long ago that rushing into situations like this usually got a person killed.

It didn't amount to skill; it amounted to overconfidence and underestimation of the enemy.

According to Stony Man's intelligence, this place was cranking out several thousand kilos of meth per month. It was no small operation—just what he would have expected from a high-resource organization like the RBN—with a vast distribution network that extended far beyond the borders of New York City. Not that they really needed it, since there were plenty of mules and other unsavory types willing to move the product whenever and wherever.

Bolan was about to put an end to that deal.

He was starting to turn away when the reflection of

light off metal caught his eye. Bolan raised the sight and peered through it. It took him only a moment to spot the source of the reflection: two men were on the roof. He hadn't seen them at first, as they'd been obscured by the high parapet running along the front of the warehouse.

Sentries—at least two of them, and they were armed.

At this distance Bolan figured they didn't even notice him. That's what he'd sensed before—something that was very wrong with the picture. With a nod of satisfaction, he turned and made his way back up to the parking lot. Returning the optical sight to its mount, he secured it, then put the M-16 A-3/M-203 muzzle-first on the floor. He started the vehicle, backed out and headed toward the bridge that would take him across the river and into the heart of the militarized zone.

As he drove, Bolan began to formulate his plan for taking the place down. The sentries would have to go first, no doubt about it, but the only way to do that would be with one of the grenades. Using the ordnance so early would reduce the time window significantly. He would have to rely on the element of surprise on this go-around. He had considered simply burning the place to ashes, since the amount of chemicals inside would prove a toxic combination for the enemy, but he couldn't bring himself to initiate a scorched-earth policy until he was one hundred percent vested in the viability of the target.

Bolan had always operated in a responsible fashion. He made certain to keep the bystanders well out of the way before taking on the enemy, and he never dropped the hammer on a cop. They were brothers on the same side, and the Executioner had adopted a policy of escape and evade whenever it came to potential contact with the police.

But this time it would be a hit and git. He would have to move very fast now that Volkov was out of the picture; otherwise Godunov would gain the advantage and most likely disappear into the smoke before Bolan had time to set the record straight. Whatever happened in the next forty-eight hours or so, he knew one thing for certain.

The enemy would have no corner left to hide in. They would find no escape.

The Executioner was about to turn it all upside down.

CHAPTER TEN

Mack Bolan's strategy against the enemy was simple.

Hit them with a full-on frontal assault, and if they responded in kind, he knew he had the right place. There was a small chance that the men on the roof were actually innocent bystanders, and the information he had been given was false. The Executioner wasn't willing to take that chance; he had always remained vigilant when it came to insuring the safety of noncombatants.

Fortunately, the enemy responded exactly as he had expected them to. As Bolan rounded the turn onto the single-lane road leading to the front gates of the warehouse, he steadily increased pressure on the accelerator. By the time he reached the gates, the SUV was traveling at better than 60 mph. The chain-link gates—secured only by a simple lever mechanism—proved no match for the velocity of Bolan's vehicle. The latch gave on impact and the gates imploded with the wrenching sound of metal on metal.

The pair on the roof immediately brought their weapons to bear. Bolan could now see they were toting H&K submachine guns as they began to rain a hailstorm of lead on his position. The soldier continued across the parking lot until he managed to get the SUV close to the warehouse. He continued on, driving full speed parallel to the building. The steel-and-aluminum exterior raced by a mere foot from his window. As soon as Bolan reached a point where he believed it would cover him adequately, he jammed on the brakes and put the vehicle into a power slide. Simultaneously, he jerked the wheel and sent the rear of the vehicle spinning until the nose now pointed in the direction from which he'd been traveling.

As Bolan climbed from the vehicle he brought the M-203 grenade launcher into play. He leveled its muzzle at approximately a thirty-degree angle and squeezed the trigger. The shotgun-style report of the weapon masked the plunk of the 40 mm HE grenade as it left the launcher. The grenade performed a graceful arc, traveling well past the gunners, who now scrambled to get some sort of decent firing solution on their enemy. Their enthusiasm was admirable, but would ultimately prove to be the chief cause of their demise. No amount of resolve could defeat the destructive force of the modern weapons of war. This was something those two aggressors learned the hard way as the grenade landed just a few feet from their position. The red-orange explosion and resulting fireball instantaneously burned the skin from their bones, and the concussion blew limbs from torsos.

Bolan didn't wait to observe the totality of the effect, but focused on the door that led inside. He tried the knob but it wouldn't budge, so he stepped back a foot or so and kicked it with enough force to break it off the door. He then withdrew one of the quarter-pound sticks of C-4, which he had already primed with a blasting cap for just such an eventuality. Bolan applied it in the hole left by the broken handle, yanked the pin back on the M-1 fuse igniter, and then crouched behind the relative safety of the SUV.

It took the burning fuse only a few seconds to reach the blasting cap and detonation cord wrapped around the C-4. The heat and pressure did their job, the deadly combination setting off the plastic explosives. The force blew the door completely off its hinges and left a jagged frame of molten metal and scorched wood in its wake. Bolan rose and advanced into the fiery, smoke-filled interior of the warehouse on a simple mission: search and destroy.

YURI GODUNOV looked at the clock on the wall.

He hadn't heard from Volkov, who was now more than forty-five minutes overdue on his scheduled check-in. Had something gone wrong? This wasn't the way they had planned it, and although Volkov had disappointed him on occasions, he was still a professional. He wouldn't have missed a check-in unless something was amiss.

Then again, even if they hadn't accomplished the mission of kidnapping Eduardo Capistrano's kids, it didn't necessarily mean Godunov couldn't go forward with his plans. Capistrano had already agreed to cooperate, and the threats against his family would probably be enough to keep the financier in line. If nothing else, Godunov knew he had the option of exploring other avenues to achieve his ends. Still, he felt it would be better if he could talk to the Wolf and ensure that things were going exactly as he'd planned.

And then there was Bogdan Lutrova. A young genius to be certain, but one who Godunov knew he couldn't trust; at least, he couldn't trust him *completely*. Since he'd ransomed Lutrova from the man who claimed his name was Frankie Lambretta, Godunov had noticed Lutrova grow increasingly distant and isolated. He didn't seem the least bit grateful that Godunov had paid money to secure his release, not to mention that Godunov hadn't opted to use more direct means of interrogating him. *Trust*. It wasn't a word used casually by Godunov or his superiors. It wasn't just a catchword of the day; the ability to trust those who worked around you, and to know their loyalties with certainty, was the mainstay of the Russian Business Network.

That was something else that bothered Godunov, although a minor irritation in contrast to his many other worries. Internally, they didn't refer to themselves in this way. They had been called by many names: the RBN, the Russian Mafia, and a half-dozen other monikers—none of which described the true nature of their organization. The Brotherhood of Social Justice had managed to maintain a certain amount of secrecy and anonymity among their ranks. It was part of Godunov's responsibilities to protect the traditions of the organization; his master in Russia expected it and had no reservations about visiting punishment on anyone who violated that code. So the answer seemed simple enough: after the mission was finished, Bogdan Lutrova had to die. For now Godunov would have to keep one eye on the young computer hacker at all times, while keeping his other eye on the mission objectives.

Oddly, a feeling of dread crept into Godunov's gut in the form of a cold, hard knot. It was almost certain the feeling had something to do with the fact that

Volkov hadn't checked in yet. Something had gone terribly wrong with their plan, and Godunov knew deep down that he could be left without any support. If that turned out to be the case, and at this point he had good reason to think it was, then he would have to exploit his own resources in order to ensure security on the operation.

He reached to the phone on his desk. "Send Stepan in here immediately," he told the young secretary who answered.

Stepan Godunov had become chief of security for his uncle three years earlier, and with very good reason. Like Volkov, Stepan had been involved in a number of the skirmishes that occurred in Russia during the nineties, along with participation in advanced military training conducted by former members of the Russian special forces. Stepan had demonstrated his talents on more than one occasion and proved himself as competent as Volkov—if not more so—when it came to applying his very unique talents. He wouldn't have been Godunov's first choice to take Volkov's place, particularly given the danger and increased possibility of them being discovered every minute they remained in America. But Godunov knew these were special circumstances that called for special methods in order to accomplish the goals of the Brotherhood of Social Justice.

Stepan was tall, lean and muscular, nearly six foot six, with a body hardened by years of physical and mental training—a force to be reckoned with. After entering his uncle's office and waiting a respectful amount of time, he said, "You called for me?"

"Yes," Godunov replied. "The Wolf has missed his check-in and I'm very concerned he may have been compromised."

"I can understand your concern," Stepan said. "However, his failure to contact you cannot be casually construed as either a failure of his mission or an indication something has gone wrong."

"You assume I have already written him off?"

Stepan's eyebrows rose. "I would think you know me well enough by now to know I assume nothing. All I'm saying is that we should not panic merely because the Wolf has missed one check-in. There are any number of viable explanations, and until we have something more definitive, we can only go on what we know."

"And exactly what is it we know?" Godunov asked.

"We know that we have not heard from him, which means we can assume he is either unable or unwilling to contact us. Anything more than that, based on the facts and evidence, would be presumptuous, and only serve to increase panic. Panic leads to mistakes and mistakes lead to failure. If it will make you feel better, I will send two of my men upstate to find out what's happening."

Godunov sat back in his seat and chuckled. "You never cease to amaze me, Stepan. The tutors and trainers who oversaw your education earned their exorbitant fees. You are a logical and reasonable individual, not without empathy or compassion, and yet still decisively effective whenever the situation calls for it. So yes, you are absolutely correct, and I would appreciate you sending your men to determine the Wolf's position."

"You may consider it—"

The phone on the desk rang, cutting off Stepan's statement. Godunov snatched up the receiver and said, "I'm in a conference."

"Sir, I'm very sorry to interrupt you but the call is urgent. It's from the plant manager at the river. I told him you were in a meeting, but he insisted I tell you that they have a major import issue on their hands."

Godunov's feeling of dread increased a hundred-fold. Every one of the shell companies operated by his investment firm—or at least what the rest of the world *thought* was an investment firm—had been given as list of code phrases. They had been instructed to use those phrases under very specific conditions and for very specific situations. In this instance, a "major import issue" was an indication that the location calling had been compromised by law enforcement or competitors, and that there was imminent action in progress requiring armed response by the small security forces Stepan had trained to protect each location and its assets. This was the first time any personnel within America had called to declare such an emergency.

It left little doubt in Godunov's mind that the Americans were onto their scheme. He couldn't help but wonder how much of this had to do with the fact that Yan Volkov hadn't checked in.

"Tell them I understand, and I will be sending some-one immediately."

"I would be happy to do that, Mr. Godunov," the secretary said. "But he does sound rather panicked. Are you sure you don't want to speak to him personally?"

"Just do as I say!" he snapped, before slamming down the handset.

"What's wrong?" Stepan asked.

Godunov looked him in the eye and said, "I believe that the trouble some of the Wolf's men ran into up in Boston may now have found its way here."

"Our mysterious enemy?" Stepan replied with a mocking tone. "This man who generates stories of seemingly appearing out of nowhere and taking on a group of trained soldiers as if they were first-week recruits?"

"The killing of the Wolf's team was anything but a random act," Godunov said. "And given the fact that he has not checked in, and I now have one of our people at the riverside facility calling to say they've been compromised, I can only assume our entire plans have been, as well."

"What do you want to do?"

"Send as many men as you feel are necessary to protect the remaining locations," Godunov said.

"You believe they are in danger, as well?"

"It is my turn to use the same logic that you used a minute earlier, nephew. We can only assume that if one location was compromised, more may become so. We cannot afford that, particularly since part of our plan depends on our ability to move the liquid assets out of the country at a moment's notice. They are counting on us back in Saint Petersburg. We cannot fail. If we do, it will not only mean the end of our lives, but might well mean sending the brotherhood into social anarchy. We cannot have that. Ever."

"I understand," Stepan replied. "I will leave immediately. But what about the warehouse? You do not want me to send anyone there?"

Godunov shook his head. "I fear by the time you arrive, there will be nothing left. We can consider everything at that facility as being forfeit. Even if the hit was not the handiwork of the mysterious agent our men encountered in Boston, it is most likely police or FBI, or even their Homeland Security. In any case, we can no longer count on the facility as a point of income or refuge. Let's take care of what remains rather than what is already lost."

"Consider it done," Stepan replied.

Godunov gave no consideration to the fact that within twenty-four hours this entire facet of the operation would be gone. What he had neglected to tell Lutrova, a purposeful omission, was that the computer hacker would be here when the place actually went up. Lining the room was a disbursement system connected to pipes containing hydrochloric acid and ammonia gas. When the two were mixed, the toxic combination would destroy not only everything in the room but everyone, as well. The doors were self-sealing, which meant that once the system was activated nobody would be able to leave or enter. Hence, it would be some time before anyone knew something was wrong.

By that time, Yuri Godunov would be long gone and the enemies of the Brotherhood of Social Justice would be destroyed.

WHAT YURI GODUNOV didn't know was that the Executioner planned to confine the destruction to the enemy, and he had a lot of experience doing that very thing.

This was something the Russian Business Network had come to learn at some cost.

Two gunmen tried to pin the soldier down in the hallway leading from the back offices to the warehouse proper. He took the first one out with two shots from the M-16 A-3. The 5.56 mm rounds punched through the man's head, one entering the fleshy part of his neck just below the jaw, while the second left his skull in fragments. The remaining RBN terrorist tried to kill Bolan with a fusillade of submachine gun rounds, but the big American threw his body to the floor at the last moment and the 9 mm stingers burned the air overhead.

A cluster of gunners burst through the door at the far end of the hallway. Bolan realized taking them with small-arms fire was no longer practical. He triggered a steady salvo to neutralize the immediate threat, his shots ripping a bloody pattern in the RBN gunman from crotch to sternum.

Bolan then turned his attention to the new arrivals, who took up firing positions from whatever meager cover they could find. He estimated the distance at thirty feet, leveled the muzzle of the M-203 to a suitable angle and squeezed the trigger. The 40 mm grenade traveled the distance in under a second and exploded just above the door frame. The high-explosive charge rained a powerful, concussive blast onto the gunmen. As the thunderous reports from the explosion died out, Bolan could hear the screams of dying enemies. He rose and advanced down the hallway, putting mercy rounds into two men who were moaning from terrible wounds that were fatal but hadn't rendered instantaneous death.

Flames began to consume the hallway, licking up the walls, and somewhere behind Bolan a fire alarm went off. If he didn't miss his guess, it wouldn't be long before firefighters began to arrive, and with them would come New York's finest. Especially if some casual observer had reported the sounds of explosions and gunfire coming from his area of operation. An encounter with the boys in blue wasn't something he could afford right now.

Bolan continued through the warehouse at a brisk clip, encountering only one other resister in his sweep. The guy appeared from around a massive support pillar with a pistol in his hands. He spotted the Executioner and attempted to cut him down, but appeared to fumble with the weapon. Obviously he wasn't a professional, and even as Bolan swung the M-16 A-3 into target acquisition, he realized the guy would never get a shot off in time.

The Executioner's shot blew the pistol out of the man's hand, taking a finger in the process, effectively disarming him but not inflicting a fatal wound. The guy let out a shout of agony. Bolan moved over to him and ripped a battlefield dressing from his jacket pocket. He tore into the thick, plastic package and held it out to the man, who was now on his knees. The guy, obviously Hispanic, looked uncertainly at Bolan for a moment before taking the offered bandage.

"What's your name?" Bolan asked as he crouched beside him.

"Alfonse."

"Who do you work for? Who owns this warehouse?"

"I do not know," he said. "I know that it is an investment property, nothing more."

"You know a man named Godunov?"

The man nodded. "Yes, that is right. Mr. Godunov."

"Did you know they manufacture drugs here? Drugs that are shipped off and sold to the people of this country?"

The man's eyes grew wide and Bolan could tell from his reaction that he hadn't been aware of this. He was just a hardworking stiff trying to defend his workplace from a violent intruder. Bolan extended a hand to help him to his feet.

"Get out of here," Bolan said. "As soon as the cops and firefighters arrive, tell them to make sure the fire doesn't spread, but that they shouldn't attempt to put it out. The chemicals here are highly flammable, and they'll only be risking their lives for no reason."

"Wh-what fire?" the man asked.

"The one I'm about to start," the Executioner replied.

A fire of destruction and justice. Yeah.

CHAPTER ELEVEN

Storm clouds had gathered across the sky by the time Bolan reached the neighborhood of his next target.

He knew this operation would require a different kind of touch, one defter than that applied to the warehouse at the river. Human trafficking was a key source of income for the Russian Business Network, and in Bolan's mind, it was the worst kind of criminal activity. Much of it involved young boys and girls—children snatched right off the streets and out of schools under the nose of officials, to satisfy the lust of rich perverts. Bolan considered acts against kids and the elderly as some of the most heinous crimes one human being could perpetrate against another. Those segments of society were incapable of defending themselves most of the time, and it spoke to the animal nature of those who thrived on such exploitation.

According to Bolan's intelligence, Godunov had acquired an abandoned tenement building that he was restoring, if only partially, to serve as a clearinghouse for their human merchandise. The tenement turned out to be a three-story complex comprised of eight units per floor. According to the building diagram he'd seen, there were no elevators in the tenement, and only two stairwells provided entry, at the front and rear of the building. The plans Bolan acquired also showed that the units surrounded an open-air courtyard in the center.

He knew a hot zone designed like this wouldn't provide a significant amount of cover, never mind that he would have to sweep the building unit by unit in order to free whatever involuntary residents might be there.

The clouds obscured the sky, which was in his favor, shrouding the neighborhood in a premature dusk. Bolan's luck seemed to hold out as he rolled past and noticed that the entire structure had been enclosed in construction scaffolding; probably just another way for Godunov to imitate an improvement project in the works.

While it might have fooled members of the building and zoning commission, the Executioner knew the only construction going on inside was building an empire of greed and degradation.

He found a strip mall with about six businesses, only half of which appeared to still be operating. He figured his vehicle would be safe enough parked there while he performed a recon. Retrieving his weapons bag, he entered an alleyway behind the strip mall and followed it back to the target location. He'd noticed another tenement across the street from Godunov's, and managed to find an unsecure back door that led inside.

The odors of filth and urine and a half-dozen different drugs combined to produce a stench so foul it stung his nostrils. The innermost halls of the building were dark and cold; the slumlords were obviously unconcerned with keeping the common areas warm. Bolan wondered if even the rooms had heat. He wasn't naive enough to believe that the denizens of many of America's inner cities didn't still live in squalor.

Bolan followed a rickety stairwell to the top floor of the tenement and quickly located a deserted unit. He closed the door behind him and drew his Beretta 93-R. It took him only thirty seconds to clear the abandoned apartment, which consisted of two small bedrooms, a bathroom, a stripped kitchen and a cramped living area. An old couch, most of its stuffing ripped away by what appeared to have been the antics of a very large dog, was the only piece of furniture in the entire apartment. That was okay with Bolan, since he was only here for the singular purpose of assessing his target.

The Executioner took the opportunity to strip down in the rear bedroom, which had no windows. He traded his slacks and polo shirt for the skintight blacksuit. This time, he donned the load-bearing equipment harness from which dangled his weapons of war. In addition to various combat pouches, Bolan wore a Ka-bar fighting knife, garrote and several grenades of varying types.

Once he finished lacing up his combat boots, Bolan grabbed the M-16 and secured the advanced electric-optical sight. He then went into the living area and moved over to the one window that looked upon Godunov's project. Locking the stock of the M-16 against his shoulder, he flipped the switch on top of the electro-optical sight and positioned his eye at just the right point to provide optimum focus. The green-white haze of the advanced infrared proved advantageous in picking up the heat signatures of potential targets.

The first two sentries were immediately apparent to Bolan. Their heat signatures registered on the scope as the RBN guards strolled along the exterior balcony. A casual observer wouldn't have been able to see them due to the thick clear plastic that lined the railed walkways, but Bolan was able to make them easily through the sights. He scanned the rest of the second-floor balcony that ran the length of the building, but didn't see any other signatures. Adjusting the sights, he did the same along the first floor, and detected only one sentry.

Bolan was about to retract the rifle when he caught a movement in his peripheral vision. It was fleeting enough to have almost escaped his notice, but the fact that he hadn't seen anything amiss as he drove past just ten minutes earlier gave him reason to pause. The movement came from the dark interior of a vehicle parked at the intersection nearing the tenement. Godunov's site happened to be set back a fair distance from the street, and the open area in front provided Bolan with a clear line of sight.

The Executioner redirected the muzzle of the M-16 toward the vehicle and looked through the electro-optical sight once more. The infrared picked up four heat signatures inside, at one point even brightening some at the edge. That brightening could have been the result of only one thing: someone in the vehicle was smoking a cigarette. Bolan considered this new information and knew almost immediately what it meant—the occupants in the vehicle were waiting and watching. But watching for what? And were they reinforcements, additional hard cases that he would have to deal with, or undercover agents keeping Godunov's dirty little secret under observation?

If the last, the Executioner knew it would make his

job much more difficult. It might even require a change in tactics at a moment's notice, which wasn't something he wanted to do if he could avoid it. If they were the enemy, then at least he had some idea of their position, and could neutralize them before hitting the tenement. Either way, he would need to have a closer look before he could determine the best course of action.

A sudden creak in the floorboards drew Bolan's attention toward the entryway. Spotting a brief flash of light in the crack beneath the door, he removed the M-16 from the window and slung it at the same time he unsheathed the Ka-bar. He rose and crept to the door, the neoprene soles on his shoes facilitating his silent passage. Bolan sidled up with his back to the wall and held the knife at the ready. His eyes had adjusted to the gloom; he could both see and hear as the door handle started to turn.

He waited until he heard the catch release, then reached down and yanked the door open.

As he hoped, the person on the other side came sailing through the door and nearly fell prone. Only because of his lithe condition was the intruder able to recover from the swift maneuver, Bolan figured. It didn't matter in any case, because he didn't intend to give the newcomer a chance to fight back. The Executioner put all his momentum behind a follow-up punch to the individual's right shoulder blade. Unfortunately, the majority of the impact seemed to skim off the surface, allowing Bolan's target to escape the full brunt of it.

The figure was dressed in black pants and a tattered gray sweatshirt with a hood. Cleverly using the momentum generated by the punch, Bolan's opponent executed a forward shoulder roll and came to his feet. In the course of the roll, the hood came away to reveal a torrent of dark hair that seemed to spill from the sweatshirt and cascade violently across the intruder's shoulders.

Bolan had no time to recover from the shock of seeing she was a woman, for she immediately launched a side kick directed at his midsection. It was a classic tae kwon do move, one the Executioner had seen many times before and knew how to counter. He sidestepped the attack and drove a hammer fist into the woman's right thigh. She yelped in pain as Bolan's jab landed on a bundle of nerves in that area. The blow not only created a significant amount of pain, but also tended to have a numbing effect on the leg.

The woman landed on her feet somehow and followed with a spinning heel kick that managed to connect with his wrist. The Ka-bar flew from Bolan's fingertips and skittered across the old, dilapidated floor. She made the mistake of underestimating Bolan by attempting to follow the disarming move with the back knuckle punch to his jaw. He evaded by performing a slip, an effective technique that involved crouching just enough to clear the punch, without lowering his other defenses.

Bolan knew if he didn't end it quickly the situation would escalate, and that wasn't something he could afford right now. The mission was his priority, and he couldn't worry about the potential risks of killing his unknown assailant. It didn't appear she was willing to discuss terms of surrender, so he would have to find an alternate method of subduing her.

As he finished the slip, Bolan saw his opening and delivered a one-two combination to the woman's kidney. She stepped in and dropped her elbow in the natural guard stance, but consequently exposed the back of her leg. Bolan snapped a low front kick to the crook of her knee, not hard enough to tear away tendons or snap joints, but it proved more than effective in taking her to the floor. At the last, it turned into a contest of simple strength, of which Bolan obviously possessed the advantage. He wrapped her neck in a rear naked choke hold and his biceps and forearm muscles clamped across her carotid arteries. He pulled back and tensed his muscles as he twisted his body and braced his hip against her back.

The woman proved no match for Bolan's experience or strength, and within fifteen seconds he felt her body slump. He released the hold immediately and eased her unconscious form to the ground. Bolan stepped back and realized the fight had winded him considerably. Whoever she was, she was full of spunk and an extremely tough customer. Bolan quickly moved to his combat knife. He picked it up, secured it in its sheath and then returned his attention to the woman.

Something told Bolan this was no agent for the enemy.

Yeah, something about her shapely figure and classic good looks signaled that there was a lot more to her than met the eye.

Or the body, Bolan thought as he rubbed his wrist.

Several minutes elapsed before she started to come

around. At first, it sounded as if she was mumbling something, but none of it was intelligible so Bolan dismissed it as delirium. The rear naked choke hold, a hand-to-hand-combat technique first developed by the USMC, was particularly effective in neutralizing an opponent when applied properly. The secret of the technique was in the speed with which it was applied, coupled with good targeting on the carotids. Unlike the standard choke hold, the sudden crushing force of the muscles against the windpipe and the arteries was a shock force to the system and caused an immediate flooding and shunting of blood to protect the other vital organs. This had a deleterious effect on blood pressure and was one very good reason it incapacitated a subject so quickly when done properly.

The woman's eyes fluttered open, and at first sight of Bolan, she sucked in a deep breath. It didn't take more than an instant for her face to transform into a tough mask, but Bolan had detected a flash of shock mixed with fear before that happened.

He raised a hand. "Just take it easy. I'm not here to hurt you, and I'm not your enemy unless you give me a reason to be."

At first the woman didn't say anything, and then her breathing started to slow and her eyes seemed to clear a bit more. Finally she reached up to take the hand he offered, and allowed him to assist her to her feet. Bolan kept one hand free just in case she tried anything, but as soon as she was able to stand under her own power she released her grip. The Executioner didn't think he could trust her yet, but he felt some of the tension leave as she stepped a respectful distance away.

"You mind telling me who you are and what you're doing here?" Bolan asked.

"Funny," the woman replied. "I was just about to ask you the same question."

"Why don't we stick to me asking the questions and you answering them? I'm not really in the mood to play guessing games right now."

"And I'm not really interested in *what* your mood is, mister."

The Executioner considered his options. His first thought was that maybe she needed some retraining on why it wasn't particularly wise to antagonize him. He quickly dismissed that tactic in favor of trying a more sensible approach. She seemed well-spoken, and her accent was definitely that of a native New Yorker. If he didn't miss his guess, she was probably a cop, maybe a detective or narcotics agent who had observed him surreptitiously entering the building.

Before Bolan could say another word, the woman went to the door, leaned into the hallway and picked up something. His hand went to the butt of the Beretta, but he relaxed when he saw she'd only been going for a mini flashlight. She turned, noted his reaction and shook her head.

"What? You were going to kill me over a flashlight?"

"It seems we've gotten off on the wrong foot," Bolan said. He extended his hand and continued, "My name is Cooper. I'm an agent with Homeland Security."

She stared at his hand a moment, then put her palms on her hips. "Yeah, sure, and I'm the kid sister of Queen Latifah."

Bolan shrugged and dropped his hand. "Well, either way, I don't have time for small talk, so I'm going back to my original question. Who are you and what are you doing here?"

She reached inside her sweatshirt and withdrew a wallet. She flipped it open to reveal the credentials card and badge of a New York City police detective.

"Justina Marquez," she snapped. "Organized Crime Unit—OCU."

Bolan nodded. "A gold badge, Detective First Grade. Impressive."

"How did you know that?" she asked.

He smiled again, this time a bit warmer. "I've been around the block a few times. I know a little something about something. But what's more important right now is that you walked right into the middle of a very sensitive operation, and I can't have you milling about. So if you don't mind, it would be best if you turn around, walk out of here and forget you ever met me."

"Just like that," she said.

Marquez looked in the direction of the window and spotted Bolan's equipment bag, along with the other gear barely visible in the fading light. She then looked at the harness he wore, with the various tools of his trade dangling from the OBE in plain view. "So here you are in an abandoned apartment, dressed up like G.I. Joe, and you think I should just tell you to have a nice day and split. That about sum it up?"

"I'd say you nailed it," Bolan replied.

"Let's just suppose I do decide to walk out of here, which of course I'm not going to do." She took a respectful step back and said, "At least, not voluntarily. You can be sure I'd be back here in five minutes with about a dozen detectives. You want to take that chance or do you want to show a little interagency cooperation?"

Bolan considered his options and realized she hadn't really left him any. He needed to get things moving, get his assault against Godunov's site under way, and he couldn't afford to have the cops involved any more than they already were. Beside the fact it wouldn't take someone with even half of Marquez's skills to figure out Bolan had had something to do with the incident at the warehouse less than a half hour earlier.

"All right," he finally replied. "The long and short of it is that members of the criminal organization known as the Russian Business Network are using that building across the street as a front for human trafficking. I'm here to shut it down once and for all."

Marquez folded her arms, shook her head and replied, "Well, what the hell took you so long?"

CHAPTER TWELVE

"Come again?" Bolan asked.

"I've been trying to get somebody at the federal level to pay attention to what's been going on here," Marquez said, putting her hands on her hips again. "I was told by my boss, his boss and the chief of d's to leave this thing alone. I even filed a formal protest with the deputy chief, which bought me a three-day rip and a notation in my personnel file that I tended to violate the chain of command with wild conspiracy theories. Can you believe that shit? They think I'm a conspiracy nut!"

Bolan sighed. "Look, Marquez, I'm sorry for the trouble you've had, but it's not my concern. I have a job to do and I'm going to do it."

"All by yourself?" Marquez replied with a challenging smile.

"That's the way I operate."

"Well, there's no way in hell I'm going to give this up just on your say-so. I worked entirely too hard on this case, not to mention your very presence here is what I need to clear my name. So you either count me in or you count me out. But if you do that last, Cooper, I can pretty much guarantee you'll have a wall of blue down on you before you can get inside that place. I still have a few friends left in the department."

Bolan considered what she was saying. The Executioner didn't really enjoy operating this way, but he couldn't justify putting his mission at risk for the sake of advancing Marquez's career. Still, a part of him realized that she wasn't really interested in making a name for herself. This wasn't a reporter for the *New York Daily Herald*. Marquez was a highly competent police officer who'd gotten short-changed.

"Okay, I'm willing to give you any intelligence I have about the group so far," Bolan said. "I'm also willing to let you play the part of observer. But there's no way I'm going in there and letting you tag along. I mark four men in the vehicle parked at the corner, at least two sentries on the ground floor and another two walking the balconies."

"You're forgetting the six heavies sitting in the courtyard smoking cigars and playing poker."

Marquez's statement surprised him. "How do you know that?"

"Well, to put it in your own words, 'I know a little something about something.'"

Bolan folded his arms. "Okay, you have my attention. I'll give you two minutes."

"Two minutes? Where do I start?" Marquez stuck out her lower lip and blew the locks of dark hair out of her eyes, her expression becoming thoughtful. "About eight months ago, I was on a case being run by a colleague of mine. We were taking down a small drug house not too far from here. The only problem was that when we hit the place, it seemed someone else had been calling the shots and we were blown before we even got through the front door. My colleague lost his life that night, and of the two other casualties, one will never walk again. Some of the mutts in Internal Affairs were convinced that someone on the inside had let the dealers onto our little plan."

"But you didn't agree," Bolan interjected.

"Hell no! I mean, sure it raised a lot of questions in our minds that we might have somebody inside the unit spying on us. It's not like detectives in the NYPD make a whole lot, and there's no doubt some guys take it personally. But what got me thinking about this was how well organized and well armed our reception committee was. It was no mere accident they were prepared for us. Local drug dealers might have the guns and guts, but these guys were way too organized and well equipped to be dopers. In other words, this wasn't local gangbangers. These guys were the real deal, professionals all the way."

"What makes you think so?" Bolan asked.

Marquez snorted, although it wasn't in derision as much as a prelude to the obvious. "We went into that house with nearly a dozen trained detectives and officers. We went against three men, possibly four, and we barely got out of the deal with our asses intact."

As soon as she said that, Bolan knew it was the unadulterated truth. He also suspected that Yan Volkov had been in charge of the reception committee. "Okay, but that doesn't explain how you know it's the Russian Business Network behind it all."

"I figured it was more like Russian Mob, but I'm sure I came to that conclusion the same way you did… or whoever it is you work for. Do you know the name Yuri Godunov?"

"I know it."

"Then you also know it's his holding company that oversees the management of most of the criminal fronts in this city," Marquez said. "It was a foregone conclusion that this Russian Business Network would be behind the whole problem. But when I took that up to the brass, they didn't want to hear it. Frankly, that surprised me. It almost seemed like they wanted me to drop the whole case, put my attention on other things instead of trying to figure this out. But the fact is I wasn't going to drop it no matter what." Marquez's eyes narrowed. "I don't go soft on cop killers."

"I'm glad to hear it," Bolan said. "But the situation is a lot bigger and more insidious than you might think. And I'm here to put an end to it. Now."

"You promised to hear me out."

"And I have. Within the next twelve hours, Godunov plans to try to collapse the New York City financial system by blackmailing the top financiers across the state. He's doing everything he can to make that happen, including attempted kidnappings of children and young girls, the manufacture of methamphetamines and money laundering."

Bolan jerked his thumb in the direction of the tenement. "As I said, that building is a front for human trafficking, and it's my guess there are a whole lot of 'missing' women, boys and girls inside. If I let you get involved, you're going to try to do it the official way, and I don't have time for warrants and SWAT teams. I need to go in and I need to go in now. And I'm going to go in hard."

Marquez stared at Bolan for a very long time and

the silence weighed heavily as each of them pondered the situation. The Executioner didn't want to spend any more time explaining or arguing, while Marquez felt she had a right to an explanation. In fact, Marquez knew she didn't have a leg to stand on. When it came to foreign criminal organizations operating on U.S. soil, the FBI and Department of Homeland Security had jurisdiction.

Bolan knew, as Marquez did, that by the time she actually got someone in authority to protest the situation it would most likely be over.

"Well, if you can't beat them, join them," Marquez said.

"No dice."

"Look, mister, I don't know where you come from, but in my profession you don't leave a fellow cop out there by himself. You back him up and to hell with the consequences. Several good officers are dead or badly wounded because of these people, one of them a friend of mine. And I'm not going to sit on the sidelines and watch someone else take all the risks. I have to do something, and doing something with you is better than doing nothing with the rest of the whole goddamn department."

Bolan sighed, frustrated with the time he was losing and the additional time he would lose if he bothered to continue arguing. Finally, he gestured for her to follow, and returned to the window. He picked up the rifle, put it in her hands and pointed her toward the vehicle parked at the corner. Marquez seemed a little awkward with the weapon at first, but she quickly caught on and looked through the scope. Something told Bolan it wasn't the first time she'd held an assault rifle.

"Looks like you know your way around that thing," he observed.

Marquez didn't take her eyes from the scope as she replied, "I spent four years in the Army with the supply unit in Fallujah."

She didn't have to say anything more. Mack Bolan was quite familiar with Iraq, having been there many times throughout the course of his career. As Marquez studied the vehicle, Bolan said, "I'm guessing there are four sitters inside that car. They're obviously doing some kind of observation because I saw one of them smoking. Seems like they're waiting for something, although I'm not really sure what yet. I'm also not sure if they're friends or foes, and if I try to take them out before I hit the tenement, there's a pretty good chance that any element of surprise I might have had will be gone."

Marquez turned and studied Bolan a moment, her expression making it pretty clear that she was searching for some sort of deception in his eyes. The Executioner remained impassive, knowing that if he tried to protest she would only be more suspicious of his motives. Sure, he wanted to keep her out of the line of fire if possible, but he also knew she could see the logic of his argument.

"What do you want me to do?" she finally asked.

"I want you to keep them at bay," Bolan replied.

"And how would you like me to do that?"

"I'll leave that to your own devices," Bolan said. "I already have enough to do without worrying about that.

Mostly, I need to make sure that I don't get flanked by whoever they are. So I need you to make sure that doesn't happen. You up for that?"

Now Marquez smiled. "You bet."

BOLAN GAVE MARQUEZ five minutes before he cut loose on the tenement.

The warrior brought the pair of heat signatures on the second floor into acquisition, waiting until they were nearly on top of each other before squeezing the trigger. The first green-yellow target collapsed in a flash even before the report from the M-16 thundered through the cold air. Bolan followed immediately to the second target and squeezed the trigger again. The 5.56 mm slug left the barrel at a muzzle velocity of 975 meters per second. The target collapsed to the floor in a heap, the heat already beginning to dissipate from the motionless lump.

Bolan turned his attention to the pair on the first floor, whose signatures had brightened with the rush of adrenaline. He poured on the heat by flipping out the rangefinder sight for the M-203, estimating the distance to the target and squeezing the trigger. The 40 mm grenade sailed to the target in just over a second and landed midway between the two sentries, who'd had enough foresight to split up upon realizing they were taking sniper fire.

The Executioner never saw the end effect of the grenade, only hearing it as he raced out the door and made his way down the hallway. He descended the steps two at a time and emerged from the front of the building, M-16 held at the ready and now set for 3-shot mode. Bolan sprinted across the street and reached the perimeter within seconds. He didn't even break stride as he leaped onto the chain-link fence, scrambled its height and vaulted over the top. He landed gracefully on the other side, shoulder rolling through the landing to minimize impact, and came to his feet in a flat run.

A shot came from his right.

He scanned the vehicle to find one of its occupants now outside and pointing a pistol in his direction. He heard two additional shots, these coming from a different weapon. The gunmen who had drawn on him abruptly disappeared from view behind the sedan. Bolan knew that although he couldn't see Marquez, there was no question she had his back.

Confident that the young detective could handle herself, Bolan continued his charge. As he drew near the tenement, he could hear the screams of women and children coming from somewhere inside. The shouts were more like cries of shock than terror. Bolan didn't think his enemies were attempting to remove the evidence of their crimes. They would still be busy trying to figure out exactly what was going on.

Bolan tried to get inside the head of whoever was in charge of the operation. In all likelihood, they would figure this was a rival gang, since it wasn't typical for SWAT teams or FBI units to simply start shooting without some kind of warning. Bolan intended to use every precious moment to his advantage, hopeful that Marquez's assessment about the lax attitude of those in the courtyard would hold up. Beside the fact, most of the first-level men guarding the RBN assets didn't seem to be highly trained like Volkov and his mercenaries;

these were more thugs who would do most anything to make a quick buck.

Bolan knew his assessment was spot on, merely given the fact he made it as far as he had without being cut down.

The Executioner came through the front archway, passed beneath an overhang that was actually the second floor of the tenement, and emerged into the courtyard. A small gate served as entrance to the open-air yard. He put his foot to the shabby wooden gate and it gave immediately under the force of the kick. Bolan's eyes followed the sweep of the M-16's muzzle as he looked for targets.

The first RBN hood appeared from behind a large column, one of many that formed a colonnade surrounding the courtyard. The man held only a pistol and snapped off two quick shots before running away from Bolan. The warrior started to raise the M-16 to his shoulder, but movement in the corner of his eye alerted him to a greater threat. He changed direction with the assault rifle, verified his target and squeezed the trigger. All three rounds found their mark—an RBN thug holding an antiquated Ingram MAC 10—the first two punching through his stomach and the third cracking his sternum before mangling the soft tissue behind it. The guy's body went airborne and he landed on the concrete with an audible crack of his skull.

Two more of the RBN gunners appeared from one of the rooms on the second floor.

That was the one factor that had given Bolan cause for concern; it was hard enough to do battle in a confined space with a limited amount of running room, but more difficult when the enemy had the high ground. He sprinted for cover behind a column just as the two hoods opened up with their pistols. Fortunately, the two men were largely inexperienced and obviously used to doing business with innocent children and bystanders who couldn't fight back. Yeah, apparently these guys were used to drive-bys, because they fired repeatedly at Bolan even though he managed to secure the protection of the column.

The response ate up their ammunition in short order. The gunners realized their mistake much too late when Bolan emerged from the other side of the column, brought the M-16 into target acquisition and unleashed a volley of 5.56 mm hell. One of the gunners took a round to the groin and two more to the stomach. He staggered backward, drawing his partner's attention. Bolan seized the advantage and swung the weapon in the second man's direction. He squeezed off one more 3-round burst, and the RBN thug's head disappeared in a fountain of blood, bone and brain matter. The headless corpse was so close to the edge of the flimsy metal balcony that it crashed through and sailed to the concrete. The lifeless missile struck with a loud, grisly smack. Bolan was already on the move.

A young girl of about six emerged barefoot from one of the ground-floor rooms and nearly caught Bolan off guard. At the same moment, two more RBN gunmen rounded the corner—probably coming from an apartment slightly recessed in an alcove. The pair raised their guns to fire. Bolan scooped the crying girl under his left arm while swinging the M-16 into action. The report from his assault rifle flooded one eardrum as the screams of the girl flooded the other. The pandemonium wasn't anything he hadn't dealt with before, and it didn't affect his aim.

The 5.56 mm man-shredders drilled the two hoods. The impact slammed one backward hard enough that his body cracked the glass window behind him. Only the black plastic covering its interior prevented the shards from flying into the apartment. The second gunman keeled over, clutching his stomach where Bolan's rounds had nearly disemboweled him. Sticky entrails combined with blood protruded from the man's gut. The Executioner finished the job with three more mercy rounds that decimated his enemy's skull.

Bolan pushed through the apartment door the girl had come from, and gently deposited her on the bed. Movement attracted his attention and he swung the M-16 in that direction. A girl who couldn't have been more than six years older than the younger girl screamed and threw up her hands. She sat in the corner, back pressed to it and an expression of fear on her dirty face. Bolan could see she had a black eye. Her skimpy dress was torn and hung on her, a filthy rag. She'd obviously been abused by her captors.

The sight of this battered child kindled fierce flames of anger in Mack Bolan.

CHAPTER THIRTEEN

Justina Marquez wasn't having a good time of it.

When the guy called Cooper said he was going up hard against the Russian Business Network and their human trafficking stronghold, Marquez hadn't been entirely sure what that meant. And why would she have? Marquez lived in a world where everyone was concerned about the rights of criminals more than those of honest, hardworking American citizens. She needed warrants in her world and the approval of the chain of command before acting against the criminal element. She hated the bureaucracy of the department, but she also understood the need to maintain order.

Apparently, her new ally wasn't under any such restrictions. She could see that after he took down two of the sentries with the M-16, and immediately followed that up with some type of heavy explosive. Marquez had noticed the M-203 grenade launcher, and she assumed that's what Cooper had used to produce the fireworks.

Her job was pretty simple in comparison. All Cooper had asked her to do was keep an eye on the four men inside the sedan. But when the shooting started, it turned into something more than that. She'd watched Cooper as he left the apartment and ran across the street to the tenement. One of the guys in the sedan—the one sitting in the backseat on the driver's side—climbed from the vehicle when he observed Cooper emerge from the apartment. It seemed odd to her that none of the other men left their seats; neither did they seem overly concerned about the destruction being rained upon the tenement.

So who the hell were they?

Marquez knew it probably didn't matter when she observed the lone gunner pull a pistol and aim it in Cooper's direction. The guy managed to get off two shots before Marquez could clear her weapon from its holster. She'd been observing them from the shadows in the alley, her only cover a large garbage bin just far enough away from the wall that she had been able to wedge her body between it and the side of the building.

Marquez sighted down the slide of her Glock 21, took a breath to steady her grip, then squeezed the trigger. The pistol produced a booming report as a .45-caliber slug left the barrel and traversed the distance to strike the gunner in the side. His pistol clattered onto the roof of the sedan as he collapsed in a heap next to the vehicle. None of the other occupants had apparently seen where the shooting was coming from, but they immediately bailed from the car and turned their weapons on Cooper.

Marquez delivered two more shots, but neither of them hit, and she realized her mistake even as the trio of Russian hoods turned their attention toward her position.

"Uh-oh," she muttered.

The detective didn't have time to react beyond that

as the air around her came alive with a hailstorm of autofire. It was at that point she realized she'd come up against men armed not with simple semiautomatic pistols, but machine pistols that were fully loaded and in the hands of practiced combatants. Marquez realized she had only one option available to her, only one other tool in her arsenal that would be effective here: her police radio.

She whipped the radio from her belt, put the microphone close to her mouth and pressed the transmit button. "This is 3-oh-5 to Central, repeat 3-oh-5 to Central. Do you read?"

"Central Dispatch to 3-oh-5, go ahead with your traffic."

"I am 10-33. Repeat, I am 10-33. Shots fired! Officer needs assistance!"

Marquez repeated the address twice before signing out. She knew Cooper didn't want her brothers in blue involved, but at this point she didn't see that she had much choice. There was no way she could take on three Russian enforcers, no matter where they were from or who they worked for, with only an 8-round magazine and one reload. But at the same time she had no intention of leaving her post. The reinforcements would arrive soon enough. She was certain she didn't have to tell the dispatcher the seriousness of the situation, especially given the cacophony of shots from the machine pistols.

Marquez waited for a break in the fire before returning it with two shots of her own. One round grazed the front-seat passenger, who had moved into the open and was indiscriminately spraying the area with rounds from his machine pistol, as if he were holding a bullet hose. Marquez could tell she'd only clipped him, because he didn't fall, so she followed with two more rounds, and one of them shattered the guy's skull. He dropped his machine pistol and collapsed.

Her response only served to fuel the anger of the remaining two gunners, and they continued to flood her area with a metal storm of high-velocity rounds. A couple ricocheted and bits of metal and stone lodged in her neck. Marquez reached for them, wanting to scream at the burning sensation, but she thought better of it and took her hand away from her neck. At least they would stem the bleeding. If she removed them, it was possible she could hemorrhage to death before help arrived.

At one point a break in the firing permitted her to drop her magazine and insert a fresh one. She let the slide come forward, then bit her lip, realizing she might have betrayed her position. It was dark enough now that her enemies couldn't see her, and if she could simply outwait them, it would buy her the time she needed for reinforcements to arrive. As she pressed her body as close to the pavement as possible, Marquez heard the echo of gunfire coming from inside the tenement. She hoped Cooper could accomplish his mission before the place was bombarded by uniform squads, but she also didn't want to wait that long for help.

A moment later it didn't matter, as the two remaining gunners opened up on her position with fresh salvos from the machine pistols. It almost seemed to Marquez as if these guys had an unlimited supply of ammunition. One thing was certain—they had been waiting for Cooper. They'd known he was coming in much the same way they had known her unit was coming to storm the drug house, which would have pointed more toward some type of intelligence network than a spy inside the OCU.

When sirens wailed in the distance, they were the sweetest sounds Marquez had ever heard.

IT TOOK MACK BOLAN only a couple of minutes to sweep the remaining rooms in the tenement for his enemies. He didn't find any, and assumed the rest had run when they realized the odds weren't in their favor. What he did find were at least two dozen boys and girls, along with some teenagers and four adults who'd been recruited to keep an eye on the younger ones. Bolan didn't have time to question them, find out if they were there voluntarily or otherwise, but he figured it was better to leave that to the police in any case. His mission here was done, and before the sun set in New York City this night, a whole lot of very happy parents would be reunited with their kids.

Bolan gathered the group and covered their flanks as he ordered them out of the tenement and into the parking lot. Once they were assembled there, he led them to an area far enough away that the police—their arrival now imminent, as evident by the sirens that wailed in the distance—would have no trouble spotting them. Bolan ordered one of the adults to see that everyone was accounted for and that they remained where they were until taken into protective custody by the authorities.

The soldier left the group to make his way across

the parking lot. He was nearly to the fence when he realized a couple of the gunmen from the sedan were still alive. And they were pouring a merciless hail of fire onto Marquez's position. Well, at least he had some hope that she was still alive. They wouldn't be shooting at mere shadows.

Bolan crouched, realizing the gunners were so occupied with Marquez they hadn't taken notice of him or the group of shattered souls he had just liberated from an incomprehensible future. The Executioner loaded a 40 mm HE grenade into the launcher, sighted on the vehicle and squeezed the trigger. The high explosive missile hit the sedan a moment later and erupted into a fireball, the concussion knocking both men to the ground. Bolan didn't let up on them, immediately loading another 40 mm grenade and delivering it. The entire area was consumed by the quenching fire of justice. The explosion ripped arms and legs from the pair of RBN hostiles and ignited gases hot enough to char flesh off their bones.

The remainder of his enemy was neutralized and the RBN hostages safe. Godunov's human trafficking front was now in shambles, along with the factory where they had been producing the methamphetamines. That left only the money laundering operation, which Bolan surmised would be the primary way for Godunov to move all the cash they planned to siphon out of the New York financial system. The numbers may have been running down, but Bolan was confident he could push the Russian crime ambassador to exactly where he wanted him.

Godunov's estate in the Hamptons.

"THAT'S YOUR STORY?" Captain Stan Dagum asked. "Some mysterious federal agent named Cooper, no first name and no way to validate his identity, tells you that he's with the Department of Homeland Security and is going up against the Russian Business Network?"

Marquez put her hands on her hips. "It's not my story, sir, it's the truth! Why is it so hard for you to believe? When it comes down to things like this, why is it always *me* you doubt?"

Marquez waved at what remained of Cooper's handiwork. She hadn't seen him disappear into the night, but she would always be grateful that he'd rendered aid when he saw she was in peril. It wasn't that she agreed with his methods so much as she understood them. Well, maybe that was bullshit and maybe she did agree with his methods—more than she wanted to admit, perhaps. But it wouldn't do any good to tell Captain Dagum that. While he wasn't just another bureaucrat, and had recommended she be accepted to the Organized Crime Unit, he'd always been tougher on her than on her colleagues. Maybe it was because he expected more from her—something that came from his loyalties to her father. Maybe it was just the fact that she was a woman, and Dagum came from an old school that believed men should be cops and women should stay home and take care of their cop husbands.

"Why is it hard to believe?" Dagum shook his head and then encompassed the area in a sweeping gesture of his own. "First of all, because you came to me, and then went to the chief of d's, and then to the deputy chief with this story about the Russian Mafia. Now you claim that it's actually some group called the Russian Business Network. For your information, Justina, the Russian Business Network is a cybercrime organization. There is no evidence they've ever been linked to anything but electronic embezzlement, spam bots and e-mail fraud. And of course they run a lot of the overseas pornography sites that steal people's money by charging hundreds of dollars a shot to credit cards so that perverts can watch little girls and boys do unspeakable things. Okay, so they're a bad lot and I don't dispute that. But there's no way you can make me believe that some nutcase is running around here shooting up the interests of this group because he's on a government-sanctioned mission to disrupt their operations. And what about your ridiculous story that Yuri Godunov, who we have investigated and found to be an impeccable businessman and member of the community, is somehow tied into a plot to destroy the financial system of this city? Listen to yourself, Justina! If you were me, wouldn't it sound ridiculous?"

"If I were you," Marquez replied, narrowing her eyes, "I would believe what my detectives had to tell me. Did I make up all those people over there being loaded into the ambulances and buses? Did I make up all those children who've been abused and abandoned? Did I make up all the bullet holes or explosions that are quite obviously the result of military grade explosives?"

"I'm not saying you made it up," Dagum replied. "That's not what I'm saying at all. What I'm telling you is that your explanation for all of this doesn't hold water. You haven't submitted any evidence whatsoever to back up your claims that this is anything other than an extension of the drug wars we've been fighting in the city for the past twenty-five years! Now, both I and the chief of d's ordered you to back off from the situation. But no, you had to push and push, and now we've got an overblown disaster on our hands."

Before Marquez could say anything else in her defense, another officer ran up with a thick sheaf of papers. Marquez's initial glance told her it was some sort of a status report, and that based on the size of the folder, it was obviously contained data on a matter of some importance. Dagum held up his hand to indicate he needed a moment, then opened the folder and began to read.

In the dim light of the streetlamp overhead, Marquez saw Dagum pale.

"What is it?" she asked.

"It's a report from the East River district commander," Dagum replied. "Apparently, there was some sort of trouble in a warehouse there. A number of unidentified persons were found dead, apparently the direct result of some kind of assault that involved automatic weapons and high explosives. The place was burned to the ground, and there was only one witness left alive, who'd been shot by a man claiming the factory was actually a meth lab."

Dagum looked up, and Marquez could see the light of realization in his eyes. "The perp got away, but he left the witness, who gave a pretty good description," he added. "The details match your description of this Cooper nearly verbatim."

"You see?" Marquez nodded, experiencing a moment of clarity. In fact, she had never been so clear about anything in her life. Everything had transpired just as

Cooper had told her it would, and she knew at that moment that the U.S. government really *had* gone to war with this criminal organization, be it the Russian Mafia or the Russian Business Network or the Russian Cooking Club. She suspected Dagum knew the same thing.

It didn't really make any difference now.

"I guess that explains it," Dagum said. "And it also gives significantly more weight to your theory that there really is a foreign crime organization operating in New York City."

Marquez raised an eyebrow. "What was your first clue, Captain?"

"Watch yourself, Detective," Dagum warned. "Your father and I might be old friends, but I won't tolerate any sort of insubordination. You've shown yourself to be a trustworthy officer, there's no question there, and I'm going to make sure they pin a commendation on you for your work here. But don't think you can push me on this issue. We're going to let this thing run down exactly the way the brass wants it, and I don't want any arguments out of you."

"Fine. But you can skip the commendation, because it's not awards and decorations I'm interested in, sir."

"Then what *are* you interested in?" Dagum queried. "I swear, some days I don't even think I know you!"

Marquez thought fast before replying. "Has it occurred to you that the way to clear this whole thing up would be to actually *catch* this Cooper? I'm sure he could resolve any questions about his identity or the authority behind his activities in just a few minutes. Why put the focus on the crooks, when we can potentially solicit the cooperation of the federal boys?"

Dagum looked genuinely interested now. "What did you have in mind?"

"One of the things Cooper told me was that they knew, or at least *he* knew, that Yuri Godunov was using the businesses held by his firm as fronts for various criminal operations. Cooper specifically mentioned a meth lab, which we now know he destroyed, and the human trafficking ring that he broke up here."

"So what?" Dagum's tone was laced with impatience.

"But there was a third operation he mentioned to me, however briefly."

"What kind of operation?"

"He said something about Godunov having a money-laundering business somewhere in the city. Cooper said once he finished his mission here, Godunov wouldn't have anyplace to go, and most likely would have to flee the country."

"I don't see how that helps us, Justina." Dagum furrowed his brows and added, "This money-laundering operation could be anywhere, and I don't have the resources or manpower to start combing the city on a mere whim."

"No, you don't," Marquez replied. She smiled. "But you do have me, and I've done quite a bit of research on Yuri Godunov. I don't think it would be too difficult for me to narrow down the list of possible fronts where he could run such an operation. With your permission, I'd like to pursue whatever leads I can find. If anything, I can assure you that whatever target Cooper has in mind, he'll probably come at it as hard and fast as he did these first two."

"I'm not certain I'm comfortable with this," Dagum said. "I don't want to put you in the line of fire."

"I understand, Captain. But you have to remember that Cooper will trust me. Maybe I can dissuade him from doing something stupid before anyone else gets hurt. Maybe, just maybe, I can get him to come in peacefully and work with us instead of going off on this insane path of guerrilla warfare. I'm no more interested in seeing a war start on the streets of this city than you are. So if you trust me, this is your chance to prove it."

Dagum didn't reply immediately. Marquez could see the wheels turning in his head. Dagum was a decorated officer and a fine commander, but he had a pension to think about. Marquez was new to the force, a young hot-shot who cared little about making a name for herself. Despite their relationship, cops like Marquez were extremely dangerous to career-minded guys like Dagum. Although in the end, Marquez had proved herself, and that kind of thing went a long way.

"All right, I'll give you a shot." He jabbed a finger at her and added, "I swear to God, Justina, you don't stay in touch and I will bust you down to traffic beat, where you'll stay for the better part of your career. Hear me?"

"I hear you," Marquez said, mustering as serious an expression as she could.

But inside she was smiling.

CHAPTER FOURTEEN

Mack Bolan rolled past the club in upper Manhattan twice.

To the casual observer it would look like he was trying to find a parking spot, but Bolan, of course, had an entirely different agenda. There were two possible spots for Godunov's money-laundering operation. Bolan had already gone to the first one, and after a careful recon that included spending some time inside the establishment, he'd realized the place was neither large enough nor busy enough to cover up the kind of operation Stony Man's intelligence concluded Godunov had in place.

This left the Lisbon Social Club as the only viable option.

On both passes, Bolan noticed quite a line to get inside. He considered contacting Kurtzman to see if the cybernetics wizard could attain information that might help Bolan gain access to the club without drawing attention. While the warrior was confident this was the place, he knew it wouldn't be feasible to just hit the club with guns blazing. A more subtle approach was required in this case, as it stood to reason a large number of the occupants were simply innocent New Yorkers out for a night on the town. After all, it was

Friday night, and there would be a large crowd at a place like the Lisbon Club.

This presented the largest tactical challenge to the Executioner. Cutting out the heart of Godunov's money-laundering operation inside this club wouldn't be easy, especially when the place was crowded with innocent people. Bolan suspected that most of those inside *were* innocent, not knowing that the money they paid for the music or the liquor or even the drugs was being used to supplement operations and defray Godunov's expenses. But that was the way of organizations like the RBN. They preyed on those who wouldn't know what was going on.

Just like with the methamphetamine factory and the "renovation project" that actually disguised the inhumane exploitation of American citizens, America's children, the Lisbon served as a reminder to Bolan that groups like the Russian Business Network were nothing more than great deceivers. Not that the social mores of America were so pure and honest, or that he thought all U.S. citizens were perfect and untouched by corruption. The one thing he did know about the American people was that a good number of them were honest and hardworking, just struggling to get by on a daily basis while the brokers of corruption and power sowed seeds that were designed to destroy the fiscal stability of the country.

Bolan pushed the indignity of it all from his mind and forced his concentration onto the mission at hand.

The warrior parked his vehicle in a lot three blocks from the club. He'd earlier stripped out of his combat gear and dressed in the slacks and polo shirt. The leather jacket creaked during his walk to the club, but protected him from the biting winds. A dry, powdery snow had begun to fall, and his shoulders and hair were blanketed with it by the time he reached the club.

Bolan looked at the line in front of him, considered his options and then bypassed the group by shouldering through them to the head of the queue. He started to accompany the two women the bouncer had just admitted, but then felt a heavy hand clamp on to his shoulder.

"Hold up there, partner," a deep voice said.

He turned to see a giant of a guy wearing a dark button-down shirt and bow tie. The man had a butch cut, and his dark hair and dark eyes looked part Asian; Bolan figured he was likely a mix, Caucasian and Chinese. The button-down shirt was tailored, but clung to the bulging muscles in his chest, shoulders and arms. Bolan saw he stood at least a half head taller, putting him somewhere around six feet seven.

"What's the problem?" the soldier demanded, putting as much righteous indignation into his tone as possible.

"The problem is this is a members-only facility," the bouncer replied. "Plus we have a dress code here, and that includes shirt, tie and jacket. And looking at you, I'm afraid you don't come close to passing muster."

"Are you an idiot or something?" Bolan asked. "You think I don't know there's a dress code here? Exactly who is it you think sent me here at this time of night, dressed this way? I'm on an errand for Yuri, and I don't really have time to explain myself to the help. Got it?"

Bolan began to advance, well aware of how things would play out in the next minute, because he had intended it that way. Role camouflage took more than simply looking the way someone expected him to look. He also had to act the part—in this case, in a way that would imply someone of importance, or at least self-importance, who could present an aura of arrogance and petulance. Bolan could do pompous ass well when he had to.

It was the key to pulling off a convincing performance.

The big man maintained his grip on Bolan's shoulder as he reached over and clamped his other hand around the back of Bolan's neck. Unfortunately, he had failed to realize that while a show of strength was enough to deter the majority of men, Bolan wasn't an average man. The bouncer realized his mistake at that point—the mistake of tying up both his hands—when Bolan twisted out of his hold by pivoting on his heel and raising both palms to shoulder level.

The Executioner continued to spin, bringing his arms close to each other as he dropped them onto the bouncer's outstretched hands. The impetus of his movement caused the man's top-heavy physique to lose its center of gravity. As his upper torso pitched forward, Bolan reversed direction and caught his opponent in the throat with a ridge-hand strike. The blow wasn't fatal because it wasn't intended to be, but it had enough behind it to make the man's larynx spasm and his breathing became difficult.

A second guy off to one side, whom Bolan had marked as an RBN heavy at first sight, stepped forward and started to reach inside his jacket. Bolan turned and shoved him off balance with a palm strike to the chest. He followed through with the blow until the hood's back contacted the outside wall, while he simultaneously reached beneath his jacket and whipped the Beretta into play. Bolan got in close and pressed the barrel of the pistol against the man's belly, keeping it concealed from the eyes of the observers.

"I don't think Mr. Godunov would appreciate that," Bolan whispered. "So keep it in your pants and don't get in my way again. Otherwise, the next one to show up here will be the Wolf, and I don't think you want to cross him. Got it?"

The guy's eyes went a little wide and he nodded rapidly in understanding.

Bolan smiled and returned the Beretta to its holster as he slapped the man's cheek and said, "That's a good boy. In fact, I think we can just forget this unfortunate little incident ever happened."

The soldier turned and waited for the bouncer, who had recovered and was rubbing his tender throat, to clear the rope blocking the heavy wooden door. The bouncer looked at the gunman, who straightened his jacket and tie while nodding curtly as a signal they should permit Bolan to pass. The Executioner stared expectantly at the bouncer, who glared back but complied, detaching the rope from the waist-high stanchion holding it and nodding for him to enter. Bolan tossed the bouncer a sloppy salute with two fingers, then opened the wooden door and stepped inside.

Loud, raucous music assaulted his ears and flashing strobe lights threatened to disorient him. Despite the indoor smoking ordinances established for clubs with certain occupancies above some random number Bolan couldn't recall, the air was thick with cigarette smoke. With each beat of the music, Bolan's eardrums throbbed, and he couldn't remember a single firefight that had threatened to drown his senses like this place.

He moved easily through the club, keeping his eyes on every person who stood out as more than a simple partygoer here to blow off some Friday night steam. Most of the RBN heavies were easy to identify; they kept to the corners of the club and were dressed like the one Bolan had met outside. For a moment, the Executioner wondered if he would even have to bother making contact with someone. If he was right about his suspicions, the activity that had just occurred out front was being reported at that very moment. He decided to wait it out and order a drink—at least as close as tonic water on ice with lime could pass for a cocktail.

Bolan kept his eye on the six separate figures he'd identified as RBN gunners. True to form, one or two casually brought their hands to their ears, then their eyes rolled over the club as they spoke into microphones on their sleeves. To any observant person, it would be obvious these men were security. Then again, Bolan realized, they really had no reason to hide the fact. After all, a club of this size with a clientele of this nature would have call for a security force that acted as inconspicuously as possible, but was readily identifiable for the patrons.

True to Bolan's assessment, it didn't take long for one of the dapper men to make an appearance. He tapped

Bolan on the shoulder, and the Executioner was careful to keep his hands visible. He knew that one false move would likely result in either a gang of security escorting him out the door, or trouble of a more serious nature. Bolan knew the key to getting out alive would be to make it look like he had every business being here.

"I understand you're here on orders from the top."

Bolan searched the man's eyes a moment as he took a large swallow of his tonic water, sized him up over the rim of his glass and replied, "That's right."

"We haven't seen you before."

"That's because I'm the newest member of the Wolf's team," Bolan replied. "I don't think our mutual boss feels he needs to explain himself whenever he chooses to send someone for a spot inspection. Do you?"

The man produced a grin, although Bolan sensed no warmth in it. "The strange thing is that he's never sent anybody to inspect before. What makes you so special?"

"I'm not special, pal. He didn't send me because I'm special, he sent me because there's some freak shooting up our other interests. But I don't think that here and now is the best place for this conversation. Best we take this to a more private setting. Right?"

The question obviously threw the man off guard, because he appeared uncertain how to reply. It was true that Bolan was gambling at this point; he often gambled in situations like this, where things could deteriorate quickly. He didn't want to go hard, but if that was the hand he got dealt, he wanted to be able to respond without putting innocent people in jeopardy. Even if it meant he had to step deeper into the bowels of enemy territory, that was preferable over risking the lives of those who couldn't protect themselves from whatever conflict might ensue.

The man finally jerked his head ever so slightly, then turned on his heel, obviously expecting Bolan to follow. The Executioner downed the remainder of his drink, set the glass on the bar and gestured for the barkeep to pour him another. Bolan's alleged escort was halfway across the club when he turned to see that Bolan hadn't moved. He came back and threw up his hands with a questioning gaze.

"I want another drink," Bolan said.

"You can get a drink in back."

The bartender returned with a fresh glass before the RBN goon could make it an issue. Bolan scooped the glass off the bar, then nodded his readiness. Once more, the man took off and this time Bolan followed. For the sake of the security watching him he took a couple of unsteady steps; it was important he put on an air of moderate inebriation. He needed them to think that he was just like any other hired gun, someone with his own weaknesses and vices. It was vitally important; it was part of the act.

Bolan's escort led him to a black door with a thin red line painted down the center. The Executioner thought this design was a little odd, and he couldn't help but wonder if there was some significance to the mark. The guy rapped twice on the door before opening it and gesturing for Bolan to step inside. The Executioner didn't wait, immediately moving past and acting with as much superiority and arrogance as he could muster. He had to make sure they believed he felt secure. This way, they would underestimate him, and he planned to use that to full advantage.

The office was large, and a massive desk occupied one wall. A man with long legs propped on the edge of the desk sat reclined in a leather chair. He had light brown eyes and reddish-blond hair that he wore in a military cut. He was dressed in Armani complete with a silk tie. A gold watch, something of European make, gleamed in the recessed lighting. A group of three men stood near him, their hands clasped in front of them. The men looked relaxed, but Bolan immediately detected the ready state of their expressions.

"Welcome, Mr. Lambretta," the man seated at the desk said. His voice was thick with a Russian accent, most probably from the northern region around Saint Petersburg. "We've been expecting you."

JUSTINA MARQUEZ watched the action as it went down outside the Lisbon Club.

The binoculars were department issue and didn't provide her with a terribly clear view of what was happening three floors below her. This was the only office she'd been able to get that provided a view of the club, and it had cost her a hundred dollars cash. The janitorial services employed people who believed in capitalism and the free enterprise system. They weren't going to let just anybody into the empty offices, didn't matter if they were flashing a badge or not.

But Marquez felt this was important enough to warrant the cost, and whether the department would reimburse her wasn't an issue. Besides, this gave her an opportunity to prove her theory and get one more chance to enter into the company of Cooper. Part of Marquez knew that name was most likely bogus.

It thrilled her to witness him operate in this fashion—first the move he used to neutralize the bouncer, followed by the minor encounter he had with the well-dressed man who didn't know how to carry himself without projecting that he had a concealed weapon. Whatever had transpired below, it went down fast, and Cooper somehow managed to say something that got him inside the club. In fact, it appeared to Marquez as if the two men were practically tripping over themselves to let him inside.

Marquez pulled her eyes from the binoculars suddenly and mumbled, "That doesn't seem right."

For the first time since meeting Cooper, the police detective began to wonder if he was a double agent of some kind—maybe he was actually working for Godunov. Then again, the entire idea seemed a little crazy. Not only had he destroyed a major factory containing methamphetamines, something Dagum told her the bomb techs had confirmed shortly after their conversation at the tenement, but he'd also freed a lot of women and children who'd been reported missing. And he'd saved her from certain death at the hands of the goons toting machine pistols, to make no mention of his killing at least a half-dozen criminals wanted for a variety of crimes that included robbery, rape and murder.

No, Cooper could be a lot of things, but an employee of Yuri Godunov seemed unlikely. Marquez scolded herself for even thinking it. And that theory didn't hold water anyway, since Cooper's encounter below looked

like a bit more than some simple misunderstanding.
There was something deeper at work here.

In fact, it looked a lot like her newfound ally was
operating undercover. Maybe that was it; maybe he'd
given them some story so they'd let him inside the club.
After all, Marquez had managed to figure out this club
was the most likely location for Godunov's money-
laundering operation, and now seeing Cooper here only
served to validate the guess. But if Marquez hadn't
missed the mark, another possibility existed. There
was a good chance Cooper was walking straight into a
trap and didn't even know it. He'd been right about one
thing—the guys in the sedan had been waiting there,
and that implied they were waiting for *someone*. It also
implied they had some reason to believe Cooper would
show up, and that could mean the RBN was actually
one step ahead of him.

Surely the word about the warehouse and the tenement would be out on the streets by now. There had also
been another very interesting tidbit that came over the
wires this morning: a car-bombing in upstate New York
very close to a Catholic school. Saint Bart's, wasn't it?
Marquez couldn't remember all the details, but one
thing seemed sure. Cooper was walking into a potential
trap.

And Justina Marquez felt duty-bound to help him.

CHAPTER FIFTEEN

Yuri Godunov had a growing sense of unease.

It wasn't so much his plan to acquire the necessary funds for the continued operation of the Brotherhood of Social Justice that troubled him, as much as the fact that he had allowed himself to be deceived. He had also learned in the past couple of hours from his sources that the Wolf and his team were no more. Godunov had suspected there might be a problem when Volkov didn't check in at the appointed time; he would never have guessed that the mercenary leader had met with his demise.

Upon learning this fact, along with the activities that had happened at both the warehouse and his trafficking center, Godunov could only assume the worst. Somehow, the man who called himself Lambretta was actually the government agent who had taken down the Wolf's hit team in Boston. That also meant that Bogdan Lutrova was either an unwitting pawn in the game—something Godunov couldn't believe was possible of someone with such a brilliant mind—or a willing accomplice.

The government had somehow flipped Lutrova, and that meant the computer hacker had become a liability to the operation.

Godunov had actually entertained the idea at one

point of letting Bogdan Lutrova escape with his life. He had even thought it might be better to keep Eduardo Capistrano alive. Now he knew that once the work was done and they had the funds secured, neither of those men would be allowed to leave his offices alive. In the meantime, he was confident Stepan would take care of the meddling Lambretta. The only thing Godunov could do at this juncture was to continue with the operation and return to his estate as quickly as possible.

He had also put Stepan's entire security force on full alert. Part of his fifty-man unit had remained at the house, part had gone with Stepan to cover the various business fronts, and the remainder now accompanied Godunov and Lutrova as they headed to the Chase One Plaza in Manhattan. While the two Russians rode in a late-model sedan driven by one of Godunov's personal bodyguards, a panel truck with approximately ten armed escorts followed behind them.

As they pulled to the curb in front of the building that housed Godunov's offices, the panel truck skirted past them and turned into a drive that descended to an underground loading area. There was a single bay designed for vans and small trucks like the one that concealed the escort team. Of course, even as he walked up the sidewalk leading to the building—Lutrova on his heels with a computer in the notebook bag slung over his shoulder—Godunov knew the guard at the entrance to the loading dock would need to inspect the back of the truck. It was too bad for him, since he wouldn't walk away from the encounter alive.

The orders were already given in very simple terms: no witnesses.

At this time of the evening only two guards were on duty at the main entrance. Godunov had decided it was best not to attempt to circumvent security with any type of firearms. While he knew where the weaknesses were, and knew he would probably be able to get away with it, he couldn't afford to draw any attention. It would already seem strange for him to go into the office at this time of night, although it wouldn't be the first time the guards had seen him work late hours.

Within a few minutes, they were through security and upstairs in the special room Godunov had constructed for Lutrova to do his handiwork. Godunov sent his bodyguard to retrieve Capistrano.

Godunov couldn't refrain from smiling at the thought of how Capistrano was probably champing at the bit by now. He'd ordered the shallow, contemptible puppet to arrive early this morning and go about his normal business until such time as he was given further instructions. Godunov noticed the clock on the wall was approaching 9:30 p.m., which meant Capistrano had been here over twelve hours. Godunov wondered, although only as a point of self-amusement, what the man had done to pass the time. He'd probably watched television on the massive plasma TV Godunov knew he had in his luxurious office.

Godunov had just seated himself at his desk when Capistrano showed up as if on cue. The man didn't waste any time. "My children okay?"

"I am a lot of things," Godunov answered. "And I am not a lot of things. But one thing I can assure you that I *am,* Mr. Capistrano, is a man of my word. As I have already explained, as long as you've cooperated and done precisely as I instructed, not only will you leave here alive but you will arrive home to find your children are perfectly safe."

"I suppose it doesn't occur to you that the fact you are a man of your word is coming only from you," Capistrano replied, not without venom. "It would seem then that your opinion is a bit on the biased and subjective side, so you'll forgive me if I'm not gushing with relief."

"I can tolerate a lot of things, Mr. Capistrano. Being called a liar isn't one of those things, and I would remind you that until our agreement has been consummated you would do best to keep a civil tongue in your head. Otherwise, I might encourage my people to simply cut it out."

When Capistrano didn't have any reply for that, Godunov considered the issue closed, and rose from his seat with a nod. He gestured for the man to follow, and led him down the hallway to where Lutrova was working. Part of Capistrano's goal had been to get the system wired in this office connected to the wireless system, which was then rerouted to the physical terminals and the accounts of Godunov's personally selected targets. It wouldn't be enough to simply transfer the funds and then take off; there were safeguards in place in the system, including the automatic alerting of federal agencies for any transactions over ten grand. Godunov would also need the list of financiers whose accounts they were compromising, so that he could ensure they didn't tell the FBI or other investigators that the transactions had been done without their knowledge. A large part of their plan depended on

Godunov's ability to blackmail individuals into keeping their mouths shut.

Capistrano immediately noted the presence of Bogdan Lutrova and looked at Godunov expectantly. "You didn't say anything about involving additional people in this."

"It doesn't matter," Godunov said. "You have your responsibilities and he has his. Your responsibility is to now give him the access codes needed to circumvent the security system. I trust you've already done the work of connecting a wireless interface to the central computer terminal by some direct physical means?"

Capistrano nodded. "I have, but it wasn't easy. The place is under constant surveillance, and more than one person saw my face. When this is through, it is entirely likely I will need to leave the country. I assume you won't try to stop me."

"Why would I? It makes no difference to me what you do once we are successful here. In fact, as soon as we are done getting the information we require, and transferring the funds, we will no longer have any need for you and you will be free to go. As I said, I am a man of my word and I have no intention of killing you."

Capistrano nodded, although Godunov could detect just a hint of skepticism. The man didn't believe him, and with good reason. Up to this point, Godunov's relationship with Capistrano had been based entirely on coercion and blackmail; it was something at which Godunov had become very proficient over the years. The Russian didn't blame Capistrano for not seeming to believe him; Godunov hadn't given him any reason to.

"You'll understand if I reserve judgment until after we're finished here," Capistrano said.

"Do as you wish and judge as you will. Just make sure that until that time, you do as you're told."

With that, Godunov turned on his heel and left the room. He had arrangements to make and very little time left in which to do so.

THE EXECUTIONER had the enemy just where he wanted them.

It wasn't the first time Mack Bolan had been in this situation, and it certainly wouldn't be the last. While to most observers it would appear Bolan was at a disadvantage, this was exactly the type of situation he considered ideal. It surprised him that this tall stranger knew Bolan's Lambretta cover name, but it also confirmed what he'd suspected from the beginning—Godunov had sent his personal team to protect the other operations. That could only mean things were going exactly as Bolan had hoped.

"You seem a bit surprised to see me, Mr. Lambretta," the man said.

Bolan decided to play the cards close to the vest until he could solicit additional intelligence. "I don't know you."

"And there is no reason that you should, since we've never met," the man replied in an almost congenial tone. He shrugged, smiled, and then rose and stuck his hands in his pockets. As he ventured around the desk he continued, "You see, I work for the same people that the Wolf worked for. You *do* know who the Wolf was, yes?"

Bolan said nothing, instead taking another sip from his glass. He knew that to give away too much too soon would only point to his guilt, and he had to convince the stranger that he was still on their side. As far as Bolan knew, he could play out the line a little bit longer. There was no reason to believe that either this man or Godunov—in fact any of the men standing here—knew he was the same one who took out the meth factory and the tenement. As far as they knew, those incidents were entirely unrelated to what had happened up north.

"It's obvious you know the answer to the question already," Bolan said. "So why are you even asking it?"

"You have a pretty cocky attitude for a dead man," the Russian replied frostily, folding his arms and staring at him with a malevolent expression.

"And who exactly is supposed to kill me? You?"

"I try not to get my hands dirty unless absolutely necessary. However, I do employ men especially trained for that kind of work." The man gestured to the others in the room. "Men like this, men with very peculiar talents. You know, it struck me as odd when Yuri told me he'd decided to bring you on, give you a chance by putting you into the employ of the Wolf. I was glad that he did not assign you to our team, seeing as though the two men you wasted in his office were *my* men."

"That was simple self-defense and I won't apologize for it," Bolan said. "And I'm only here to do the job Mr. Godunov sent me to do, so I don't understand what all this is about. Unless you're telling me that he actually sent me here just so you could kill me."

It lasted only a moment, barely a heartbeat of time, but Bolan saw the flash of uncertainty in the man's eyes. The soldier knew that the next few minutes would be the most critical and would likely determine whether he could take control of the situation or would be carried out back, stuffed into a garbage bin and set on fire.

"You trying to tell me he *sent* you here?"

Bolan took another drink, this one very large, and then smacked his lips together and dropped the tumbler onto a side table. He then walked to the desk and boldly dropped into a chair positioned in front of it. He propped his feet on the other chair, folded his hands across his stomach and made a show of yawning as if he might die of boredom.

"No disrespect, pal," he muttered, "but maybe you ought to get your hearing checked. I just said he sent me here with a message—that he wants all of us back as quickly as possible."

"Back where?" the Russian asked.

"He didn't say," Bolan said with a shrug. "He told me not to worry about it, that I was to simply come here and tell you we needed to get back, and that I was to go where you go, and do what you tell me to."

The man who had accompanied Bolan into the office took a step toward him now and put his hands on his hips. "Then what was with the big ruckus out front, telling the guys you're here for an inspection? Why all the bullshit?"

"That's what Mr. Godunov told me to say," Bolan said, throwing his hands up in mock defense. He looked at the boss and said, "I just do what I'm told and that's what I was told to do. I was told to come here and say that I was here on business for him, and that I wasn't supposed to talk to anybody but you."

The man turned to look at the Russian. "What the hell is going on, Stepan?"

That was excellent—now Bolan had a name.

"Don't ever question me, Max." Stepan looked at Bolan and asked, "What happened upstate?"

"What happened upstate is that the Wolf didn't listen to my warning," Bolan replied. The Executioner had learned long ago the best kind of lie was one that involved a grain of truth. In this case, it was the truth that Yan Volkov hadn't listened to Bolan, and it had gotten him killed. The fact he had died by the Executioner's hand didn't really play into it, but it did allow Bolan to be more convincing.

"That's not an answer," Stepan said. "You're going to have to do better than that."

"Why? It's the truth, and after I explained it to Mr. Godunov, he believed me. If you got some sort of a problem with that, then I'd suggest you take it up with him."

Stepan took a step toward Bolan, but was restrained by the hands of one of his men. Bolan's nameless savior said, "Isn't it better that we talk to the boss before going off half-cocked?"

Whoever this guy was, Stepan obviously put more weight on his opinion. Maybe he was a type of adviser, perhaps Stepan's lieutenant or second in command. Bolan didn't know if he could use the information to his advantage at some point, but he filed it away just in case. Stepan straightened his jacket, moved his head from side to side to stretch his neck, then took a deep breath and sighed. Once he had regained his calm, he looked at Bolan.

"The Wolf was a valuable ally to the Brotherhood," Stepan said calmly. "As far as we're concerned, the very fact he didn't report in, and you are the lone survivor in this unfortunate situation, gives both Yuri and me reason to suspect you're at the root of this. In fact, I was sent here with express orders to intercept whoever was shooting up our locations, and stop the threat. Up until you walked in here five minutes ago, we thought *you* were that threat. So unless you give me a very convincing explanation for what happened, my orders are to kill you."

"Okay, fine," Bolan said. He stood and faced Stepan openly. "I'll tell you exactly what happened. We went up north to do the job at the school like we were told. My instructions were to show up early this morning at the house over in the Bronx. You know the place?"

Stepan nodded.

"Fine, so we get up to this school—and remember something here, because this is important. The Wolf didn't tell me nothing about what we were doing or where we were going until we got there. So if I don't know where we're going or what we're doing until were actually there, what makes you think I could set a trap for him or something? Huh? What makes you think I could somehow betray him or get him blown up?"

"So how did he and his men get killed and you somehow manage to walk away without a scratch?"

Bolan shrugged and splayed his hands in true Italian mobster fashion. "Just a lucky Catholic? How the hell am I supposed to know? I pulled up in front like he told me to, and waited for him and Southpaw to come out. Next thing, I see this guard, right? And he's poking around and acting kind of queer. So I get out of the car and go over to him, try to find out what he knows, or see what's going on. Then the shooting starts and I watch the other two guys in the van, see? These guys, one was Igor something—I don't recall the other guy's name—anyway, they buy the farm just like that. I mean, bam, bam, and that's *it!* Gone."

"Slow down a minute. What do you mean, they bought it?" Stepan asked. "You saying somebody was shooting at them?"

"Yeah, yeah," Bolan said, in a hurried tone for emphasis. "I thought you knew all of this already."

Stepan didn't want to look ignorant so he just nodded and said, "Go on."

"So I turn and figure it's time for us to go, and I'm looking for the Wolf and Southpaw, and I don't see them. And I'm trying now to get back to the car, because I figure they're going to be coming out and I'm supposed to be there waiting for them. But there's all these kids running around, these little brats in uniforms, and the place gets mobbed by parents screaming. Then I see the Wolf and Southpaw out by the car. And I yell at them, but they jump in and don't see me, so I figure maybe they can't hear me over all the screaming brats."

"So what happened to them?" Max asked.

"They take off like a bat out of hell, and I figure they weren't doing it on purpose, you know, I figure they weren't leaving me dry. And I know I shouldn't have got out of the car but I didn't want anything to go wrong. And then the car just blew up! The thing went up in smoke!"

Before anyone could say another word, there was a heavy rap at the door. Max went over and opened it a crack. "What is it?"

Bolan couldn't hear the gist of the conversation, but he knew the implication when Max closed the door, turned on his heel and looked at Stepan with a panicked expression. It bothered the Executioner, because whatever was going down was something he hadn't planned, and such complications could make it more difficult to get out of this alive. So far, he figured the story he had spun was convincing enough that Stepan no longer suspected him as the threat. As far as he was concerned, the mysterious combatant who had taken out the Wolf's team in Boston, and now the Wolf, was still at large.

"What is it?" Stepan demanded impatiently of Max.

"There's a cop out there, a woman cop snooping around and asking a lot of questions."

And Mack Bolan felt a lead weight form in his gut.

"Get rid of her," Stepan replied. "Now."

CHAPTER SIXTEEN

Mack Bolan considered the odds arrayed before him.

If he reacted here and now, he'd be going up against at least four experienced guns, excluding Stepan, in a confined space. That didn't seem like the most efficient tactic. What bothered him more, though, or maybe even impressed him, was that Detective Marquez had managed to follow or track him here. Perhaps he had underestimated her; perhaps she knew more than he originally guessed about the Russian Business Network.

He hoped if they got out of this alive he'd get the chance to ask her. Which now begged the question of how he would react to Stepan's directive that they "get rid of her now." Taking out the RBN team here and now was something he'd already ruled out, as being impractical. Bolan thought about the alternatives. There wasn't any way they would be able to take Marquez without her putting up a significant resistance. Additionally, too many people had seen her come into the club, and there was a good chance she had identified herself as a New York police detective. That would offer her some protection while she was inside the club; beyond that, Bolan knew she was no more immune to the devices of the Russian crime organization than he was.

The Executioner needed a sufficient distraction, and he thought the best way to provide it would be getting directly involved in whatever it was she was up to. Obviously, she felt some reason to try to support his mission here, so he couldn't believe Marquez had followed him here to sabotage his efforts. No, she was here trying to help.

"She was probably following me," Bolan said.

All eyes turned toward him in surprise.

"What are you talking about?" Stepan replied.

"I knew somebody was following me. So if she's a cop, then she's not a particularly good one, because I spotted her on my tail from the first moment I picked up her scent."

"If you knew somebody was following you, why are you just speaking up now about it?" Stepan asked.

"Because I knew if she managed to follow me here and I took her out, whoever she's working for would send other people here, and they'd be looking for not only me but the rest of you. As long as she stays breathing, then nobody else comes snooping around in our business. There are better places and times to deal with her, and I didn't personally think this was one of them."

Stepan looked at the man who had stepped in before to stop him from delivering the Executioner a beat down—assuming that Stepan had intended to do that. Of course, Bolan would have never let him get away with it. But this way, Marquez's appearance had actually taken some of the heat off him. Bolan figured the smart thing would be to work that to his advantage.

He saw the other man nod at Stepan, and the Russian leader finally said, "All right, Max, just leave her be for now. We need to get over to the offices and find out what Yuri wants."

Max shook his head. "What if she follows us?"

"Well, if what Lambretta here says is correct, that's probably exactly what we *want* her to do." Stepan looked at Bolan. "That sound right to you?"

Bolan nodded.

A potential disaster now averted, Stepan and his men led Bolan out the door and through the club. Two men in the escort team dropped off, leaving only Stepan and Max accompanying the soldier. The trio walked down a center aisle, Bolan's senses attuned to the situation. He doubted they were going to kill him at this point. As far as they were concerned they were executing the orders Godunov had given.

As they walked, Bolan considered it a little strange that Stepan hadn't even bothered to call Godunov and verify his story. He wondered if that fact had to do with Godunov's heavy-handedness as a leader, or if Stepan figured Bolan's story was too preposterous to have been fabricated. That kind of failure to exercise due diligence had been the mainstay of Bolan's previous successes in situations similar to this one. Some called it ego; some called it sloppiness. Bolan didn't choose to put any label on it, since to make those kinds of assumptions could ultimately prove fatal one day. One misstep, one miscalculation of an enemy's capabilities, and Bolan's War Everlasting against the enemy would reach an abrupt conclusion.

They reached the front of the club, and Bolan's eyes flicked in Marquez's direction briefly. The young detective caught the look, realized it was intended to be a warning, so averted her eyes. Smart kid.

Outside the club a Lincoln Town Car sat at the curb, idling. Stepan climbed into the front passenger seat and waved Bolan and Max toward the back. Bolan got in and slid across the seat in order to position himself behind the driver. If something went down, it would be best for him to be in this spot, since he could exert immediate control on the one person whose actions would most affect the outcome in a hot situation. Bolan didn't surmise there would be any such trouble, but he figured it was best to take every precaution possible.

The driver pulled into traffic just as Bolan noticed Marquez making her exit. He also noticed the two escorts that had left them were right behind her. There wasn't much she could do about it. She wouldn't have seen him inside the vehicle from that distance. There was a virtual wall of traffic traveling slowly along the street, and no way she could get to her own vehicle fast enough to follow them. Instead, Marquez turned and hailed a cab.

Bolan decided to make something more of it in order to gain the attention of Stepan's men, while building additional loyalty and trust in his role. "There she is. That's the cop who was following me."

As he pointed in her direction, Stepan and Max followed his gesture. Stepan immediately withdrew a cell phone from inside his jacket and punched in two digits. A moment later, Bolan could hear him speaking under his breath, but couldn't really discern many words. He did manage to catch a phrase that led him to believe

Stepan was ordering his men to follow Marquez and take her out as soon as possible.

Killing her openly on the street in front of a hundred witnesses wouldn't have been any more prudent than doing it inside the Lisbon.

Bolan tried not to show the tension that flooded his chest and made it difficult to breathe. It seemed almost ironic that drawing attention to Marquez rather than attempting to subvert the attention of the Russian Business Network goons from her was turning out to be the one thing that would save his life. Before Stepan could hang up, Bolan decided to venture one more proposal into the works.

"It might be a good idea to just let the cop shadow us."

Stepan told whomever he was speaking with to hold on, then turned and looked at Bolan directly. "What do you mean?"

"Well," Bolan replied, "if you think about it, at least giving her a reason to follow us will also make it easier to keep an eye on her. If we know where she's at and what she's doing, we'll have a better idea of when the time is right to take her out. Just shaking her and following her probably won't be anything but a waste of time."

Stepan considered Bolan's proposal and then nodded. "Maybe Yuri's idea to bring you on was a smart one, after all. You seem to have some experience with this kind of thing."

Bolan shrugged. "I have experience with a lot of things, boss. Who knows? Maybe you'll find me useful."

"Maybe I will."

Stepan returned his attention to the phone, again dropping his voice too low for Bolan to make out what he was saying. If things went the way the Executioner planned, they would allow Marquez to follow them to wherever they were going. In some ways, Bolan didn't really have to guess on their final destination. He knew Godunov ultimately planned to tie into the financial mainframes within the building at Chase One Plaza. That was why Bolan had told Stepan only that Godunov wanted them to join him for the operation; he figured the Russian would know where that was going to happen and when.

Now all Bolan had to do was sit back and wait for his opportunity. He would have them all in one place and be ready to make his move when it seemed most appropriate. Perhaps he would be able to take all of Godunov's team at once.

Only time would tell.

BOGDAN LUTROVA SENSED Yuri Godunov had no intention of letting him leave New York City alive.

He'd never trusted Godunov from the beginning, even during his harebrained scheme to arrange for U.S. Customs officials to arrest him when he blatantly attempted to enter the country illegally. Of course, it had surprised Lutrova when the Customs people actually bought his story. Only the man named Cooper seem to know—a knowledge that seemed to come into intuitively—that Lutrova's story didn't make much sense. There were easier ways for the Brotherhood of Social Justice to get their people inside the country.

In fact, the Brotherhood often used American citizens with Russian backgrounds as a means of furthering their ambitions.

Lutrova wasn't a terribly ambitious man. He didn't have this unwavering hatred of Americans or the West; the Arabs, in fact, viewed the Russians as much imperialists and agents of Satan as they did Americans. Lutrova had to admire the Islamic view though, because at least it was consistent. Nothing about America seemed consistent, except maybe for their continued and unabated inconsistency.

Lutrova could even see it in the behavior of guys like Eduardo Capistrano. The guy had been living high off the hog. Men like Capistrano knew nothing of hardship; he'd never gone hungry, or wondered where his next meal might come from; he'd never been caught in the middle of a bloody and violent conflict like the one that occurred when the Russian tanks had rolled into Bogdan's hometown. Lutrova could remember his parents running away from the shells and the bombs. He could remember vividly the shaking of the ground.

The young hacker had never forgotten it, never forgotten the dying screams of his mother in the smoky, choking darkness that had nearly overcome him. Had it not been for the massive hole left by a mortar shell, which created a gap between the floor and the frame through which the young Lutrova had been able to squeeze his tiny body, he wouldn't be here now. It was the adoption of that young, revolutionary-minded boy—one with an uncanny intellect and incomprehensible knowledge of electronics—that changed Bogdan Lutrova's future. Lutrova admitted that he owed something to the Brotherhood of Social Justice. He meant to make good on that.

But he would never admit to owing anything to Yuri Godunov, and he realized if there was any chance of survival—any hope at all of coming through the situation alive—he would have to come up with his own alternative plan. After careful consideration, Lutrova thought he might be able to find an ally in the one other person present who held as much contempt for Godunov as he did. Lutrova wasn't sure he could trust Capistrano entirely, but he was equally sure he couldn't trust anyone else at this point. And it appeared that Cooper had abandoned him. For all Lutrova knew, the American had either turned tail and run or he'd become another mortal statistic for the Brotherhood's list.

As he tapped steadily at the keyboard, Capistrano hanging over his shoulder, Lutrova said, "He has your kids?"

Capistrano didn't say anything at first, and Lutrova could sense the hesitation in the man even though he couldn't see his face. Lutrova could understand how he was feeling. It probably sounded as if Lutrova was trying to trap him, give himself away or provide Godunov with some reason to rescind the deal. Lutrova decided the only way he could gain ground was to attempt a different tack.

"I'm only asking because surely you know he's not going to let you go." He stopped typing and turned in his chair. Looking up into Capistrano's eyes, he continued, "He's not going to let you out of here alive. He's not going to let *either* of us out of here alive."

Capistrano cocked his head. "What are you up to?

You're trying to trick me into saying something wrong so that he can back out. You're just trying to get me killed, that's what it is."

"No, because we're both in the same boat right now," Lutrova said. "I may be helping him do this, but it's not because of the loyalty toward him personally. My loyalty is toward the same people he's loyal to, and that's the extent of the relationship. I was coerced into doing this, and now that I've set it up, I am as much a liability as you are. These people…you see, I've worked with them a long time and I can assure you they do not leave any loose ends. It's the only way they can continue to operate in the way they *have* operated up until this point. Untouched."

"So because you've told me that I'm supposed to trust you now," Capistrano said.

Lutrova sighed. "You don't have to believe anything I say if you don't want to. There's very little chance we're going to come out of this alive, anyway. But there is a small chance, and you need to think about your kids. I've seen what they do and I don't agree with it. Children are helpless, and shouldn't have to be subjected to the blind greed of people with no understanding or compassion for the young and impressionable. I may be guilty of a lot of crimes, but I'm not a monster and I'm not a murderer."

"He said as long as I cooperate with him that my kids will be fine," Capistrano said. "How can you expect me to not do everything possible to take him at his word? We're talking about the lives of my children."

"Yes, we are, aren't we? Let's take a closer look at that for a minute. Do you honestly think that a guy capable of threatening your kids just to get what he wants is someone you can believe? If you don't do exactly as he says, he's not only going to kill your kids, he's going to kill *you*. If you do exactly as he says, he's still going to kill you, because you're a witness to what he's done. And then your kids will be without a father."

"I can't go to the cops after all this," Capistrano replied with a derisive snort. "This guy has me over a barrel, but good. If I roll over on him, I'll be rolling over on myself, as well. The cops will throw me in the slammer for the rest of my life and my kids won't have a father then, either. Better to take my chances that there's a grain of honor, however small, in this guy."

"Really? Have you looked carefully at this room?"

Capistrano appeared to hesitate now. "What about it?"

Lutrova threw up his hands in disbelief. "What about it? Look around you, dude. This room isn't equipped like any of the other offices. Those windows are heavy tempered glass, reinforced with steel riveting. They're also covered with a one-way, tinted film, which is not on any of the other windows in the offices I've seen. Only this one."

Capistrano shrugged. "So what? That doesn't mean anything."

"It means something when you look at the edges of the room," Lutrova replied as he swept his hand toward the walls around them. "See that ventilation system? It runs the entire length of the walls, not just the outside wall, like all the other offices. I think when we're done doing Godunov's bidding, he's going to seal us up and pump this room full of toxic chemicals."

"That's ridiculous."

"Is it? Then if it's so ridiculous, I guess that means you're willing to take the chance he's a man of his word. Has he given you any indication that he's even a halfway decent human being? He's done nothing but blackmail and coerce you from the beginning, and yet you have some grand idea that when this is through he's going to let us go. It's not going to happen, so quit lying to yourself."

"Even if you're right, which I'm not saying you are, what makes you think you can do anything about it? He's got this place locked down tight, and in a very short time you're going to give him control of nearly a third of the New York economy!"

"We have a chance to get out of here alive, but only if we work together."

"You have some way to override the transfer?"

"Oh, will you forget about the fucking money? You need to start thinking about survival and not about how much cash you're going to lose here! The same way that we're using to gain control of the financial system gives me access to just about every other system in this building."

"What are you talking about?"

"I'm talking about things like the alarm system, the environmental system and the security systems."

"I already told you, we can't bank on the cops to help us."

"Maybe not," Lutrova admitted. "But if I can gain access to those other systems, which I'm pretty sure I can, I can lock the doors as I choose. And I can probably shut down whatever he's got planned for us inside this room, since I'm assuming all of these electronics were installed in such a way as to feed into the delivery systems. Maybe he's going to flood the room with poison gas, maybe a nerve agent. Or maybe he's just going to suck the oxygen out. But whatever he does, you can be sure that he'll be long gone from here before he triggers it. That means it has to be triggered remotely, and *that* means it has to be triggered by electronics. Electronics that I will have the ability to shut down!"

Capistrano's expression showed his realization of what Lutrova was saying. "If you're right, then we'd be able to turn this room into something just the opposite of its intended purpose."

"Now you're getting the picture," Lutrova said. "Instead of it being a death room, I can turn it into a safe room. I can turn this room into a place so safe that the gods themselves couldn't break in. If we can keep Godunov out long enough, then generate some type of alarm, even the fire alarm, he'll have no choice but to leave us behind."

"So what do you need *me* to do?"

Lutrova offered his new ally a tight smile and replied, "I was just getting to that."

CHAPTER SEVENTEEN

It didn't come as a surprise to Mack Bolan when their procession of vehicles arrived at the One Chase Manhattan Plaza building.

On Stepan's orders, the driver of the Lincoln Town Car made sure he drove fast enough so as not to arouse suspicions, but slow and purposefully enough to ensure that Marquez's cabbie didn't lose them in traffic. Even at this time of night, it was surprisingly crowded on the New York streets—just another Friday night in the city that never sleeps. Bolan thought they would stop at the curb out front of the building, but instead the Town Car turned onto a private drive that descended to a garage door marked as a loading area. The driver rolled the window down halfway and made some kind of gesture at a uniformed guard who then engaged the door. As it rose, the driver pulled into the garage and followed the drive as it circled around to stop in front of the loading zone.

Stepan and Max got out, and Bolan followed suit in a manner that appeared comfortable and certain. He knew this was still dangerous territory. If he had to be careful at any point in the mission, this would be it, as senses would be heightened for Stepan and all his men. The loading zone opened up through twin sets of massive, sliding glass doors that led to a corridor. At the far end they reached a freight elevator.

Stepan stabbed the switch and the elevator arrived a minute later. The doors opened to reveal a heavily armed man dressed in black fatigues. He wore a black stockingcap and his face was smeared with combat cosmetics. A Heckler & Koch HK53 submachine gun dangled from the man's neck by a sling. Bolan noted this and realized he could have miscalculated the Russian Business Network's security precautions. The Executioner was armed only with his Beretta 93-R, and that wouldn't prove much good against trained RBN gunners equipped with heavy assault weapons.

The trio stepped aboard the elevator and the security guard pressed the button for the twenty-eighth floor. Bolan recognized it immediately as the floor occupied by the offices of Godunov's bogus holding firm. He felt the elevator move beneath his feet and watched as the numbers ticked off. None of the other men with him could have had any inkling of the irony in that moment. Bolan knew he would have to make his move very soon if there was any chance at all he could seize this opportunity to squash the RBN's plans and put Godunov on the defensive. Of one thing he was certain: Stepan and his security force wouldn't retreat without a fight.

And that was fine, because Bolan fully intended to give them one.

JUSTINA MARQUEZ WATCHED with interest as the Lincoln Town Car turned into a drive marked as a loading zone area and descended from view.

The cabbie obviously found her a little on the crazy side when she ordered him to pull to the curb and let her out. He didn't make too much noise or protest the dangers of a lone female in this part of town at this time of night when she passed fifty dollars cash through the bulletproof window and told him to keep the change. It seemed almost absurd to her how quickly money could obscure any notion or sense of chivalry in the male psyche. But she supposed that if it weren't for those things, there wouldn't be any corruption of the kind she had witnessed so many times before. That's what kept her employed, and she couldn't say she minded, although she wished she could live in a world where it didn't exist.

No such luck, she told herself as she exited the cab.

Once it departed, Marquez looked at the front of the One Chase Manhattan Plaza skyscraper and began to think furiously. She knew there were probably security guards watching the front doors, and she had no reason or cause to be there at that time of night. Chances were good they wouldn't admit her without a warrant. She also didn't have any idea what was actually going on, although she'd seen the look Cooper had given her as he made his way through the club under the escort of the Russian thugs.

Marquez hoped she had read Cooper's expression correctly, one that almost pleaded for her not to cause a scene. She'd wondered as she followed the entourage from the club if his look had actually been a call for help and not a warning to hold off alerting the cavalry. Still, she realized it was best to trust her instincts, and her instincts told her the time hadn't yet come. She couldn't see a guy like Cooper wanting to start something inside the Lisbon Club. Not that she would have, anyway, since innocent people could have been seriously hurt. That didn't seem like the way to run an undercover operation, and she affirmed for herself in that moment that she had done the right thing.

Now a new dilemma faced Marquez: how to follow and observe until it became obvious the moment had come to act or dial Captain Dagum and sound the alarm. Based on what she knew about Yuri Godunov and what Cooper had intimated the RBN planned to do, Marquez figured that whatever was going down was imminent. It also seemed probable it would happen here. The issue now, however, was how to gain access to the building and find Cooper, who could be on any one of the sixty floors. She was about to head inside and take her chances with the guards when she suddenly remembered something she had seen in Godunov's file. Marquez took her cellular phone from her belt and dialed the station house.

One of the OCU detectives on duty, a young rookie named Tommy Blaine, answered the phone.

"Tommy, it's Justina."

"What's up?" Blaine said in greeting.

"I need you to pull some information from the file I worked up on a guy named Yuri Godunov."

She heard him typing into the computer, and then he said, "I don't see a Yuri anybody in the active case files."

Marquez shook her head, even though she knew he couldn't see her. "No, this is something I was doing on my own. It's not in any of our records, although Captain Dagum knows about it."

She elected to add that last clarification because there were still some significant rumors running through the department that the OCU had a spy among its ranks. It wouldn't do her much good to make a young and inexperienced cop like Blaine suspicious. The last thing she needed right now was an Internal Affairs investigation opened up on her, however superfluous or baseless it might be. Dagum had told her she was skating on thin ice as it was for running her conspiracy theories up the chain of command, regardless of how effectively she had demonstrated there was merit to her conclusions.

"The file folder is in my desk," she said. "It's in the center drawer."

"Okay, hold on a sec," Blaine replied.

Nearly a minute elapsed, and Marquez had to wonder what the hell Blaine was doing, since his desk sat right across a narrow aisle from hers. She glanced at her watch and began to tap her foot just as he came back on the line. "Okay, I found a file labeled Godunov. What do you want to know?"

"He owns a business firm, a holding company called Vastok & Karamakov." She spelled it from memory and said, "It's located at One Chase Manhattan Plaza. What's the suite number of the address?"

She heard Blaine thumbing through several pages, and he finally said, "Um…here it is. Twenty-eighth floor, suites 101 to 105."

"You're a doll," she said. "Thanks."

"Hold on a minute there!" he said. "What's going on?"

Marquez sighed, unsure how much she should tell him. It was entirely possible that nothing would happen here, and she didn't want him going off half-cocked, bringing the entire department down on top of this place without cause. Nonetheless, she knew the dangers of not at least telling *somebody* where she was, and she didn't have the time to call Dagum personally and give him the information. Marquez decided to err on the side of procedure and fill Blaine in on what was happening.

"Basically, I followed that federal agent I told you about here to the Chase Manhattan building. I think something's about to go down, but I don't know exactly what. I'm going to go inside and see if I can somehow bypass the security people. As soon as I know something I'll call you back, but don't do *anything* in the meantime until you hear from me. Got it?"

"Yeah, sure I got it. But do me a favor, Justina."

"What's that?"

"Be careful. I don't need you getting yourself killed while I sat here on my hands," Blaine said. "Not when I know I could have brought help."

"You're a good cop, Tommy," Marquez said. "Don't worry about it, I'll be fine."

She closed the cover of her phone, placed it into the holster on her belt and then surreptitiously checked the action on her Glock 21 before heading purposefully toward the front doors. She'd nearly reached them when she heard the shuffle of footsteps behind her. Marquez started to turn, but something hard and thin pressed against the small of her back and a big hand grasped her shoulder.

"Don't turn around and don't say anything," a gruff voice told her.

"You're one stupid bitch," another voice added. "Aren't you?"

A knot formed in Marquez's throat and nearly choked off her reply. "I don't know who you are, but you're making a big mistake."

"The only one who made a mistake was you," the first man replied. "Now move."

The small object at her back—Marquez could only assume it was the barrel of a gun—exerted enough additional pressure to force her in the direction of the front doors. Marquez knew whether she wanted to or not, she was about to see exactly what the RBN was up to.

And she wondered this time if anybody, including Cooper, would be able to help her.

THE DOORS OF THE ELEVATOR opened onto an empty hallway, and Mack Bolan breathed a quiet sigh of relief. He didn't want to make his move quite yet. As they stepped off the elevator and headed down the hallway— Stepan took the lead while Max and the guard grabbed flank—Bolan began to formulate his plan. It would take split-second timing to exploit the element of surprise, but there was little doubt in his mind that the moment was closing.

All that remained was how soon that moment would come.

They arrived at Godunov's office. Stepan rapped

twice on the door, and then opened it and stepped inside, with Bolan close on his heels. The Executioner waited until all four men had cleared the doorway and Godunov, seated behind his desk, looked at them. The soldier waited until Stepan started to speak, and gauged Godunov's reaction before he made his move.

The Executioner whirled on his heel and grabbed with both hands the HK53 slung around the guard's neck. He yanked down, then stepped behind the man as he flipped the barrel and stock into a position where he could control it. Bolan pulled backward with all his might, effectively using the canvas sling as a makeshift garrote while maneuvering the muzzle into target acquisition on Max. The Russian goon had only time to look at Bolan with surprise before his face disappeared under a burst of close range autofire.

The 5.56 mm slugs blew Max's head apart with singular effect.

Godunov rose from his chair and began to scream at Stepan even as Bolan backed out of the office with his human shield. Stepan disappeared from view, and the soldier pulled tighter on the sling, while reaching beneath his coat and drawing the Beretta 93-R. While nearly as big as Bolan, his RBN hostage couldn't get the leverage necessary to escape, and his only choice was to back-step quickly, hands clutching desperately at his throat as Bolan half dragged, half walked him down the hallway.

Stepan emerged from the door with his pistol in hand, but ducked for cover when Bolan aimed the Beretta at him and snapped off two rounds. The soldier hadn't necessarily intended to kill Stepan as much as keep him off balance until he could gain some running room. He retreated another fifteen feet before untwisting the sling from the weakened sentry's neck and relieving him of his SMG. The man slumped to his knees and Bolan lifted a knife from him as well, before sending his unconscious form to the floor with a swift kick to the back of the head.

Bolan turned and sprinted down the hallway, now out of direct line of sight with Godunov's office. He knew he had maybe five seconds to formulate a plan before the RBN security responded in force. A man with dark hair and eyes and dressed in an impeccable suit emerged from one of the office doors and nearly collided with Bolan.

The Executioner raised his pistol and pointed it at the man's head. "Who are you?"

The man immediately raised his hands and stammered, "Ed-Eduardo Capistrano."

Bolan waved his pistol in the direction of the doorway from which Capistrano had come, and ordered him back inside. Before the Executioner could follow behind him, he heard the elevator doors open. He whipped the muzzle of the HK53 in that direction, but was taken off guard at the appearance of none other than Justina Marquez. Behind her were the two RBN gunners who had been with Stepan at the Lisbon Club. They had to have been following Marquez and taken her into custody at the first opportunity.

The men looked surprised to see Bolan standing there with an SMG in hand. Their hesitation proved fatal. Bolan took the first one with a short burst to the belly. The man danced backward under the impact, eventually landing inside the elevator just as the doors began to close. Marquez smartly went prone and Bolan made the most of it.

The other gunman managed to clear his pistol from leather before Bolan's rounds found their mark. A trio of 5.56 mm rounds struck the man in the chest, puncturing his lungs and heart. The short-range volley proved devastating and spun the enemy's body into a nearby pillar. He glanced off the column and toppled to the linoleum.

Marquez jumped to her feet and stepped back into the elevator. Bolan checked the rear while simultaneously wondering what the hell she was doing.

"Let's go!" Bolan finally ordered Marquez even as she reemerged.

The detective rushed to him and held up a pair of pistols. "Figured we could use all the firepower we can get."

Bolan looked at her in surprise, a little irritated with himself that he'd jumped down her throat. Maybe she had complicated the situation by following him in spite of the fact that it put her as well as the mission in danger. But at least she was thinking clearly, something he had to admit he admired under the circumstances.

He inclined his head toward the open door where the man named Capistrano had appeared, and followed behind her. Once they were inside the office, Bolan slammed the door behind them, and then turned to find the last person he had expected to see.

"No!" Bogdan Lutrova said. "You stupid bastard!"

"Excuse me?" Bolan replied, taking a few steps in his direction.

"You heard me," Lutrova snapped. "Do you have any idea how long it took me to get that damn door unlocked?"

"What're you talking about?" Marquez interjected.

Lutrova looked at her only a moment and then returned his attention to Bolan as he jerked his thumb in her direction. "Who the hell is she?"

"She's a New York City police officer," Bolan said.

"You can call me 'Detective,'" Marquez added sharply.

Capistrano took a hesitant step toward them and said, "I didn't have any choice in this stuff. Godunov blackmailed me into—"

"I know who you are and how you were involved in this," Bolan interrupted. "And your kids are going to be safe, so you have no further reasons to cooperate with the Russian Business Network."

Capistrano shook his head with disbelief and then said, "The who?"

"Long story," Marquez replied for the Executioner.

Bolan turned his attention back to Lutrova. "Now what's the situation with the door?"

"The situation is that this room is rigged with some sort of booby trap," the hacker said. He gestured toward the walls. "I'm assuming it's probably designed to pump a lethal gas into the room, something like a nerve agent or other toxin."

Bolan furrowed his eyebrows. "What makes you think so?"

"The room is hermetically sealed."

"How do you know that?" Marquez asked.

Lutrova glanced at her, shook his head, then gestured for Bolan to follow him to the door. He stuck his hand out and ran it along the areas where the door met the frame. "There's absolutely no air movement coming from the seams. Check it for yourself!"

Bolan did and realized in a moment Lutrova was probably right. The guy might have been a criminal, but he was highly intelligent, and the Executioner believed it was probably a good idea to pay attention to what he had to say on such things. Without a word, he turned to look at Marquez and Capistrano, who stood there with expressions of perplexity tinged by fear.

What a motley crew.

Bolan looked at Lutrova. "Any chance you can get the door open again?"

Lutrova frowned and scratched his head. "The security system operates on a rotating frequency. I'm going to have to start the algorithm over, which is going to take more time than we probably have."

"Any way you can stall?" Marquez asked.

Lutrova looked at her with disbelief. "You're kidding, right?"

"Just get to work on the door," Bolan said.

"Why don't we just shoot our way out?" Marquez asked.

"No dice," Bolan said, shaking his head. "Godunov is smart enough to think of that, and I'm sure it's reinforced with heavy steel. All we'd do is waste ammunition."

"And what happens if he can't get the door open again?" Capistrano asked, his voice rising in pitch.

Bolan looked him square in the eyes. "Then we're dead."

CHAPTER EIGHTEEN

While he didn't intend for his words to be prophetic in any fashion, the Executioner saw no point in mollycoddling Capistrano, or any of them, for that matter.

As Lutrova began to hammer at the keyboard, Capistrano standing over him and breathing down his neck, Marquez covered the door with the two pistols she'd lifted. Bolan went about the work of attempting to communicate with Stony Man. He walked to one of the open terminals, sat down and attempted to gain access to the internet. He was hopeful that if Lutrova couldn't come up with a plan to get them out of there in one piece, perhaps Aaron "the Bear" Kurtzman and his team of wizards might be able to crack the security system.

If anybody could get inside of whatever booby trap Godunov had implemented, it was Kurtzman. Unfortunately, it didn't take Bolan long to realize the limits of connectivity were confined to the internal network; there was no mechanism for getting out to the external world without reconfiguring the wireless system Capistrano had rigged so Lutrova could transfer the money. Bolan muttered a curse beneath his breath and rose to join Marquez, who stood vigil at the door.

"What's the matter?" she asked.

"There's no way for me to help," he replied. "If I

could get word to my people, they might be able to shut the entire system down. But we would need external access and we don't have it."

"What about the cell phone?" Marquez asked.

Bolan shook his head. "Damaged in the last engagement. It's completely worthless."

With a grin, Marquez reached to the phone on her belt and held it up. "Mine works."

Bolan nodded and took the phone from her. He stepped over to where Lutrova was working and got a two-minute brief on how to get the phone hooked into the computer system. Lutrova assured the Executioner that as long as the phone had a clear, wireless signal it could be plugged into the computer and interface in such a way as to gain internet access.

"Probably won't be superfast," he said. "But it should work."

Bolan moved over to the computer terminal, with a USB interface cable Lutrova had provided from his bag of equipment, and immediately plugged into it. Once he was hot, Bolan dialed in a special code that would connect him directly to Stony Man's authentication and control system.

"I was beginning to wonder if you'd decided to stand me up permanently," Kurtzman cracked when the connection was made.

"You know how much I hate to be tied down," Bolan replied. He changed his tone at that point to signal there wasn't time for additional banter. "I have you patched into the computer systems at the One Chase Manhattan Plaza building. Are you ready?"

"As ready as I'll ever be, now that we know the exact

programming parameters," Kurtzman replied. "We're standing by to revert the transfers."

"I'm not worried about the transfers right now. Lutrova is convinced this place is booby-trapped with some sort of chemical weapon that we believe Godunov will deliver through the ventilation system in the room."

"No way you can get out?"

"Not without risking the lives of everyone here," Bolan said. "If I try to blast out of here and leave them behind until I can get it done, there's a pretty good chance Godunov will set off whatever trap he has planned, before I can clear a path to the nearest exit."

"Windows aren't an option?"

"Not on the twenty-eighth floor. Lutrova's trying to get the door open right now, but we're not hopeful. In fact, the transfers have already begun, and as soon as they're done, I imagine Godunov will release the hounds."

"Well, I guess we better cut through all the red tape then," Kurtzman said. "How long can you leave this channel open? My system shows this is a pretty slow connection, and without broadband speed it's going to take some time, since I'll have to overrun the entire platform rather than implement a targeted solution."

"I can leave it open as long as necessary," Bolan said. "The phone belongs to Marquez, a detective with the New York Police Department."

"All right, I'll get to work on it immediately. Any idea how much more time you have?"

"I wish I did," Bolan replied. "Just do your best and I'll worry about the details on this end."

"Good luck, Striker," Kurtzman said.

Bolan set the phone on the desk, which was actually a very long table facing the back wall. He climbed out of his seat and moved over to the windows, inspecting them for any sort of weaknesses. He rapped his knuckles on the glass and grunted with satisfaction.

"Excuse me," Marquez said, interrupting his train of thought.

"What?"

"What are you doing?"

"Testing to see if the glass is bulletproof."

"Why?" Capistrano asked. "Even if it isn't and you can shoot it out, what good is it going to do us? I don't see any parachutes in here, and I don't think you can fly."

Marquez fixed Capistrano with a furious gaze. "He's hoping that in the worst-case scenario he could blow out the window and maybe vent whatever toxins they might pump in here." She looked at Bolan and added, "Right? That *is* what you were testing for?"

Bolan smiled down at her. "Yeah, that's what I was testing for. The only problem is if Godunov is using some kind of chemical weapon, it might be a bio agent powerful enough to affect people outside the building. I can't have that on my conscience."

"Oh, that's great," Capistrano said. "That's just great. Better that *we* die than take a chance of others getting contaminated, however remote that chance might be."

"Why don't you do us all a favor and just shut up!" Marquez countered.

"Easy," Bolan said, putting a hand on her shoulder. "Save the fight for the bad guys."

She returned her gaze to him. "Why don't we just get out of here and take on the Russians? At least we could have a fighting chance against them."

"Let's be patient a little longer," Bolan said. "I've got faith that my people can shut it down before the transfers and information download Godunov is running are completed. Either that or Lutrova here will manage to get the door open."

Lutrova didn't look in their direction, but he did acknowledge the conversation by saying, "I'm working on it, I'm working on it."

With that, the room fell silent.

"IDIOT!" Yuri Godunov spit.

Stepan winced as Godunov slammed his fist on his desk. His nephew obviously had found it extremely difficult to explain how he'd allowed Lambretta to dupe him with such an absurd story, but then to also overpower an armed man and kill one of Stepan's closest friends…! If the young, impetuous man standing before him hadn't been a relative, Godunov probably would have pulled the pistol from his desk and shot him point-blank between the eyes. Instead, the Russian crime leader withdrew the weapon and tucked it into the holster at the small of his back.

"We have no time for this right now," Godunov said. "But I assure you that we're not finished. The transfer has already started, and as soon as it is complete the system I put into place will activate and the room where our enemies have stupidly clustered themselves will flood with ammonium chloride."

Godunov saw the look on his nephew's face. He had learned after many years of working with the Brotherhood of Social Justice not to be squeamish about such things—though many of those around him couldn't see it in the same way he did. For Godunov, such things were subjective. He wasn't entirely inhuman, and understood why the thought of subjecting the human body to such a horrific death might turn the stomach. Hydrochloric acid and ammonia in combination produced a highly caustic substance that crystallized much like salt. However, it took only a small amount of water to separate the two, and when sprayed aerially under high pressure, ammonium chloride would coat everything in its path including mucous membranes and respiratory passages, with corrosives. Usually victims of such exposure in a confined space died from swelling of the tissues around the lips and nose, where the mucosa burned, or they drowned in their own fluids.

Godunov had seen such a reaction only once before, when studying at the library in Saint Petersburg. It was there he had learned a very similar reaction occurred around volcanic sites, where essentially fissures of great heat filled with sulfuric, molten rock combined with the natural ammonia gas that was produced with the combustion of one nitrogen molecule and three hydrogen molecules. The hydrochloric acid then combined with the ammonia, to produce a saltlike substance so caustic it would burn through any material other than those known to be nonreactive: essentially glass, PVC, plastic and lead. Most all other substances couldn't resist the highly volatile nature of this deadly combination, least of all human tissue.

Godunov saw no point in dwelling on such things. "It is time for us to go. Our mission is done here, and I must return to the Hamptons. We will have to leave the country very shortly, I would think."

"I do not understand," Stepan said. "If we have what we need, why do we have to leave?"

"If I am correct in my suspicions, Bogdan is working for the American government," Godunov said. "That means the presence of Lambretta—who I believe actually probably works for a covert agency—not to mention the involvement of the local police, clearly demonstrates we are no longer able to operate with any level of anonymity."

Stepan's jaw tightened and his voice became quiet. "I mean no disrespect, Yuri, but I am not accustomed to running. You should let me deal with this Lambretta personally."

"Phah! You had your opportunity to do that and failed. Now, I don't want any more arguments. Round up your detachment, leave only a couple of guards to ensure those inside the room don't find a way out, and let's get out of here. And make sure that you eliminate those guards in the downstairs security area before leaving."

Godunov then scooped the portable computer notebook off his desk and headed for the door.

SWEAT POURED DOWN Bogdan Lutrova's face as he beat on the keyboard. "No, goddamn you! No!"

Capistrano ran a hand across his eyes, muttering beneath his breath and shaking his head.

Marquez raised an eyebrow and said, "Problem?"

"Too much of the computer's processing power is being taken up by the ALU."

"The ail-a-who-what?" Marquez retorted.

"The arithmetic logic unit," Lutrova said. "It's a microchip inside every computer system that's designed strictly to perform mathematical calculations so more of the other functions requiring memory can be delegated to the central processing unit...the brains of the computer."

"Can't you fix it?"

Lutrova looked at her in utter amazement. "It's not a car I'm working on here! Why don't you just sit over there and be quiet, and let the men work on what we know best."

"Look, friend," Capistrano interjected. "There's no reason to talk to the lady like that."

Before it could go further, the Executioner said, "All of you put it to rest."

Capistrano opened his mouth as if to protest, but a quick hard look from Bolan made him think better of it. He shut his mouth, shoved his hands in his pockets and turned to gaze out the window.

Marquez stepped away from Lutrova and sidled close to Bolan. The much shorter detective looked up at him, and when she managed to get his attention she gestured for him to accompany her out of earshot of the other two. It wasn't really that easy to have privacy in a room that size, but Bolan figured, as Marquez probably did, that the other two men were too wrapped up in their own thoughts to worry about what she wanted to discuss.

"Why don't you just let me call the department?" she asked quietly. "I can have a whole army down here in just a few minutes."

Bolan shook his head with a grim expression. "And if they break us out of here just as the delivery system goes off?"

"We don't really know there's any danger at all from those things," Marquez argued, as she nodded toward the vents lining the walls. "The only thing we have to go on is the word of this guy over here, and if you ask me, he seems pretty high-strung. I'm not sure I'd put that much weight in what he's saying."

"But you can't be any more sure there isn't a danger," Bolan countered. "And I'm not willing to risk the lives of civilians or even rescue personnel on a maybe. Are you?"

Marquez pulled her head back a little, as if surprised at the strong tone in his voice. He didn't like coming down on her, but he also knew she wasn't thinking clearly at this point. Marquez might be tough, but she was as susceptible to panic and irrational thinking as anybody. Bolan had learned valuable lessons, spending as much time in perilous situations as he did. He'd walked on every continent and faced the most dangerous odds any single human being might encounter. Such experiences had taught him the most logical way through any potentially fatal encounter was to remain calm and clear-thinking.

"The best thing we can do is continue to work the solution and hope the clock doesn't run out," he said.

Marquez appeared to think it over another moment, then nodded. "Of course. You're right."

As if on cue, a loud and steady beep began to issue from the terminal into which Bolan had plugged Marquez's cell phone. He exchanged hopeful glances with her before turning and rushing to the terminal, the detective and Capistrano on his heels. Both of them began to inquire as to what was happening at the same time but Bolan simply held up his hand to signal for silence.

After thirty seconds or so of studying the screen, Bolan put the cell phone to his ear. "What's the story?"

"We found some code in the security system that was designed for emergencies," Kurtzman said. "If we trip a building-wide power loss, the door locks will automatically detach and all doors will open. It'll be dark and you won't have elevators, but at least you'll be able to get out of there until a haz-mat team can get in."

"We'll take it."

"All right then, get ready. The door should open in three, two, one…now!"

A soft buzz emanated from the door, and then a click, and it popped ajar. As well, every light winked out, and visible through the opening was the orange-yellow glow of emergency lights. Capistrano let out a cheer and rushed for the door, obviously having no consideration for the others in the room. It also didn't appear he'd given any thought to the fact that the enemy might be waiting right outside. Bolan had considered it and he shouted a warning.

It fell on deaf ears.

Capistrano whipped the door wide, rushed into the hallway and was immediately cut down by a hail of bullets. High-velocity slugs smashed into his chest and sent his body crashing into the wall behind him. Marquez started for the door, but Bolan grabbed her by the shoulder and turned her toward Lutrova.

"You get him. I'll worry about them."

Marquez snapped something in reply, but did as he instructed. Bolan rushed to the door and peered around the corner. Two shadowy figures silhouetted by the emergency lights raised their SMGs and fired on his position. Fortunately, they directed their fire high, and in doing so exposed their positions through the muzzle-flashes. Bolan went out the door low, gained momentum, then shoulder rolled to concealment behind one of the pillars. He snap aimed around the near corner and sent a quick volley in the enemy's direction, then doubled back and came up on the opposite side, partially concealed behind a large planter.

Bolan now had a clear sight on the pair, but the gunners were still focused on where he'd been.

The Executioner took the advantage by raising the HK53, acquiring his targets and squeezing the trigger. Three successive bursts of 5.56 mm bullets reduced the odds by one hundred percent. One burst caught a gunner full in the face and ripped bone, skin and soft tissue from everything below eye level, chopping most of the man's face into mush. His partner tried to evade Bolan's rounds, but instead of escape he walked right into the field of fire. He took slugs in the belly, chest and neck before toppling to the floor, his weapon leaving his fingers and skittering across the polished linoleum.

Bolan watched as the weapon tapped the foot of a small, familiar-looking figure. Justina Marquez reached down, scooped up the SMG and tossed a salute in Bolan's direction.

The Executioner smiled, but it quickly turned to a scowl when he saw Lutrova grab her around the neck and put the barrel of a pistol to her head.

CHAPTER NINETEEN

"What the hell are you doing, Bogdan?" Bolan asked.

"There's no way you're going to let me go, Cooper," Lutrova replied. "The way I see it, my only possibility of getting out of here alive is if I take a little insurance along with me."

"Don't let him do this, Cooper!" Marquez shouted. "Just kill this bastard. Kill him right now."

Bolan had stepped into view and now held his Beretta 93-R leveled in Lutrova's direction. He knew he couldn't miss—he'd made much tougher shots at much greater distances. But the warrior in him, an instinct he had learned to listen to over the years, convinced him Lutrova didn't really mean to harm Marquez. Sure, he was a criminal and hardly trustworthy, but in Bolan's experience only men who were desperate and had nothing to lose would make good on such threats.

"Just be quiet, Detective."

Marquez looked at first as if she might argue with Bolan, but remained silent.

Bolan peered intently at Lutrova over the slide of the Beretta. "I don't know that much about you, Bogdan. But I'm willing to bet you're intelligent enough to realize that if you shoot her I'll kill you where you stand. I think you're smarter than that, and I think you know you have something to lose here. Get wise. Don't force my hand and don't do anything as reprehensible as murdering an unarmed woman."

"What reason do I have to believe you?" Lutrova asked, the initial resolve in his eyes beginning to waver.

"Would you rather trust Godunov? That's worked out for you real well so far, hasn't it? Where exactly do you think it is you're going to go? Godunov knows by now that you betrayed him, and if you run, the Russian Business Network will find you. I think your chances are better with the United States government."

"Ha, that's a joke! The American government that blows up villages in Afghanistan, the same country they trained to resist the armies of the Soviet Union? A government that tortures prisoners of al Qaeda or funds its intelligence agencies to execute the high-ranking members of sovereign governments?"

"I'm not here to argue politics with you," Bolan replied. "But there's one thing I can guarantee. If you use your head and agree to work with me, there's something I can do to help you. But if you take this woman's life, even if you manage to escape from me now, I will hunt you down. I will find you. And if I don't, you can bet Godunov and his men will. You'll be on the run for the rest of your life, always looking over your shoulder, always wondering and waiting for the bullet to come. So if that's what you want, go ahead and pull the trigger. But remember this and remember it good. I rarely miss."

The Executioner knew he was taking a chance, a big chance, actually, but he didn't see he had much choice. The numbers were running down quickly, and the more time he spent wasting words with Bogdan Lutrova the better the chance Godunov would escape. Even if Bolan knew where he was headed, his full-court press was on. In all likelihood Godunov had moved to a defensive posture. It was difficult to fight the enemy while retreating, and Bolan knew a large part of his success in this mission would be to keep Godunov and his people on the run. It'd gone from a fire-and-maneuver tactic to the full-on Bolan blitz.

"What guarantees do I have from you?"

"No guarantees, Bogdan," Bolan replied. "I don't think I need to give any guarantees, anyway. I think I've done enough to prove that I'm as good as my word. The only question is whether you're smart enough to take what's being put on the table. Are you smart enough to live?"

Lutrova met Bolan's gaze, but wasn't equal to the challenge, so he finally relaxed and stepped away from Marquez.

Bolan moved forward, but before he could reach them Marquez turned and slugged the Russian hacker hard in the chest, hard enough to knock the breath from him. She followed with a kick to his shin, then kicked aside the weapon that he'd dropped and began to flail at him with the butt of the submachine gun.

Bolan stepped in quickly and pulled her off. "Calm down, Marquez. I said calm down!" Marquez took a couple more swipes at him even after Bolan had restrained her.

When he felt her body relax, he released her and she turned on him. "Who the hell do you think you are?"

"We're not getting into this right now," Bolan said.

He bent and retrieved the pistol, shoving it into her palm. "You have handcuffs?"

She nodded and produced them almost instantly. Bolan took them from her, gestured for Lutrova to turn around, then clipped them onto his wrists. He grabbed Lutrova by the crook of the Russian's elbow and steered him toward Marquez. He then grabbed Marquez's hand and placed it on Lutrova's arm.

"This guy is now your prisoner and an asset to the United States government," Bolan said. "Congratulations on capturing him, Detective."

He wheeled and headed for the stairwell.

"Where are you going?" Marquez demanded.

"I have a pressing engagement to attend."

"Well give my regards to Godunov and his goons," Marquez shouted after him.

"I'll do that," the Executioner replied.

BOLAN KNEW when he reached the lower level of the loading area that his quarry didn't have much of a head start. He went to the guard shack and found the "real" security officer lying prone on the floor inside, a bullet hole in his back at about the level of his heart and a second in the back of his head. The poor old guy hadn't even seen it coming.

Bolan wondered how he could pursue Godunov and his men when he didn't have wheels, but then he spotted a key dangling from a hook. A quick inspection revealed it belonged to a vehicle. Fortune smiled on him and he found a security patrol car parked in an alcove near the loading area. The door was unlocked and Bolan climbed behind the wheel.

Within a minute the Executioner reached street level and headed uptown, away from the Manhattan business district. His first stop would be the Lisbon Club, where he'd left his car. Then he would head for Godunov's estate in the Hamptons. There was a good chance the Russian would make reasonable speed at this time of night. The traffic had lightened considerably, and Bolan thought through his options as he closed on the club.

There were a lot of people who might have considered Bolan's mission a failure, since he had failed to take down the money-laundering operation at the Lisbon Club. The Executioner didn't see it that way. He'd put Godunov on the run, and without leadership there was a pretty good chance those operations would now crumble on their own. If nothing else, Stony Man could make sure that the information got dropped into the laps of Marquez and her people. Bolan smiled when he thought of the spunky young detective. She had definitely proved herself throughout this particular mission, and he had to admit he admired her tenacity and strength.

Bolan parked the security vehicle in the spot directly across from his SUV.

As he left the lot in the SUV and pulled into traffic, Bolan's eyes flashed to a vehicle that nearly crashed when it pulled into traffic to the blaring horns of several irate drivers. Bolan thought at first it was coincidence, but he knew there was no such thing in situations like this. For just a moment he searched his memory, thinking about where he had seen the vehicle before. Had it followed them from some other place? He couldn't recall anybody on his tail other than Marquez, and even then he had learned she hadn't followed him to the Lisbon Club; she'd just managed to guess where he would hit Godunov and make it hurt the most.

Bolan headed down Sixth Avenue and turned left onto Thirty-fourth Street. Directly ahead he saw signs for I-495, the road that would take him toward Godunov's residence in Sagaponack Village. Bolan checked his watch and saw it was approaching midnight. It would take him nearly two hours to reach his destination, possibly three if he hit any traffic or construction. He knew it might take even longer when he discovered a troubling sight just ahead.

The soldier immediately recognized the panel van approximately four car-lengths ahead of him on Thirty-fourth Street. He'd hit a logjam of traffic, probably partyers out for a night on the town, now headed toward parts unknown. Many businesses were still open, but most of the restaurants and bars were nearing closing time.

It was only here along Thirty-fourth Street—with the Empire State building looming like a giant, spire-topped shadow in the distant streetlights—that Bolan encountered any sort of considerable traffic. He could see over the smaller profiles of the cars ahead, noting where a lighted sign indicated traffic needed to merge into a single lane. But it was that panel van, the one he had seen in the loading dock of the One Chase Manhattan Plaza building, that gave him cause for concern.

The moment he detected the potential threat, Bolan also looked in his rearview mirror and noticed the vehicle that had positioned itself behind him. He had to wonder how they had managed to follow him; in fact, he had to wonder how they even knew he was still alive. Had there been cameras in the building? Had he somehow been observed by sentries posted on the street or at the club, and had they reported him? Bolan couldn't be sure what the situation was, but the fact that the vehicle on his tail looked familiar continued to bother him.

Bolan had to let it go when the rear door on the panel truck rose upward and a dozen armed men emerged. The soldier looked around and realized he'd allowed himself to be penned in by the rows of merging traffic. His eyes flicked to the rearview mirror again, watching for any movement from the tail vehicle, but didn't see any. As his eyes faced front once more, Bolan realized his time had run out. One of the panel truck occupants had knelt and raised a cylindrical object to his shoulder; the muzzle of a rocket launcher was pointed in Bolan's direction.

The soldier snatched the weapons bag off the seat and went EVA. He barely managed to make the safety of the far side of the vehicle in the lane next to him when he heard the whoosh of the rocket's trail and felt the superheated gases that passed over his head nearly close enough to singe hairs. Oddly, it seemed Bolan never heard the explosion, but he exposed his head long enough to see the interior of the SUV now awash in bright flames, with thick black smoke pouring from every opening.

Fortunately, the vehicle's sturdy walls and safety glass windows had contained most of the explosion, and it didn't appear that any bystanders had been injured. Bolan didn't have time to check more closely, because rounds were buzzing past his head and ricocheting against the pavement. The Executioner couldn't see the team that had burst from the panel truck, which meant they couldn't be shooting at him—at least not from that angle. The shots were coming from a higher vantage point, and Bolan couldn't determine exactly from where, given the darkness.

What he did know was the enemy had somehow managed to devise a strategic ambush against him, and Bolan realized right now wasn't the time to attempt to determine how they'd done it. He would figure it out later, if he managed to come through it alive.

He scrambled to his feet and raced out of the fire zone, getting to the sidewalk and searching for cover. Nearby windows shattered as a storm of autofire wreaked havoc around him, a couple of the rounds coming so close he could hear them buzz past his ears. Through some miracle, he managed to avoid being hit, Seeing the broken glass, he realized he had only one place to go. Bolan vaulted the dais supporting a cluster of mannequins and rushed past them into the darkened interior of the building, alarms already audible.

The Executioner pushed onward, seeking cover. He knew that hiding from his enemies was out of the question, which meant his only choice would be to seek a point of refuge where he could take them down one or two at a time. Bolan reached into the weapons bag as he traversed the wide, main corridor of a department store.

There were only a couple of lights at various work-stations, probably left on for safety reasons, and Bolan was thankful they provided adequate illumination to negotiate any potential trip hazards. At that moment, a fresh salvo came in his direction and sought his destruction. He had to hand it to Godunov's men. They were devoted to ensuring the success of their masters, and were obviously not going to give the Executioner any quarter.

Bolan angled to the left and entered a clothing area, maneuvering through the racks of dresses, blouses and pants like a dog through an agility course. His choice to go this way hadn't been an accident, but rather a matter of tactics. The clothing racks not only provided a veritable maze in which Bolan could lose some of his pursuers, it would also force them to fan out. While they outnumbered him twelve to one in manpower and ammunition, they weren't capable of covering every fire zone at every moment.

The soldier found concealment in a changing room with a back wall, facing the entry point for two of the team members. Given the darkness and their focus on the immediate area ahead, the pair of RBN gunners never stood a chance against the Executioner's assault. By the time they heard movement behind them and managed to bring their weapons to bear, Bolan already had acquired his targets and committed to engage them.

A short burst of 5.56 mm hardball rounds did the trick nicely. The first man took two shots to the chest, one of them passing completely through him and blowing a chunk of his heart against the inner wall of his shoulder blade. Blood gushed from the man's mouth as the shock wave from his ruptured heart traveled through his lungs and esophagus. Bolan blew the second man's head off even before the corpse of the first dropped to the carpeted floor with a loud thump. The second body followed the first in like fashion a moment later.

"Nice shooting," said a raspy voice behind Bolan.

The soldier whirled and leveled his weapon in that direction, but held off pressure on the trigger at the last moment. It was then he realized where he'd seen the vehicle following him. It was the one parked in Tom Remick's garage. The aged veteran now stood there in an old set of camouflage fatigues, jungle boots with an M-16 A-2 nestled in the crook of his arm. Bolan also noticed the butt of a Colt M1911 A1 .45-caliber pistol protruding from a beat-up leather shoulder holster under Remick's left arm.

"What are you doing here?" Bolan whispered.

"Never fear," Remick said. "The cavalry has arrived."

CHAPTER TWENTY

Mack Bolan didn't have time to reply.

Godunov's men began to pour the heat on their position, forcing Bolan and Remick to seek cover. The tree racks of clothes provided a decent obstacle course for the RBN hit team, just as Bolan had expected them to, forcing their opponents to fire above the tops of the racks. The Executioner didn't think such a tactic would cause hitters to run out of ammunition anytime soon, but surmised that in the darkness it would continue to cause confusion.

Remick crawled to Bolan's position even as a fresh maelstrom of high-velocity rounds burned the air over their heads, some traveling lower and shredding clothing. Occasionally they could hear one of the bullets zip past as it ricocheted off of the wall or broke the glass on the doors of the dressing rooms.

Remick shouted to be heard over the onslaught. "Looks like I got here just in the nick of time."

"You weren't supposed to be here at all," Bolan retorted.

"Nuts to that. You've always been a glass half-empty kind of a guy, Coop!"

As the initial retorts from enemy weapons died off, Bolan detected the hammer of boots on the floor—probably a group coming up the wide main aisle to their left. He quickly ran down tactics and realized that even if he told Remick to take a hike there was little chance the old vet would comply. Remick had been itching for action for a long time, and Bolan had to admit right at the moment his help would be welcome.

"You showing up here gives us an advantage," Bolan whispered.

"How so?"

"They followed only me in here," Bolan said. "They're not expecting a second person, especially not one who is both trained and armed."

"It's your show," Remick replied. "What's the plan?"

"I'm going to see if I can get into the main mall. Once they've made some distance you come up on their flank."

Remick smiled. "Catch them in the cross fire. Nice."

"Two minutes," Bolan said. "Then you go."

The Executioner climbed to his feet, surprised when the enemy didn't immediately respond. He managed to get to the edge of the clothing department and then moved parallel to it until he reached another aisle perpendicular to the main one. He stopped there and knelt, using a shelved rack of T-shirts for cover. He poked his head out and looked in both directions to clear his flank before bursting into the aisle and rushing for the double glass doors ahead.

As he reached them, he risked a glance behind him toward the sound of running men. He heard shouts and curses in Russian, followed by the stuttering reports of several submachine guns. Bolan ducked in time to avoid being perforated by an enemy salvo. The autofire shattered the glass and blew most of it out of the metal frames. Bolan returned fire with a few short bursts of his own before scrambling to his feet and pushing through the opening they had provided for him, careful not to catch his frame on the jagged remains.

Once out of the store he sprinted down one side of the mall corridor, keeping as close to the edge as he could. Occasionally the enemy would trigger a fresh volley and he would duck into an alcove or get behind a pillar. He would then wait for a lull in the firing before returning a few bursts from the FNC—here and there to keep the enemy busy and their minds off the surprise that would be approaching their flank in short order.

It didn't take long for Bolan to reach the far end of the mall, which happened to be a dead end. He looked around and noticed that one hallway branched off toward the restrooms, while another descended slightly and appeared to open onto a food court. The Executioner knew he had only one logical choice—he and Remick would make their stand in the food court and hope the element of surprise was enough to secure victory. Bolan took off once more, and not a moment too soon, as his pursuers had closed the gap considerably. Rounds danced off the walls and floors and a few passed much too close for comfort. Bolan had just reached the end of the hall and was making for a cluster of tables to his right when a round burned through his leather jacket and bit a small chunk of flesh from his forearm.

Bolan gritted his teeth and looked at the wound while in motion, knowing that to stop at this point was tantamount to suicide. Reaching the cover of the tables, he crouched and took a moment to inspect his arm.

The soldier realized he'd been lucky, the slug had only grazed him, and then traded out the nearly expended FNC magazine for a fresh one. Bolan waited in the shadows, the only sounds the thudding of his heart and the coursing rush of adrenaline-rich blood through his head. He could only hope he'd bought Remick enough time to get into position, because he was sorely outgunned and outmanned from a tactical perspective.

It looked as if the hunter had become the hunted, and there wouldn't be any second chances.

Tom Remick was in his glory.

To actually have Cooper involve him in this kind of operation was nothing less than a pure testament to the big guy's honor. Remick had always felt betrayed by his government, in a lot of respects. They had washed him out of the service with little more than a piece of tin dangling from a ribbon, and a kick in the pants, while they said, "Here's your hat, what's your hurry?"

Well, Remick had the privilege of fighting alongside his friend now, a man of superior skill and honor. Remick would show these bastards exactly what kind of damage an old man could still unleash. He had brought more than just an assault rifle in his bag of tricks. He also carried a couple of fragmentation grenades and one AN-M14 TH3 incendiary grenade, and he damn well planned to use them.

Remick counted off sixty seconds before leaving his position and heading in the direction Cooper had taken. He heard the reports from the weapons, most likely enemy fire, but resisted the urge to engage in a pursuit action. He trusted Cooper implicitly. The guy knew what he was doing, and Remick didn't plan to screw it up by jumping the gun. Somebody had to be the quarry, and Remick knew it wouldn't have made sense for him to take up that role, no matter how much he might have wanted to.

Cooper had made an astute observation in pointing out that the enemy's lack of knowledge about his very existence would provide both men with a tactical advantage. Remick saw that advantage as he half trotted and half limped down the darkened walkway of the mall. At first, he didn't hear what he'd expected to— there were no sounds of weapons fire and no sign of the Russian goons. Remick had to wonder if he'd gone past them, perhaps taken the wrong path, but he quickly dismissed the thought. He'd passed through the broken glass of the double doors, the surest sign in the world his targets weren't too far ahead.

The echo of autofire reached his ears a moment later and Remick followed that sound, a sound he knew all too well. He reached a point in the main aisle that branched in two directions, and he veered to the right, breaking into an easy trot when he detected the shadowy forms of his enemy directly ahead. Remick was a trained combatant and knew the senselessness of giving away his position before absolutely necessary.

When he got in close enough, he knelt behind the cover of a column protruding from the wall, raised the rifle to his shoulder and squeezed the trigger. The ten or so RBN gunners whirled on him with such surprise that three of them fell under the hailstorm of 5.56 mm rounds before even realizing they'd been flanked. The remaining others recovered and dived for cover even as the trio that had been hit stumbled into one another due to their proximity and collapsed to the floor.

Remick had to duck behind the column because the seven left now had adequate distance to make taking them out en masse no longer an option. He cursed as a vicious fusillade chipped paint, drywall, linoleum and concrete from the walls around him. The firestorm they rained on his position filled the air with a choking cloud of dust. Remick waited for a lull in the firing before ripping the AN-M14 TH3 from his belt and yanking the pin.

At only thirty-two ounces, the incendiary grenade was still a formidable weapon and a bane of terror among experienced fighters. And with good reason, since those familiar with this particular ordnance understood exactly what it could do. When deployed, a portion of the thermate mixture inside the grenade was converted to molten iron. It burned in excess of 4000°F, more than hot enough to weld itself to any metal object. The chemical nature of the thermate caused it to burn in any environment where there was adequate oxygen, including underwater, and it was capable of searing through a half-inch of homogenous armor—this variant had a burn rate of nearly sixty seconds.

Remick didn't wait for the grenade to cook off, as he might have done with a frag; only an idiot would do something like that. Unfortunately, he wouldn't have any stories to tell, since he couldn't throw it effectively from his current position. Making the AN-M14 TH3 grenade worth a damn meant that the bearer had to be able to get it in a tight zone. Without a confined space in which to work, he would have to fall back on proximity.

"Well, God favors the brave," Remick said, even as he climbed to his feet and burst into the hallway. He thought of the irony as he popped the spoon and rolled the grenade underhanded directly toward the enemy position. He thought about how it was the first time he could recall using God's name in more than twenty years.

Just before the enemy opened fire, he whispered, "'Vengeance is mine, sayeth the Lord.'"

As soon as Mack Bolan realized the attention of his enemy had been diverted by Remick's flanking action, he burst from cover and circled around the food court. He kept to the shadows, the ones provided by the low wattage, twenty-four-hour lighting that ran along the walls and was diffused toward the ceiling. Bolan heard the shouts of at least two men and realized Remick had taken the enemy by surprise.

Bolan made it into a position where he could provide a decent cross fire. He raised the FNC to shoulder level, calculated the most effective field of fire and began to ease back on the trigger. A bright flash stayed him, and Bolan brought his face away from the stock to look around the barrel of his weapon. It took him only a moment to determine what had happened, because the acrid stench of burning flesh and the screams of men painted a picture as clear as crystal. That kind of carnage and misery could only have been produced by an incendiary grenade—Bolan knew, because he'd used them many times himself.

It didn't take long before the first target came into view, a human torch flailing about like a decapitated fowl. Bolan sighted in on him and pumped three mercy rounds into the flaming, screaming man. The cries of agony died and the body collapsed to the floor face-first, the flesh and clothing continuing to burn. Bolan verified that the body wasn't close enough for the fire to spread; the last thing he needed was to burn the entire building down.

The Executioner waited at least thirty seconds before proceeding into the hot zone, realizing that if Remick had used one grenade and it hadn't produced the desired effect, there was a better than good chance he would use another. Maybe even a frag. But as Bolan rounded the corner and looked, he saw that Remick wouldn't be doing much of anything. The rest of the Russians had gone down and we're definitely dead or incapacitated, one of them smoking and charred so badly it looked as if he had spontaneously combusted.

Only the fact that nobody else was moving directed Bolan's attention to his friend's writhing form. Bolan rushed to Remick's side and knelt, but knew at once he'd come too late. Remick's entire body shook violently, not so much from the throes of death as from shock and trauma of blood loss. There was so much blood covering him that Bolan couldn't tell how many rounds he'd actually taken. Before the warrior could decide on his next action, Remick reached out and grabbed his hand, clutching it so that their palms were pressed together and their thumbs interlocked. It was the handshake of two soldiers, of brothers in blood.

"Did we g-get them?" he stammered in a hoarse voice.

"We got them," Bolan said. "*You* got them."

Remick managed a smile. "I'm sorry it didn't work out like you hoped, Coop. I know you were just trying to protect me."

"You should've got out while the getting was good."

Remick smiled again as he spoke his last words. "I hope you won't hold it against me after I'm gone."

Bolan closed his comrade's eyes.

BOLAN MANAGED to get past the wall of police officers and emergency unit personnel arriving on the scene. He'd lifted the keys from Tom Remick's coat along with the man's wallet. He wanted to make some distance, and hoped it would take time for the police to identify Remick. Of course, there wasn't anything to really tie him to Bolan, but the Executioner didn't want to take any chances. He still had a mission to complete, and the longer he could keep the police in the dark, the better his chances of getting his mission accomplished, and vacating New York before they put out a statewide dragnet.

Of course, he knew as soon as one particular police officer heard about it she would know exactly who was at the center of the commotion. He'd have to contact Stony Man on that count, buy a little more time.

Bolan considered his next option and realized he needed to proceed on it. It bothered him that Godunov had managed to throw one of his hit teams against him, putting bystanders at risk. It spoke to how dangerous

Godunov had become, and the reach of the Russian Business Network.

Yet something bothered Bolan even more, something time hadn't permitted him to dwell on until now. During their time inside the offices at One Chase Manhattan Plaza, Bolan remembered Lutrova mentioning "the Brotherhood" when referring to the RBN. The thought had been clawing at Bolan's mind as he tried to understand what Lutrova had meant. Bolan would have to see what he could find out about this Brotherhood.

As the police directed his car, or rather Remick's car, around the area blocked off, and he picked up speed to head toward I-495, Bolan knew that even if he managed to shut down Godunov, the chances were good someone would rise and take his place. Maybe it would be the man he knew only as Stepan, maybe someone else. Whatever the case, Godunov's demise wouldn't topple the RBN regime. But the Executioner would see this through to the end. He'd take down Godunov and deal with the upper echelon later.

First Sergeant Tom Remick had been a tough old bird with the warrior spirit if there had ever been one. Yeah, someone needed to pay for the loss of Remick—someone named Yuri Godunov.

And the Executioner would make damn sure he collected the debt.

Personally.

CHAPTER TWENTY-ONE

Detective Justina Marquez couldn't concentrate, mostly because the images of a tall, dark-haired avenger filled her thoughts.

A mound of paperwork on her desk didn't help the situation. Her sleep-deprived mind was unable to focus on the task ahead, leaving her unable to complete all of it. She didn't bother to look at the clock because she had already observed the little hand pass midnight and push into the a.m. She had at least three to four hours to go before she would finally be able to head home.

Marquez had already caught an earful, and she wasn't in the mood for hearing any more. Dagum had yelled at her when he found out she'd ventured into the downtown building without backup or a warrant. Only because she'd observed suspicious activity and followed Godunov's men to the building, coupled with the fact that she had entered under duress, managed to save her badge. While her superiors still weren't buying a conspiracy theory, Dagum had managed to get them to loosen the leash some.

It bothered Marquez that they still didn't trust her even after her theories about Godunov and a Russian crime syndicate operating in New York were proved valid. There were times the bureaucracy and red tape aggravated her so much she wanted to pack it in. But one thing remained in her favor: New York City would never forget it was the site of the first foreign terrorist attack on American soil. The brass was always concerned whenever criminal activities came close to even mirroring possible ties with terrorists. Nobody could argue that the Russian *mafiya* might be in bed with terrorist organizations. In a sense, the blackmail and subsequent embezzlement—hell, it was downright *theft,* she knew—could be viewed in itself as an act of terrorism.

What bothered Marquez most of all, however, was how Cooper had cut her out at the end of the deal. She had come after him in the belief he might be in trouble. Now all he'd done was dump in her lap a big mess to explain. And then there was this young Russian hacker who to her knowledge hadn't committed any crimes, at least none she could prove in court. What the hell was she supposed to do with him?

Well, he was currently sitting in a nice comfy cell, and she knew they could hold him only twenty-four hours tops. Maybe something would surface on the guy in that time. Marquez blew hair away from her face, wiping the curls from her eyes as she set one stack of finished work aside and started into the next. She looked at the clock and groaned; it would be three more hours before the coffee vendor showed up with his cart down the block from the precinct. She didn't want to wait that long, but she wanted to drink some of the rotgut purchased by the department even less.

Better to wait.

Marquez had barely put a dent in the witness statements when the phone on her desk rang. She looked at it with irritation at first, considered not answering it. Ostensibly, she was off duty, and it probably wasn't anything the night shift couldn't handle. Then again, they had incoming calls allegedly being forwarded to their cell phones since they were currently on a tactical observation run. That meant the call was coming through on her direct inward dial, and there weren't many people other then her sister or two brothers, along with a couple of close friends, who even had the number.

The phone rang six times before she finally reached for it, but when she picked it up nobody answered. She slammed it into the receiver, adjusted her seat and started on the reports again. The phone rang once more and this time Marquez picked up on the second ring.

"OCU Unit, Detective Marquez speaking."

A low, gritty voice replied, "Detective Marquez?"

"Yes, this is Detective Marquez. I already said that. Can I help you, sir?"

"Cooper was right," the caller said. "You are a sassy one."

"Who is this?"

"My name is Hal Brognola. I work for the U.S. Justice Department, and I'm calling because I understand that you have a federal prisoner in your jail. I would like to arrange to take him off your hands, if it's convenient."

"It's not convenient at the moment," Marquez replied. "I would've definitely liked to know where you were a few hours ago when he got dumped in my lap."

"Detective Marquez, you do understand that Mr. Lutrova's involvement with the Russian Business Network makes this a federal case. I'm sure you also understand he has always been under the custody of the federal government, and it's your duty to release him back to us without delay."

"Look, Mr. Brognola," Marquez said. "I have no intention of getting into a turf war with you or the Justice Department. You are more than welcome to take Mr. Lutrova out of here, since I basically have no reason to hold him other than the fact he's a material witness to murder. But I'm equally sure you understand it will be at least nine or ten o'clock tomorrow morning before we could finish his outprocessing. I'm also sure you'll be notified soon enough that he is not to leave the country or preferably even New York City while this case is open and pending."

"We've been informed that you are an outstanding officer and a first-rate detective. Cooper vouched for you personally, which is something I can assure you happens rarely. Bogdan Lutrova has vital information that we must protect, particularly if we expect to stop Yuri Godunov from doing any further damage."

"So Cooper works for the Department of Justice?"

"I didn't say that," Brognola countered. "All I told you was that I work for the Department of Justice. Cooper is, shall we say, an associate, and not under my direct control. However, those who had custody of Bogdan Lutrova before he agreed to accompany Cooper to New York City *do* work for the same people as me."

"And what people are those?" Marquez asked.

"The kind whose address begins with 1600. Need I say more?"

Marquez felt as if a part of her throat had just dropped to the bottom of her stomach. Apparently, this went *well* above her pay grade, or that of anyone in her department, for that matter. It made sense, actually: the high-powered weapons, military grade ordnance and brand-new credentials for Homeland Security never did really mesh with her. Cooper had seemed more like a commando, some kind of urban soldier or military specialist than a federal agent. Marquez had met plenty of federal types in her time, guys in suits and sunglasses—oh, they weren't the kind stereotyped in the movies or on television, but if Cooper fit the profile for an agent with Homeland Security or the FBI, then Marquez fit the profile for royalty.

"Okay, I kind of figured something like this might be going on. So you can't really tell me who you work for, but it sounds as if you're telling me I'm better off not knowing. And perhaps Cooper didn't tell me everything because he couldn't tell me anything, or at least only half-truths."

"I can assure you that he told you the truth, Marquez."

"So the story about the Russian Business Network is true?"

"Yes," Brognola said.

"Then what about this Brotherhood of Social Justice. Where do they fit in?"

"The what? Where did you hear that?"

Marquez snorted. "That loudmouthed Russian genius of yours we have locked up. Lutrova. He claims that while the outside world knows these guys as the RBN, they're really called the Brotherhood of Social Justice.

He claims they're actually run by some mucky-muck in Saint Petersburg, a politician or something."

"He give you any names?"

"No, because I thought he was just a crackpot and told him to shut up."

"Maybe that's for the best," Brognola replied.

"What do you mean?" Marquez asked, sitting back in her chair and arching her spine to stretch off some of the ache.

"Knowing even what you know is enough to get you killed."

"I can take care of myself, thanks."

"Like at the tenement building on the Upper East Side?"

"How did you know about that?"

"You really have to ask?" Brognola inquired, although his tone sounded almost good-natured, as if teasing.

She laughed. "I guess not."

"Look, Detective," Brognola said, "I know the situation hasn't been ideal for you, and I also know you've taken quite a number of hits on our behalf. We appreciate it. But I'm afraid I'm going to have to ask you for one more favor."

Marquez sighed quietly and shook her head. She had already violated a number of interdepartmental regulations relative to Cooper's activities. She was also withholding a fair bit of information as to the exact nature of Bogdan Lutrova's involvement, confident that if she could release him he would either leave the country or get picked up by the feds. Either way, the guy wouldn't be a thorn in her side anymore.

"I don't want to sound like a bureaucrat here, Mr. Brognola."

"Hal."

"Excuse me?"

"Why don't you call me Hal?"

"Okay, fine…Hal, then. But I think you should know I feel I've done my bit for king and country, and I'm not particularly fond of having my captain or any of his superiors take a piece out of my ass because I'm playing hardball with them while I jump to help the Feds at a moment's notice. I do have a job to do here, and I'm sure you can appreciate that."

"I do appreciate it," Brognola said. "And I know that Captain Dagum can be a bit of a ballbuster at times. But he's an awfully good cop, and you can learn a lot from his example."

"I didn't know you knew him," Marquez replied.

"I know a lot of people. But understand that there's a lot more at stake here than the financial system of New York City. The information the Russian Business Network has managed to abscond with targets not only people with significant financial influence, but also those with political influence. In some cases that influence reaches as high as the individuals who happen to work at that address I told you about earlier. This is no longer just about money or power, Detective. This is an issue of national security and may possibly extend even to the international interests of the United States. I have to know that I can count on you and that you'll give me your full cooperation. So I'm going to ask one more time if you're willing to hand Bogdan Lutrova over to our people."

Marquez thought about Brognola's words and made her decision before even thinking about it. Cooper may have been a lot of things, but he was no criminal, which was essentially what her chain of command had called him. No, if Cooper was anything he was a patriot and a man dedicated to far more than the pursuit of glory. Marquez believed it had something to do with duty and honor, and those were things she wouldn't have tried to take from anybody. Maybe the bureaucrats at the department could question Cooper's methods, perhaps even his motives or morals. But nobody had a shred of evidence that Cooper was anything but unswerving in his love for America and the innocent people who suffered under the machinations of a bastard like Yuri Godunov.

"What exactly is it you need me to do?" she finally asked.

"Are you aware of the incident that occurred on Thirty-fourth Street?"

"No, nothing's come over the wire yet."

Brognola sighed. "Maybe that doesn't mean much at this point, since the police units dispatched to the scene have no reason to think this is tied to your case. But I can assure you that information is about to change."

"I'm not sure I get the point here, Mr. Brognola." She quickly added, "I mean…Hal."

"Cooper nearly bought the farm when he discovered Godunov had reinforcements waiting for him. We're not sure how they even knew where to find him, but the fact that they did means the RBN is definitely onto our game plan. There was a man who helped Cooper, an old friend who followed him and managed to provide backup at the cost of his own life. If his identity were to be discovered and investigators in your department took a deep enough look into his background, there's no question they would initiate a statewide manhunt for Cooper. We need to make sure that doesn't happen for at least the next four to six hours. After that, it doesn't matter."

"I don't see how I can help you with that," Marquez said. "I have no influence over anyone in the forensics area or in the crime lab, even. And I'm not sure that I'd do anything to sabotage or stall an investigation if I did. You're asking me to do something that could cost me my badge."

"I'm asking you to do anything," Brognola replied. "I believe that each one of us has to follow our own conscience. That's something Cooper taught me once, as a matter of fact, a long time ago. Look, we're going to manipulate the situation and get the case assigned to you. I'm only asking you to sit on the identification for six hours. That's it, six hours and then you can proceed full force."

"And how exactly do you expect me to do that?"

Brognola chuckled. "Well, if anything that Cooper has told me about you is true, I'm sure you'll figure that out on your own."

"You know, that's exactly what he said to me at the tenement building. Then again, that shouldn't be any surprise to you, either, should it? I have a feeling you stay in pretty close communication with him."

"You assume right."

"All right, Hal, I'll do what I can to put it off, but don't expect any miracles. These people down here are watching me like a hawk right now, and I can't afford to get caught playing the cards too close to the vest."

"Don't sweat that," Brognola replied. "Believe it or not, I actually have quite a number of connections in the NYPD. In fact, I suspect if you got into any trouble on this at all I would need to make only one phone call and suddenly your problems would disappear. I'll do that if I have to but, I'd rather not get directly involved unless it becomes absolutely necessary. Just help us buy Cooper some time, that's all we're asking."

"All right," Marquez said. "I'll give you the time you need, but I want something in return."

"Name it."

"I want the full story on this RBN."

"What do you mean 'the full story'?" Brognola asked. "You know practically as much as we do about them."

"No, that's not what I'm talking about. I want to know exactly what it is they're planning to do. I can't very well keep the kibosh on certain things if I'm out of the loop on what's happening. Otherwise I'm utterly directionless and groping in the dark without knowing what's real and what's not, what's important to keep under wraps and what isn't. Surely someone in your position can appreciate that."

"Fair enough, I'm willing to break the rules and tell you what I know. Most of it you have on the surface, and your catching that name Lutrova dropped, the Brotherhood of Social Justice, may very well help us to identify other players in the game. But the bottom line is that the RBN has operated with impunity in this country for far too long, and Cooper is somewhat of a troubleshooter for us.

"The short story is that some time back we identified increased criminal activity centered on the financial industry, particularly around New York City and outlying areas. At first we didn't know what it meant, until we got a report that Customs officials had caught Bogdan Lutrova attempting to sneak into the country illegally. Just as soon as we asked Cooper to investigate, a hit team penetrated the federal law-enforcement offices in downtown Boston and tried to kill Lutrova. Or so we thought, until Cooper discovered they were actually there to retrieve Lutrova and smuggle him across state lines into New York."

"Okay, that sounds like a pretty solid story, but I'm not quite sure what all of it means. Why the hell would the RBN go to so much trouble? Why not just bring the guy in through their trafficking network?"

"We asked ourselves that same question and what we came up with was that they didn't want Lutrova attached in any way to the RBN. You see, he was given a cover story by Godunov, a story that he was actually fleeing to the United States. This way, when the RBN sent a group of independent mercenaries to steal him away, our people would start looking overseas instead of worrying about anything that was happening internally. The idea was to make us think the threat was coming from outside the United States, which would buy them the time they needed to implement their plans."

"I think I get it," Marquez said. "By the time anybody realized what was actually happening, they would already have been here and gone. No muss, no fuss."

"Exactly," Brognola replied. "The only problem is they weren't counting on Cooper. He was our ace in the hole, so to speak. We knew if we could get him inside their system it would result in a disruption of their plans. We just didn't realize how deep it went and how far it expanded. You heard about the explosion in upstate New York?"

"You talking about the one near the Catholic school? Yeah, I not only heard about it, I was the first to make the connection between that incident and what was happening down here. Again, though, my people didn't believe me."

"Then they're fools," Brognola said. "Listen, Marquez, I have to run. I want to thank you for your assistance on this and your competent actions. Whether you know it or not, you have just saved a lot of lives. You have every reason to be proud of that. And when this is through, I will make it my personal mission to set things right with your higher ups."

"I'd appreciate that," Marquez said, "but I can fight my own battles. It's not necessary."

"It is."

"Fine, I'm too tired to argue. But do me a favor, will you? Tell Cooper to be careful and not get himself killed. We need more men like him."

"That we do," Harold Brognola replied.

CHAPTER TWENTY-TWO

Anger seethed in Stepan Godunov's gut as he listened to the report.

His connection inside the NYPD mechanically recited details that were of no real consequence, while paying no heed to the fact they had just lost a dozen good men. Stepan wasn't naive enough to think that sacrifices weren't part of war. This was a war of its own kind, a war on foreign soil that at times Stepan almost felt might be unwinnable. Of course, he would never have told this to his uncle, but it didn't change the fact that his forces were dwindling.

Stepan issued some basic instructions to the caller, made sure the man understood, by having him repeat them, and then disconnected the call.

He stood on the portico outside Yuri Godunov's mansion. He wanted to finish his cigarette before going inside to inform his uncle of the call. As he stared into the early morning sky, a biting wind cut through his clothing like a frozen knife, but it didn't really bother Stepan. He'd traded his business suit for a pair of black fatigues and combat boots. A military web belt encircled his waist, supporting the weight of a .45-caliber semiautomatic pistol, two spare magazines and a small radio with a wireless headset linked to the tactical frequency of the security force guarding the estate grounds and mansion.

Stepan had put the entire security force on alert, leaving approximately twenty men to guard this area and dispatching another half dozen or so to the nearby airfield. He'd also called ahead to the crew that attended the private jet belonging to his uncle—or rather it belonged to the Brotherhood, who had provided it for Yuri's exclusive use. Stepan didn't think the crazy American who'd managed not only to deceive them twice, but to elude and ambush his men, would actually attempt to assault the grounds here.

Still, better to be prepared for the worst than be caught utterly off guard.

Stepan turned to go inside the mansion and find his uncle, but then thought better of it and decided to walk the grounds one last time. He trusted his men for the most part, but sentries could get lax if they were allowed to let their guard down. Stepan had learned from his instructors in Russia, as well as from the many lessons he'd been taught by the Wolf, that men were still men no matter how dedicated to the cause. They were still subject to the same weaknesses that had plagued the foot soldier for thousands of years. Flaws such as carelessness, lack of physical discipline that allowed them to fall asleep or miss potential breaks in a perimeter, or just plain laziness.

Stepan prided himself on the fact that his men were some of the best trained in the world. Many had learned from the same instructors as he had, so were trained in the art of covert operations and what Stepan liked to call focused war. He knew they wouldn't let him down no matter what happened, but as a leader, part of his job was to instill that discipline and confidence. Soldiers could be trained well, and given every possible tactical advantage in a combatant's arsenal, but without firm leadership they would fall apart in an encounter instead of coming together as a fighting unit.

What concerned Stepan most was that many hours had passed since the first team to engage the American agent had been destroyed. Stepan wondered exactly what his enemy had in mind. Had he given up? Had he gone into hiding to avoid the cops, or was he gathering reinforcements before coming after Yuri and himself? Stepan knew very little about the man who called himself Lambretta, but what he did know was that this individual wouldn't give up without a fight. The man had demonstrated that much with his bold move at the office building in Manhattan.

Stepan tried to consider all the possibilities, to assess weaknesses in the defense as he moved about the grounds and spoke with each of the sentry teams. In addition to the manpower, which he'd divided into four teams of three to guard the perimeter, with the remainder inside at specific points throughout the mansion, Stepan had also put the electronic surveillance unit inside the house on full alert. The grounds were saturated with infrared cameras and motion detection sensors, configured to provide a mesh topology that wouldn't create any issues or trigger false alarms, since they were designed to evaluate only objects of a certain size and mass.

Additionally, the system accounted for the sentries patrolling the grounds through the provision of a special transmitter worn on the arm of each man. That transmitter effectively neutralized the signal provided by the electronic surveillance, and made the sentries virtually invisible to the system. It was a clever and effective way of helping technicians to coordinate a defense in the event the perimeter was breached.

Once Stepan had finished his inspection of the grounds, he returned to the house and proceeded to Yuri Godunov's study. The double doors were closed—Yuri's signal that he didn't want to be disturbed—but Stepan approached anyway. As his uncle's chief of security, he had unconditional access. This wasn't because they were related as much as a matter of rank privilege. Stepan had always conducted himself as a professional, never taking the familial relationship for granted.

He rapped once on the study doors and then entered. The interior was dimly lit at Stepan's insistence, and the curtains were drawn. All the drapes in the house, in spite of their very ornate patterns, were constructed from specialized materials designed to do two things: not let any light out, and prevent snipers with heat sensitive scopes from looking through. They were also shielded from hypersensitive eavesdropping equipment and radar or microwaves. Stepan felt confident the American wouldn't have any such equipment with him, but he'd felt when designing the security of the house that such measures were only prudent.

"Report," his uncle said.

"I just got off the phone with one of my contacts inside the New York City police. I'm afraid the news isn't good."

Godunov scowled. "It seems these days that we are

quite short on good news. In fact, it saddens me to say that I'm getting used to it. I take it from what you just said that the American is alive."

Stepan lowered his eyes, not sure what he could say that wouldn't sound like a pathetic excuse, so he settled for a nod.

Godunov rose slowly from his seat, and even in the dim light the bulging veins near his forehead were visible. The situation had only become worse with this news of the strike team's failure to kill Lambretta. Stepan checked for any sign of forthcoming vitriol from his uncle. To his surprise, it didn't come. Godunov looked merely defeated, his mood foul and brooding to such a degree that Stepan felt it roll off in waves. He'd seen Yuri Godunov like this only once before, early in their relationship, and what had followed was something Stepan had tried to forget. When Godunov became enraged to the point of silence, it typically meant that a stack of dead bodies wasn't far behind.

"What happened?" he finally asked.

Stepan took a deep breath before replying. "The tracer I had planted on his vehicle did the job of tracking him. That was a very good suggestion you had made, and we were extremely fortunate to be able to locate his SUV near the club before he could escape."

Godunov shrugged. "It was an educated guess, at best. I had no way of being certain that it would do us any good, and I was wholly confident they wouldn't escape from that sealed room."

"You're being overly modest, Yuri. It was nothing less than a stroke of pure genius, and somehow my men managed to fuck it up. I would have preferred to be reporting their complete victory, but in their defense, there was a variable none of us had accounted for."

"And that was?"

"Apparently, somebody was following our American friend."

"You're talking about the woman?"

"No." Stepan shook his head. "This was somebody we have not seen before. At first when I heard about his interference in the ambush we set for Lambretta, I thought it was another agent backing him up. But now I'm convinced that even Lambretta didn't know this man was going to show. Not that it matters at this point, since it's my understanding he was killed in the skirmish that followed."

Godunov took his seat, propped his fingers together in front of his lips and said, "And the American?"

"Escaped," Stepan replied.

"I think based on what we now know it's obvious the next place Lambretta will come is here."

"You think that he's actually insane enough to launch an assault against a position as well fortified as this one?"

"I don't know about his sanity, but I can tell you that to this point he has shown considerable courage and ingenuity. He is a cunning enemy, and it would be absurd for us to underestimate him. Three times he has managed to deceive us, and three times we have succumbed to his deceptions. Only a fool would continue to make the same mistake while expecting different results."

"What do you want me to do?"

This brought a chuckle from Godunov that dripped

with disdain. "You're in charge of security and I would not presume to act like an expert in this area. I'm sure you can handle this. The only point I am trying to make is that we would do well to remember how much damage this son of a bitch has already done to our organization. He's destroyed millions of dollars' worth of effort and killed many of our men. Remember, he was even able to neutralize the Wolf and his team. It takes an individual of great skill to outperform warriors of that caliber. In short, he's a dangerous man, and the very fact that we think he would not attempt to assault these grounds convinces me that's exactly what he *will* do."

"Then we will be ready for him."

"I believe you." Godunov rose from his desk. "All the same, I want you to contact the airfield and advise them to prepare the plane."

"You're leaving?"

"I think we've accomplished everything that we can here. It's time to return to the base in Saint Petersburg. That will give us a chance to regroup and decide on our next move. It is difficult to plan if we must worry about defending ourselves at every moment. Wouldn't you agree?"

"I would, Yuri. But I am not going to let him win this time. I will destroy this bastard if I have to hunt him down to the ends of the earth."

"Don't be foolish, Stepan. While I have every confidence in your own abilities, I must also weigh the consequences of inaction. If we prove victorious here, it will be a war as that called by the enemy of our predecessors. Was it not Viacheslav Konstantinovich

Plehve who said, 'What this country needs is a short, victorious war to stem the tide of revolution'? There is no true victory or honor dying in vain. It is better, far better, to implement a tactical retreat than to allow your forces to be destroyed."

"I do not disagree with your general assessment," Stepan said. "But I must point out that in all of the previous circumstances we were unprepared for this American devil. This time we are ready and alert, and if he does in fact bring an assault against our fortifications—" Stepan's last words were spoken coldly and evenly "—he will be destroyed."

"Let us hope that the gods who watch over the Brotherhood are in agreement," Yuri Godunov replied.

SINCE ITS establishment in 2005, Sagaponack—just one of many villages and hamlets that made up the Hamptons—had earned a reputation as the most expensive address in America.

Mack Bolan regretted the fact he was about to treat its denizens to a concert of death and destruction. He hoped the police had better things to do at this time of morning than be patrolling his immediate area of operation. There was no question he would look strange attired in the blacksuit, never mind the bag of heavy weapons on the seat next to him. Moreover, when Bolan had stopped at an abandoned service station to change, he'd inspected the trunk and found a considerable arsenal from the personal armory of Tom Remick.

As Bolan drew closer to Yuri Godunov's estate, his thoughts went back to Remick. It seemed no matter how hard Bolan tried to keep others from getting embroiled in his War Everlasting, there were select individuals unwilling to stand on the sidelines and let him go at it alone. In one sense, Bolan could understand their feelings, because they were the same feelings he'd experienced himself. It was selfish of him to think that he alone deserved to swing the hammer of duty and honor while excluding others from the same.

In the case of people like Tom Remick and Justina Marquez, Bolan realized they were just as qualified and indebted to their sense of justice as he was. Remick had gone down and out with style—something the man had always longed to do—and nobody, least of all Mack Bolan, planned to deprive him of wearing the warrior's ultimate badge of honor. It was just how Bolan hoped he would go out, defending those who couldn't defend themselves, and fighting enemies that considered their own ends above the life and liberty of others.

Bolan turned onto the road that corresponded to the address of Godunov's estate, according to the GPS coordinates provided by Stony Man through his cell phone. The soldier looked to his right and barely made out the whitecaps of waves rolling in from the Atlantic. Remick's car was ancient, an old Chrysler K Series that despite its relatively decent condition didn't have the best heater. Occasionally, a draft brushed across Bolan's legs where the blacksuit tucked into his combat boots.

One thing seemed certain: it would be one cold morning for an assault.

Bolan glanced at the analog clock on the dashboard, realized it was nonfunctional and checked his watch. It was closing in on 0330 hours, and he figured he had another forty-five minutes at most before making his move. He turned onto a side street down the block from Godunov's estate and searched for a logical place to stash his car. He didn't want to park too close to the estate, and to simply roll past would have likely put the defense teams on high alert.

Bolan held no illusions about the risk of this op. After what he'd seen of Stepan, and given that someone within the organization had had enough forethought to ambush him in the event he managed to escape from the bank building in Manhattan, there was little question in Bolan's mind that the RBN security force would be supervigilant. But he also knew that sentries were susceptible to being most tired the hour or two preceding dawn. And even if they were prepared for his arrival, their all-night watch in this chill weather would have taken its toll.

Bolan finally located a small park that had an outbuilding and shelter overlooking a public beach. He pulled into one of the spaces on the back side of the building; this would prevent his vehicle from being observed by a passerby or patrol car. Once he had completed his mission here, he would need a way to get out quickly, and he hoped the numbers were with him. The sooner he launched his assault against the estate, the sooner he could escape under the cover of darkness and get out of the area before the police cordoned it off.

The one thing that worried him was that Sagaponack wasn't exactly a sprawling metropolis. It wouldn't take long for law enforcement to seal up the area as tight as a drum. Bolan would have to count on split-second timing and a tactical plan to escape via the route least likely to get blockaded. If necessary, he would move out of the area on foot and contact Stony Man for some type of pickup.

In the end he would simply have to find a way to softly withdraw. He had civilian clothes, and now a mechanism, given the ocean at his back, to ditch all the weapons currently at his disposal. He also planned to hide Remick's large arsenal.

Bolan killed the engine and went EVA. He had already planned on what he would need to do the job. His equipment included the load bearing equipment harness that sported a fresh supply of M69 HE grenades, the Ka-bar fighting knife and a medipouch. The Beretta 93-R rode in its customary shoulder rigging, and a holstered Desert Eagle .44 Magnum semiauto pistol rode leather on Bolan's hip.

He traded the FNC for an M-16 A-3/M-203 and a half-dozen 40 mm HE grenades. He slung the over-and-under assault rifle/grenade launcher across his back. Bolan considered leaving the plastic explosives behind but decided to take a few sticks just in case he needed to create entry or exit points at a moment's notice. To round out the arsenal, he selected a Beretta 7.62 mm sniping rifle. The rifle featured a free-floating barrel fitted with a muzzle brake. It had a 5-round detachable box magazine, and this rifle was fitted with a night scope of 9 x 64 power. While the weapon was rare—something that wasn't at all out of the realm of Remick's sometimes eclectic tastes—it would do the job at a muzzle velocity of over 800 meters per second.

Once Bolan had completed his task, he removed the remaining arsenal from the trunk and located a copse.

He didn't bother to camouflage the weapons since he knew they wouldn't be spotted in the dark. The only camouflage he opted to provide was an olive-green plastic tarp he'd found in Remick's trunk to protect the weapons in the event it began to rain. His job done, Mack Bolan set off toward the hunting grounds.

It was time to bring the final chapter of his new war against the Russian Business Network to a close. It wouldn't be the end of the war, perhaps not even the end of this battle, pending on the outcome. But it would mean certain destruction of the plans of Yuri Godunov and his Russian masters. Bolan was about to throw back some of the heat he'd been taking.

Yes, the Executioner was about to give the enemy a war they wouldn't believe.

CHAPTER TWENTY-THREE

Concealed behind the base of a hedgerow directly across the street from the gated entrance to Godunov's estate, the Executioner peered through the night sights of the Beretta 7.62 mm sniper rifle. The scope didn't feature anything as advanced as the electro-optical sight mounted on the M-16 A3/M-203 Bolan had procured from Remick during their initial meeting. However, it did illuminate the area in a green haze, and the movement of the two sentries at the gate provided all Bolan needed.

As he studied them, counting off the seconds between the times they appeared at the gate and then moved out of view, concealed by the walls of the estate, Bolan put his next move to the test of the best tactics. He considered beginning the ceremonies with a couple of well-placed 40 mm grenades, but he wasn't sure how far he'd have to travel from the perimeter to the house. The grenades would do well for blowing the gates and neutralizing immediate opposition, but since Bolan had no idea what was beyond that point he didn't want to risk it.

Conversely, attempting a soft probe provided many of the same disadvantages as a full-on blitz. Chances were good Godunov had nothing short of an army guarding the grounds; the Russian wasn't stupid by any means and had shown time and again his penchant for planning ahead. Additionally, Stepan acted as Godunov's head of security, according to information provided by Bogdan Lutrova. Stepan had apparently been trained by veterans of the former Soviet Union's Spetsnaz commandos, its elite paramilitary group.

Bolan definitely had his work cut out for him on this one. These weren't fanatical terrorists he was pitted against. This time the Executioner was up against a highly trained, disciplined and well-armed paramilitary unit. It would be like conducting an offensive against a fortified bunker held by members of the Army Rangers or Delta Force. Bolan also surmised there were electronic countermeasures in place, not necessarily booby traps but most certainly high-tech surveillance and alert systems.

Yeah, someone like Godunov would spare no expense to ensure the security of his American base of operations.

Bolan ran the scenarios through his mind once more and came to a decision. He would hit them quietly at first, take down the sentries and then make his entrance through the gate. His first objective after sniping the enemy would be to create a diversion as far from that location as possible. Stepan and his men might see it for what it was, but the diversionary tactic provided by Marquez at the tenement building had worked before, and Bolan hoped that such a ploy would work once more. He would know soon enough.

The soldier took several deep breaths and waited for his enemy to show again. He tried not to shiver against the icy wind that ran across his back, and he counted it fortunate the ground was hard and dry. If he'd had to lie in snow or rain, it would have sapped the body heat from him quickly instead of buying him the luxury of waiting to implement his assault. Bolan tightened his grip on the Beretta rifle, aligning the scope to about the height he would need, and awaited acquisition of his first target. It came to him less than ten seconds later and Bolan eased back on the trigger. Unfortunately, the weapon wasn't equipped with a sound suppressor, so the Executioner knew at the most he might get off three to four shots before the enemy could pin down his location. The first 7.62 mm round burned a path straight on target and impacted at chest level.

The body hadn't even hit the ground when Bolan slammed the bolt forward to load a new round, sighted on the second target and delivered another message of death. This one struck the sentry's skull and blew his head apart. The darkness concealed the effect, but Bolan could almost imagine the man's head exploding under the tremendous force of the high-velocity bullet. The round would cause a cavitation effect, and smash the soft tissue of the brain as it exited the other side with enough force to leave a hole the size of a tennis ball.

The muzzles of two more automatic rifles flashed and rounds buzzed far overhead. They weren't even remotely close to his location, and Bolan pushed from his psyche any fear of being hit. His next target aligned in the crosshairs of the scope, Bolan squeezed the trigger and worked the bolt yet again. Experience made him confident he would score a hit every time; even in the dark and at a fair distance, the initial panic of the enemy, plus the bitter cold air that reduced pressure and enhanced effective range, would bode well for this type of engagement.

Bolan's fourth target took a 7.62 mm slug to the heart and landed on his back. Bolan put the sniper rifle to rest, shoving it into the concealment of the hedgerow, trading it for the over-and-under, which he'd already primed with a 40 mm HE grenade. He flipped the leaf sight into acquisition, settled on an appropriate range based on the approximately thirty-degree angle of the launcher, and engaged the trigger. The grenade left the tube with the pop of a firecracker and a kick equal to a 12-gauge shotgun. Bolan rocked the launcher breach up and the auto extractor spit the shell away. He put a second grenade into the tube and locked it back once more. The launcher now in battery, Bolan sighted on the same point again, confident it would lob the second grenade into proximity of the first one. There would be hell to pay on the other side of the wall.

Before the second grenade exploded Bolan was in motion and headed toward the gate, the M-16 A-3 muzzle held at the ready.

He reached the perimeter, hugged the wall adjacent to the gate and acquired one of the sticks of plastique. The C-4 explosives were a valuable tool in the soldier's arsenal. The composition reacted based on a combination of heat and pressure; lacking one or the other, the substance was relatively harmless. But in the hands of a trained combatant with a detonator molded into the block of puttylike substance, it was a killer. Bolan quickly and carefully secured it to the metal hinge of the ten-foot, wrought-iron gate and stepped back. He

produced the detonator attached to a thin wire that ran
to the blasting cap. Bolan turned his eyes away and
flipped the detonator switch. A rush of superheated
gas charged the air around him and a wrenching sound
followed the blast. Bolan blinked and watched as the
gate rocketed into the street and collapsed with a clang.
Nodding in satisfaction, he inched up to the smoking
remains of the wall. He peered around the corner, en-
sured that there was no movement in his immediate
path, and then advanced into the waiting darkness.

WHEN THE ATTACK came, Stepan Godunov was ready
for it, but it aggravated him that his men didn't respond
in like fashion.

Even as he began to bark orders over the tactical
communications frequency, he could see the place erupt
into pandemonium through the closed-circuit feeds of
the control room in the basement. In addition to control-
ling all the sensitive electronic equipment and providing
both the grounds and internal security monitoring, the
space doubled as a safe room. It had only one entrance
point, which boasted a door constructed of a titanium-
nickel alloy coated by a special polymer resin that could
dull the blade of any saw in existence save for diamond-
tipped. Outside of that, only a laser could penetrate the
door. It was impervious to bombs, blowtorches and any
other conventional means that might be used by law
enforcement. Not that Stepan was concerned the enemy
would get that far.

Despite their less than professional reaction when
the first explosion took place, there were enough men

on the grounds that the chance of the American getting inside the house was almost nil.

Almost.

Stepan thought of Yuri's counsel that the fastest way to defeat would be underestimating Lambretta's resourcefulness. Whatever Stepan might think about the American, his personal feelings had nothing to do with legitimate action, and that was something Lambretta was obviously not short on. Stepan knew as sure as his enemy did that indecision would lose this battle. They were now joined in a mortal combat. This was no longer a mere conflict of attrition; Stepan had no political or social ideologies like the Brotherhood. For him this was a conflict of good versus evil, and he intended to ensure the evil deeds of this American were punished. A great number of his men had been slaughtered during engagements with this enemy. Whatever tactics Lambretta had used against the soldiers under Stepan's command, they had been without honor or decency.

This wasn't a struggle he believed would produce good results. War had never produced anything but misery and suffering, yet the soldier didn't get to choose the war, the war chose the soldier. If they had any hope of making their stand and facilitating the escape of his uncle, they would have to make it here in this battle; they would have to hold the line against the American long enough for Yuri to escape.

Stepan watched as a second explosion blew near the wall running along the east side of the property. As the light from the blast dissipated, Stepan ordered the technician to rewind the footage. The entire system was wired to digital video recording equipment, which was then stored on hard drives. This facilitated the ability to move back and forward through the footage in real time at any given point. He ordered the man to hold and then to advance forward in slow motion. Stepan knew as soon as he saw the flaming trail prior to the explosion that they were being subjected to explosive projectiles, most likely from a grenade launcher. If it *was* Lambretta behind the attack, and Stepan had no doubt of it, he wouldn't have had time to set up a mortar or ground-anchored rocket launcher. Based on the direction from which the grenade had come, Stepan surmised the attack was initiated from the south, most likely the main entrance from the street.

Stepan ordered his men to converge on the gates. "You must protect that sector of the property."

"We're taking heavy fire here, sir!" one of his team commanders replied. "If we shift to that area, we'll have no cover!"

"Those explosions are diversions," Stepan said into the headset microphone. "Now do as you're ordered!"

The man started to reply, but was cut off in a burst of static, and for a brief moment Stepan thought he heard automatic weapons fire transmitted over the comm before signal loss. He threw down the headset, snatched his MP-5 K machine pistol off the rack and slid into the harness. As he adjusted the rigging, he turned his attention to the controllers.

"I'm going topside to get control of the situation," he told them. "Keep repeating my orders to whatever team leaders are still listening to you."

"What about the house staff, sir?" one of the men asked.

"They stay where they are. Their orders are to hold position at the points I've assigned them unless they hear directly from me and *only* from me. Make sure they understand they are not to follow the orders of anyone but me. Is that understood?"

The controller nodded emphatically, then turned to issue the directives to the grounds and house teams.

Idiots, Stepan thought as he left the control room.

THE ENEMY GUNNERS reacted just as Mack Bolan suspected they would.

His plan to create a distraction had done much to draw them away from the front gates, and with four men down and the rest running around in havoc—apparently not very receptive to the orders being shouted by their leadership—Bolan figured his chances of getting into the house had just increased tenfold.

Nonetheless, it was foolish to assume things would continue to go as planned. In most offensives, particularly when the odds were *not* in his favor, a situation could turn bad at any moment. Even as he advanced on the house Bolan could see the enemy getting reorganized. He found the cover of a large tree, knelt and aimed the grenade launcher directly at the mansion. He didn't know what kind of reinforcements he would have to face, but if he could continue with the barrage of ordnance—make the enemy think even for a little while longer they were under attack by multiple opponents—it might buy him enough time to cross the remaining distance to the house. Once he was inside, it would be more difficult to pin him down—at least he hoped it would.

Bolan raised the M-203 and triggered another grenade. As soon as it left the tube, he jumped to his feet and rushed the house. But the enemy had obviously gotten wise because gunners were now converging on his position, the muzzles of several automatic rifles winking in response to his movements. Some rounds came close enough that Bolan heard them as they passed near his head or slapped into tree trunks. He'd taken a chance, and it wasn't one that had paid off entirely, but the battle wasn't lost. He had plenty of ammunition, spare grenades and the will to use both to whatever results would shatter enemy opposition.

Bolan caught a fleeting movement to his left and realized one of the guards had spotted him. The man hadn't been facing in Bolan's direction and was still swinging his weapon into target acquisition. He didn't get off a shot. The Executioner triggered the M-16 on the run and pumped two hard-hitting NATO rounds through the guard's chest. The man's feet left the ground. His body lurched backward and slammed into the frozen rock garden behind him.

A second sentry realized his comrade had bought it, and reached to the headset, feeling a call for reinforcements was more important than neutralizing the enemy. Bolan saw the advantage as he pressed against a tree, brought the stock of the assault rifle to his shoulder and sighted on the man. The sentry got out two words before the Executioner triggered a volley that stitched him from crotch to breastbone. The impact spun the

RBN sentry with such force he tumbled into a tree and bounced off with a loud, sickly smack.

Bolan continued on a beeline for the house. He'd expected to see lights coming from the windows but he didn't. The entire grounds were still in darkness. In all of their preparations, why hadn't they equipped the perimeter with security lights? The thought came just as the grounds were suddenly splashed in bright lights, one of them glaring in his eyes.

The Executioner responded with catlike reflexes that had saved his hide many times before.

He closed one eye and threw himself to the ground, rolling over and over until he encountered his first obstacle—an elevated planter made of brick. Bolan climbed to his feet and threw himself over the top of it, burrowing into the dense, dry grass, which stood stiff and tall. He took the opportunity to eject the spent grenade shell and slam a new one into the breach, then detected the thunder of boots approaching his position. He wondered for a moment how they could have determined his location so quickly, but then remembered the grounds were most likely replete with electronic surveillance equipment.

Bolan triggered the grenade launcher in the direction of the sounds. He was rewarded a moment later with a massive explosion and the screams of several men. The blast was close enough that the heat waves generated from the high explosives caused the stiff grass in the planter to flutter back and forth as if in a high wind. Something hard landed next to Bolan, and he turned in time to see it was the stump of an arm, before every spotlight winked out.

The Executioner didn't wait for an invitation, confident that this was something ordered by Stepan. They were trying a psychological ploy with him, turning his assault into a game of cat and mouse where Bolan became the defender. Well, the big American had played that game plenty of times before, and he not only knew all the rules but exactly how to break them.

The Executioner reached the house and loaded the last of the grenades. He didn't plan to make a quiet entrance. The enemy troops on the grounds—what was left of them, anyway—were still trying to recover from the inferno left in the wake of the previous grenade. Bolan couldn't figure out why they had turned on the lights, since it had ruined their men's night vision as well as his own. It had to be part of the game, and for just a moment, even as Bolan sighted on a particularly weak looking section of the mansion wall, he wondered if this wasn't *exactly* what Stepan was hoping for.

Whether or not he was about to play into the enemy's trap was of very little concern to the Executioner. Keeping them on their toes, moving and having to defend a quarter that grew smaller and smaller by the minute, would only bring more confusion and chaos to their already shaky position. It was much like fighting a caged animal except Bolan had managed to stay out of reach.

And while his luck wouldn't hold out forever, neither would Yuri Godunov's.

CHAPTER TWENTY-FOUR

When the call finally came through to the organized crime unit, Justina Marquez tried to act perfectly normal.

Fortunately, the caller could neither see her nor be "in the know" about what had transpired over the past twenty hours or so. Damn, had it really been that long? Marquez didn't even want to know the answer as she took a few notes from the officer calling at the Thirty-fourth Street Mall two blocks from the Empire State Building. When she had the details she needed, she hung up and then picked up the phone and dialed Captain Dagum's home number.

It took six rings on the first try and three on the call back before Dagum finally muttered something unintelligible into the phone.

"Captain, I'm sorry to wake you, but we have a situation."

"Don't we always?" Dagum grumbled. On afterthought he said, "Where the hell are you? Don't tell me you're still at the house."

"Okay, I won't tell you I'm still at the house," Marquez deadpanned. "It looks like our friend Cooper is up to more of his tricks. There was an incident down at the Thirty-fourth Street Mall, and apparently there's about a dozen dead or thereabouts."

"Any bystanders?"

"Only one, possibly," Marquez replied. "They found a guy who wasn't dressed like any of the others. He had no identification on him and as far as we can tell there weren't any witnesses who came forward to confirm his involvement."

"You think he was friend or foe?"

"It's difficult to tell this early," Marquez said. "According to the description the CSI folks gave me, he sounds indigent. Quite a bit older and dressed in beat-up camouflage pants and a green T-shirt. They say they're old patterns, probably dating back to the early to mid-1970s. And he was wearing an old Army field jacket."

"Sounds like a homeless vet," Dagum said. "Maybe just a vagrant or a skel out looking for a warm place to sleep. Obviously he picked the wrong place. No sign of Cooper?"

Marquez sighed. "No, and apparently it all happened so fast that the witnesses aren't of much help. I'm not going to spend a lot of time barking up the wrong tree right now, since I'm guessing the old man is just as you say, a homeless guy or a vagrant who just got caught up in a bad situation."

"Goddamn it," Dagum said, "that Cooper is really starting to get on my nerves. Everywhere that son of a bitch goes he leaves a trail of bodies."

"I understand your frustration, sir, but one of the witnesses *did* say they saw a man matching Cooper's description. According to their statements he was on the run, not the aggressor in this particular situation. I think maybe the Russian Business Network put some sort of bug on him. Maybe they followed him from the offices at One Chase Manhattan Plaza."

"I don't give two farts what they say. That guy is creating a lot of problems for me, and now he's got you buying into this whole conspiracy theory. What about the guy you arrested, this computer hacker? He got any insight to offer?"

"I don't know, since I had to release him to federal custody a half hour ago," Marquez replied.

"You did *what?*"

"Officials with the U.S. Customs Service showed up and demanded we release him to them."

"And you just turn him over to these guys without asking any questions or raising a stink?"

Marquez had had just about enough, and she struggled to keep her temper in check as she replied, "They had an order signed by a federal judge. What did you want me to do, Captain? Apparently this guy is some sort of protected witness, or maybe he's just a scumbag and the Feds want to ask him questions. Whoever he is, I don't think we would've gotten very far with him."

Dagum groaned and finally said, "All right, I'm sorry. You did the right thing. If they had an order they had an order, so there's no use crying over spilled milk. You seem to know this Cooper's agenda better than anybody else. What do you think he'll do next?"

The question took Marquez by surprise, since she hadn't really expected Dagum to solicit any advice from her. Of course, she had a pretty good idea of exactly where Cooper was headed and what he planned to do. According to what Lutrova had told her, Yuri Godunov's address of residence was in Sagaponack, and there was a pretty good chance that's where Cooper would go. If that were true, this was her opportunity to either utterly destroy his mission or back his play, as Hal Brognola had asked her to do. It would take an act of courage, something she wasn't entirely sure she had, but she also didn't see there was much choice. After all, what support had her own people shown her throughout this entire mess?

"If I had to venture a guess, I'd say he'll hit his next target somewhere here in the city."

"Any idea where that'll be?"

"Not the faintest, since there are still a lot of businesses scattered throughout the city that are under the holdings of Yuri Godunov's bogus company."

"That's not much help, Justina."

"I wish I could be of more help, Captain, but my crystal ball is broken."

"Cute, real cute."

"Look, I don't know what else you want me to tell you, but I'm not going to make it up."

"All right, all right," Dagum conceded. "Don't get your panties in a bunch. Why don't you pack it in for now and go home. You're overtired and you've had a rough time in the past thirty-six hours. Get some sleep and come in fresh. I don't want to see you in the office before noon today. Understood?"

"Yes, sir."

After Marquez hung up the phone she sat back in her chair, arched her spine and rubbed again at her flank. She still didn't feel comfortable doing what she had, not being forthright with Dagum. But she'd made a promise to do what she could to help support their efforts. Deep down, Marquez felt as if Cooper was doing the right thing. Her ass was on the line here, and when her boss caught on to the deception, she hoped that Brognola guy kept his word and bailed her out.

WHEN THE TECHNICIANS in the control room flooded the grounds with spotlights, effectively blinding every man outside the house, Stepan had begun screaming into his radio.

"What are you doing? What in blazes are you doing? Shut those fucking lights off right now!"

It took them about ten seconds to respond, but not before the American managed to launch a grenade into the cluster of troops immediately after Stepan ordered them to form a skirmish line and advance on the American's last known position. Their failure to follow orders and spread out had gotten them killed. The blast was so close it knocked Stepan off his feet and he smacked his head against a low hanging tree branch. The blow nearly knocked him senseless and his hand went to his face in reaction. It came away slick with blood; nothing serious, but he'd definitely opened the skin near his temple.

Shaking it off, Stepan got unsteadily to his feet and watched in horror as a part of the west-facing exterior wall of the mansion exploded in a ball of red-orange flame. He couldn't see beyond the fireball left by burning bodies that had combusted with the blast of the previous grenade. It was as if Yuri had predicted with uncanny accuracy the resolve and mettle of this American.

Stepan caught a flicker of movement, a shadowy

figure silhouetted by the flames left in the wake of the grenades. He raised his MP-5 K and started to pull the trigger, but thought better of it. At this distance he would only be wasting ammunition. He meant to see the American dead once and for all, and he would do that when they were face-to-face. He would do it only when he could look Lambretta in the eyes as he was pulling the trigger.

One of his concerns had been ensuring that Yuri got away from the carnage before Lambretta could find him. Fortunately, Stepan had sent two of his men early on to retrieve his uncle and get him safely away from the mansion via a rear exit. That left only the ten house staff that remained along with Lambretta.

Stepan stormed off in search of the man who had become his archenemy in the course of just a few hours.

THE EXECUTIONER came through the charred outline of the hole left by his grenade, the fringes still a red-hot tracing of embers.

He was a ghostly, black wraith in the sight of the guards, who had been stunned by the blast but were otherwise unscathed. They were still recovering when they saw Bolan bear down on them with his M-16 ablaze. One guard managed to clear a machine pistol from a shoulder holster, but Bolan already had him pegged. The machine pistol flew from his fingers, utterly useless, as a salvo of 5.56 mm rounds punched through the RBN gunner's chest and lifted him off his feet.

A second combatant tried to flank Bolan, but the

warrior had already accounted for the position of every opponent. He switched the M-16 to his left hand and swung it toward another gunner running up the hall at the same time as he drew his .44 Magnum pistol. The booming report from the Desert Eagle operated in syncopation to the short burst from the assault rifle. The would-be flanker took a pair of 280-grain boat tail slugs in the abdomen. The man spun and crashed face-first into a low, glass-top table. The enemy gunman who advanced up the hallway, acting a little too rash for his own good, bought a pair of rounds in the face for his troubles. Even as his head exploded from his body the corpse continued in motion, an odd and grisly sight as it eventually lost momentum and skidded to a stop.

Bolan crouched and tracked the room with the Desert Eagle, watchful for additional enemies. Upon clearing all points he began to navigate the massive halls of the mansion. Too much time had elapsed since he'd begun his assault, and he wondered if it was even worth attempting to find Godunov. Surely at some point the Russian crime lord had realized the futility of his situation and opted to make his escape. The question at that point would only be a matter of where, not if.

Bolan quickly moved through the first floor of the house and cleared it. He was about to head upstairs when a flicker of light from an alcove twinkled in his peripheral vision. The soldier traversed the length of the massive kitchen until he reached the wall of the alcove. He peered around the corner and saw a stairwell leading downward. A single light fixture illuminated the stairs, but it wasn't flickering and didn't appear to be malfunctioning. In fact, the electricity in the house seemed fine, and Bolan concluded the flicker could have only been caused by human movement.

The Executioner started to advance down the steps, but heard something below that caused him concern. He opted for a tactical approach; if the quail wanted to hide in the brush, then there were tried and true methods for flushing it out. Bolan yanked one of the grenades from his LBE harness, this one a concussion type, yanked the pin and tossed the bomb underhand down the steps. He heard a whisper that turned into a shout, and then opened his mouth and plugged his ears, shutting his eyes long enough for the grenade to do its work. As soon as he felt the vibration from the concussion, Bolan advanced down the stairwell with his M-16 held at the ready.

Only one of the three men who had been waiting in the hall was still lucid enough to put up a fight. He was on one knee, holding his ear with his left hand and a submachine gun in his right. He didn't appear dazed enough that he couldn't be dangerous, and Bolan had no choice but to act on the threat. He squeezed the trigger of the assault rifle and pumped a half-dozen rounds into the RBN gunman. The impact flipped the man off his knee, and his finger, curled reflexively on the trigger, sent a bullet harmlessly into the ceiling.

The man let out a bloodcurdling groan that doubled as his final breath.

Bolan pondered why the sentries would be clustered in this hallway. He noticed only one door at the far end of the long, narrow corridor, and wondered if maybe his luck had run out. He couldn't see many details in the dim light, but it looked as if the door was pretty solid, reinforced, as might be expected for a safe room. Would Godunov have been stupid enough to lock himself in the mansion? Bolan wasn't sure he bought that, and he wondered if this was the trap he suspected Stepan had planned.

The sound of movement behind him provided his answer as a cold, calculating voice—a voice all too familiar—ordered, "Do not turn around. Drop your weapons."

Bolan froze, realizing Stepan probably had him covered. The Executioner might have been experienced, but he wasn't bulletproof. He had no intention of giving Stepan the opportunity to prove it. He had no other choice but to comply, and he slowly shed the Beretta 93-R, Desert Eagle and M-16.

"Now put your hands on top of your head and turn around," Stepan said.

Bolan again did as ordered, but as he brought his hands up he detached the Ka-bar fighting knife, raising his hands at the same moment as he began to turn. Because of the dim lighting, he figured he might get away with the deception. While the Russian had demonstrated his skill as a fighter, Stepan was susceptible to ego. He considered himself Bolan's superior. Stepan was a man used to leading others, and Bolan had noted his arrogance during their first meeting in the Lisbon Club. The soldier held his breath now as he tucked the flat of the blade between his neck and the collar of his blacksuit and his hands covered the exposed portions. If Stepan saw him make the move, he gave no indication; Bolan surmised he would most likely have been shot, otherwise.

"Get on your knees," Stepan said.

Bolan remained compliant, hopeful for an opportunity to play his hand. If Stepan didn't come any closer, Bolan's chances of pulling through this alive were slim to none. But something in the Executioner, some intuition, told him Godunov wouldn't be able to resist gloating. True to form, the Russian enforcer walked slowly and purposefully toward him and stopped just outside of arm's reach. Bolan wouldn't have been able to touch him with his fingertips, but a Ka-bar blade would more than reach vital points.

The Executioner decided where and when that would be even as Godunov opened his mouth. "You have caused us considerable damage. It shall bring me great pleasure to dispose of you."

"Why didn't you just shoot me in the back?" Bolan asked, unable to resist feeding the Russian's ego.

"Because unlike you we do things honorably," Stepan replied. "We are not murderers, we are professional soldiers. Unlike you, we do not sneak around in the dead of night and propel grenades upon our enemies from long distances. We believe in killing a man up close… personally. We believe looking a man in the eyes before taking his life is the honorable thing to do."

"So do I," Bolan replied.

Stepan's expression turned from smugness to surprise, followed by shock and pain. Bolan slapped the pistol aside with the edge of his left hand as his right came away from his neck, grasping the knife. He plunged it to the hilt in the soft tissue just beneath the tip of his enemy's breastbone. Stepan tried sucking air but realized he couldn't as the blade lacerated the phrenic nerve. He began to wheeze and panic set in, causing him to drop his pistol and step back. Bolan jumped to his feet as he scooped up his .44 Magnum Desert Eagle from where it had landed.

Stepan's eyes widened as Bolan raised the pistol and said, "Goodbye, comrade."

Bolan fired from a range of less than two feet. The bullet struck Stepan dead center in the forehead and blew his brains out the back of his skull. A fountain of blood and brain matter splashed the walls on either side. Stepan's corpse seemed to slither to the floor as his body tried to catch up with the fact that signals were no longer traveling from his brain.

As the report of the pistol died in the confines of the narrow hall, Bolan heard a faint sound take its place. A moment elapsed before he realized it was someone shouting over a radio. Bolan began to search through the bodies and found a radio attached to the belt of one of the disoriented sentries. The Executioner held the radio up to the sentry's face and grabbed his ear to make his threat implicit.

"What do they want?" he asked the man.

"They want to know if it is clear," he replied in broken English.

"Who are 'they'?"

The man jerked his head in the direction of the door.

Bolan said, "Give them the clear signal."

The man looked terrified at first, but when Bolan held the muzzle of the still-hot Desert Eagle close to his eye the Russian immediately complied. The soldier then clipped him behind the ear with the pistol butt and turned to wait for the door to open. It moved slowly, almost like a safe door, and as soon as it was open enough, Bolan stepped inside and found three technicians staring wildly at him. They weren't armed.

"Out!" Bolan ordered.

Whether they understood English probably didn't matter, since a wave of the pistol proved a consummate interpreter. Once they were out, Bolan tossed the satchel of remaining C-4 explosives onto the control panel, then stepped outside the door. He waited until he nearly had it closed, and then yanked the spoon from a fragmentation grenade and lobbed the bomb inside. He managed to get the door shut and sealed just before the thunder of destruction inside the room rumbled through the narrow corridor with such force that drywall dust sifted from the ceiling.

Bolan couldn't think of a more fitting end to Yuri Godunov's reign of terror in America.

CHAPTER TWENTY-FIVE

Weary, with bloodshot eyes and stiff joints, Hal Brognola entered the briefing room of the annex building at Stony Man Farm.

He'd abandoned his suit jacket, rumpled after he used it as a coverlet for a quick nap. Barbara Price sat and stared intently at an LCD panel, one of many that folded up from the massive table that took up a good portion of the operations center. Sometimes Brognola wondered why they'd bothered to put such a monster in the room, since the members of Able Team in Phoenix Force—the elite covert field units of Stony Man—preferred their briefings in the war room beneath the farmhouse. Whether out of nostalgia or mere stubbornness, Brognola couldn't be sure, but he had never felt the need to impose a transfer to the new facility.

Barbara Price looked up and managed a tired grin. "You feel a little better?"

Brognola held up his hand, thumb and forefinger an inch apart.

"How about some coffee?" she asked. She'd been sitting in the chair with one leg tucked under her athletic figure. She started to rise and head for the coffeepot, but Brognola waved her off.

"If I drink any more of Bear's coffee, I'll definitely be feeling worse."

"It's not that bad," she replied with a chuckle. "I could use some myself and I need to stretch my legs."

Brognola dropped into a nearby chair and yawned, running his hand over his face to revive his senses. His eyes still burned, due to the fact that his sleep had been fitful, at best. The present whereabouts and condition of Mack Bolan didn't worry him. Brognola had learned long ago not to concern himself with Bolan's status. The Executioner could look after himself.

The big Fed waited for Price to return with two cups of coffee, one of which she set in front of him despite his protests. He smiled. "Seems you know me almost as well as Helen. Even when I say I don't want something, you know that I do."

"Sometimes a look tells a lot," Price replied as she returned his smile.

She tapped the top of the computer screen loudly with her nail. "Let's focus on this."

"Go ahead and run it down for me."

Price set her untouched coffee on the table and folded her arms. She sat back in the chair. "The first thing I did was cross-reference anything in our files regarding this Brotherhood of Social Justice."

"And?" Brognola prompted.

"And I don't find anything about it. There are no references, even remote ones, of any organization by that name. We've probably questioned fifty members of the Russian Business Network, maybe even a hundred, and nobody has ever mentioned this group. Frankly, Hal, it's like they never existed. If the Brotherhood of Social Justice and the Russian Business Network are in fact one and the same, then they've done a stellar job of keeping it quiet."

"It's not that surprising, if you think about it."

Price furrowed her brow. "I'm not sure I follow."

"Well, if you consider the fact the RBN has never done anything to hide their identity *as* the RBN, it would only stand to reason they could go on with such a charade indefinitely."

"You're saying they covered their real identity with a faux organization?"

"Why not?" Brognola said with a shrug. "It actually makes a lot of sense. There's no better way to keep the attention off your actual agenda than by creating a diversion of alleged transparency. But whether they call themselves the Russian Business Network or the Brotherhood of Social Justice, their goals are exactly the same. They have stolen and exploited and black-mailed and corrupted some of the finest people in this country, and I'm on Striker's side for taking them out of the picture once and for all."

"I figured that was what you'd say," Price said.

"I hear a 'but' coming."

"Not at all. I was simply going to tell you that I've already sent Jack to pick up Striker at a small airfield in the Hamptons."

"What happened?"

"Well, he hit Godunov's estate in Sagaponack just as planned, and he was successful to a point. Apparently, Godunov had an escape plan that involved a scheduled flight out of the Southampton airport."

"How did we miss that one?"

"Well, the registration turned out to be forged, for

one thing. Somehow they managed to get it past the new aircraft recognition program as part of the Federal Aviation Administration's crackdown following 9/11. Add to that the flight plan. There was no indication the plane in question would even leave the country, so no wonder we missed it. If nothing else, it speaks to the resources wielded by the RBN or the Brotherhood of Social Justice or whatever they're calling themselves."

"So do we have any idea where they're actually headed?"

"Well, they managed to fly into Canada," Price replied. "They touched down in Toronto, and according to our information their next stop will be Anchorage. There's no question they're headed for Russia, but I don't think we'll be able to stop them. They've got quite a jump on us already. Even with Jack leaving from Dulles, he still has to touch down at the Hamptons, refuel at LaGuardia and then proceed on whatever designated flight path he can get approved."

Brognola shook his head and frowned. "Why are we going through aboveboard channels for this?"

"Well, it's not like a spur of the moment flight from Washington, D.C., to Russia won't rouse the suspicions of the FAA controllers and investigators. If we'd had Jack pick up Striker in something with a bit more range, then we would have had to deal with the major hassle of Customs at more airports then you want to count. This way, at least we can get in under the credentials of the small business jet, and inspectors won't be looking too closely when they find all of the paperwork in order."

"I guess I can see your point," Brognola said. "But

what about Godunov? Do we have any idea where he's headed? The Russian Business Network has proved quite elusive up to this point, and I don't know if you've managed to glean any additional intelligence on their operations."

"As a matter of fact we have. Thanks to our friend Detective Marquez, Customs agents picked up Lutrova several hours ago. He was apparently quite willing to cooperate with us, something I can assure you took me and a number of other federal agencies by complete surprise."

"Any idea why the sudden change of heart?"

"Near as I can tell, he suddenly feels some sort of loyalty to Striker."

"Striker?" Brognola produced a heavy sigh. "Now I'm really confused."

"Well, let me see if I can unconfuse you," Price replied with a grin. "Bogdan Lutrova apparently knows quite a bit more about the Russian Business Network than any of us had thought. He most certainly possesses information about their technical networks, which are tremendously fast. It's our understanding they are using the satellites of a couple of foreign nations for their seedier operations."

"Sounds vast."

"Indeed it is," said a voice behind him. Price and Brognola turned to see Aaron Kurtzman wheel himself into the room. He proceeded directly to the dedicated terminal against a nearby wall that provided him with an unobstructed view of the monitor mounted at the far end of the room.

"Hello, Aaron," Brognola said.

"Morning, Bear," Price added.

"Greetings, my dear," Kurtzman replied, and then with a grin he said, "You, too, Barb."

"Move on, funny guy," Brognola chided.

"I've spent the last two hours disseminating information Bogdan Lutrova provided us," Kurtzman said. He tapped a key and a massive display of the globe in the form of an oval appeared. A series of red lines were traced over it, each one interconnected to random points overlaid on a map as blue circles. "Take a good look, lady and gent, because you're getting a fairly decent glimpse of the Russian Business Network's information highway."

Brognola's eyes grew wide. "Good God."

"That's what I would've said were I a praying man," Kurtzman replied. "This RBN has one of the most powerful networks in the world today. The worst part is that it's integrated with the primary internet hubs around the world. The only satellites they don't have their fingers into are those owned by the U.S., British and Chinese governments. Somehow these bastards managed to tie into just about every other system, which is no mean feat considering that even we haven't been able to do something like that. And it isn't for lack of trying, I can assure you."

"How in the world do they get away with something like this?" Price asked.

"Somehow they've managed to infiltrate these systems the good old-fashioned way."

"Which is?" Brognola inquired.

"They've done it primarily by means of hiring insiders," Kurtzman said. "According to Lutrova, the RBN has managed to get the contracts for many of the electronic systems on the satellites. Mostly they do it by lowballing the competition, and then when they get the contract, they go into the companies bidding against them and steal the technology out from under their noses. That's the only way we can see they've been able to actually make good on this stuff."

"Ingenious," Price said.

"Maybe so," Brognola interjected. "But it also brings us to a much larger consideration. If the Russian Business Network has its fingers that deep in the cookie jar, we have a much bigger problem to face. Even if Striker has the ability to close down Godunov's operations, we're still a long way from cutting out the heart of this organization. We're faced with a massive front, and after seeing this, I'm not sure where we can start."

"Maybe Striker has a suggestion or two," Price offered.

"It's not a matter of action. It's a matter of magnitude, plain and simple. The bottom line is that the RBN has the numbers and we don't." Brognola looked at Kurtzman. "Have you explored any ways to shut this down? Would it be possible to disrupt this network?"

"I suppose it's possible," Kurtzman said. "But remember that we're talking about systems belonging to at least a dozen sovereign nations, Hal. I don't think there's any way to disrupt the network traffic flow. If we shut down the pipe at one point, the RBN's technical experts will simply open it somewhere else, like a bypass valve."

"What about a virus?" Price asked.

Kurtzman nodded and folded his beefy arms across

his broad chest. "We discussed that possibility among us, but as I've already indicated, we take the risk of downing satellites critical to the operations of a number of countries, a good many of them friends to the United States. I don't think it's a good idea."

"What about Lutrova?" Brognola asked.

Price looked up in surprise. "What about him?"

"Well, maybe I'm just being a naive, but it seems to me he's shown a pretty good willingness to help us so far. He's an expert like Bear and the rest of his team." Brognola looked quickly at Kurtzman and said, "No offense, pal."

"None taken. I agree with you. Lutrova definitely knows his business and it's my understanding he helped them design some of the system, as well as steal the schematics to the equipment-based code aboard a number of the satellites."

"You think he actually has something valuable to offer?" Price said. "I mean, can we really trust this guy beyond what he's already told us?"

"I don't see as we have much of a choice," Brognola said. "I think we owe it to ourselves and Striker to give it a try. Otherwise we stand to lose a lot and make the vast majority of our efforts to this point in vain."

"Not to mention you could be sending Striker straight into a hornet's nest," Kurtzman said.

"I'm not entirely sure how comfortable I am with this," Price said. "But after seeing what Bear has shown us here, I'm forced to agree with both of you."

"I know it's not the most solid plan, Barb, but I think it's the one that provides us the most options and presents the least number of risks," Brognola said.

"You realize, of course, that Lutrova will barter with you," Price countered. "He'll want to make a deal before he gives us any information about this. I'm sure that's why he told us as much as he did. The guy is a slimeball, we all know that, and I wouldn't doubt for a moment that he dangled this carrot in front of us knowing what Aaron would discover."

"I won't argue with your intuition. It's proved on the money way too many times." Brognola shook his head, withdrew three antacids from the breast pocket of his shirt and popped them all at the same time. "But we can't fight a war against ones and zeros. And we don't have the option of simply shutting these systems down at their source. The countries in question rely upon the satellite systems to deliver vital information that is tied to their defense, trade and even the navigation of their planes and vessels worldwide."

"There's no arguing with that," Kurtzman said. "We could take them down by force if we wanted to, but you're right, it would wreak havoc on a scale that would make what the RBN has done look like a marshmallow roast."

Brognola turned to Kurtzman. "You're authorized to make whatever deals are necessary with Lutrova to get the information you need. But he doesn't get his piece until we shut this thing down once and for all. Understood?"

After Kurtzman nodded, Brognola turned to Price. "Get Striker on the horn as soon as possible and let him know what we found."

CHAPTER TWENTY-SIX

"Your contact's name is Gregori Nasenko," Price had told Bolan via cell phone before he boarded the flight to Saint Petersburg.

"He's Russian?"

"Second generation," Price replied. "His family came to the country following the Georgian civil war when Gregori was a boy. They became naturalized citizens, and when he reached legal age, he enlisted in the Army. Military intelligence in Afghanistan and then into the National Security Agency—the NSA—upon his return. He's been a valuable asset according to my connections inside SIGINT."

"How's it going to play?"

"He'll make sure you get through Customs without any trouble," Price said. "From there, he'll escort you to a location that leads to Godunov's base. He's not going to be able to render any assistance beyond that, since the NSA can't risk exposing him. He's just too valuable an asset, Striker. I'm sorry we can't do more."

"Don't sweat it. All of you have done a great job."

Price chuckled. "You seem to have picked up another fan."

"Marquez?"

"And how. I think the girl is actually smitten with you, big guy."

"She could do better," Bolan replied with a grin.

"You should have seen the look on her face when we told her that it had been our plan all along to transfer those funds right back into the accounts Bear transferred them from. I think maybe she was a little hurt that we didn't let her in on the plan from the start."

"Those are the breaks," Bolan said.

Truthfully, nobody had been in on the exact plan except Bolan and the team at Stony Man. They had always planned to get Kurtzman plugged into the system once Lutrova had done his part. The Executioner had counted on the fact that Godunov wouldn't actually check his accounts until he reached someplace safe. That's why it had been so vitally important that once the transfer took place, and then Kurtzman reversed it over the telephone line Bolan had opened at the offices in Manhattan, that they keep pressing the offensive against the Russian Business Network. If there had been any hiccups in the battle plan, the entire operation might well have fallen apart. Bolan considered it fortunate that they were able to coordinate the efforts on such a narrow timetable.

"It's just as well if this Nasenko isn't involved," Bolan continued. "I'm not sure I want any more friendlies sacrificed. My account is already overdrawn."

"Striker." Price hesitated, and Bolan could tell she didn't know exactly what to say. He opened his mouth to tell her it was all right, to let her off the hook, but she interrupted him. "Tom Remick did what he did out of a sense of duty. Try to remember that instead of blaming yourself. The best way to honor his sacrifice is to put an end to Godunov."

Bolan didn't know what to say, so he simply remained quiet.

When the moment had passed, Price said, "Take care of yourself, Striker. And come home safe."

"You bet, lady," Bolan replied. "Out here."

Now past Customs without a hitch, Bolan sized up Gregori Nasenko. He stood as tall as Bolan, although not quite in as good a shape. His gray eyes were intense, watchful, but a mischievous smile played at the corners of his mouth. He seemed friendly enough, and when they first met he held out his hand to shake Bolan's. He had a firm grip that spoke of strength, but didn't belie a male competitiveness. Bolan liked him right off.

"Nice to meet you, Cooper."

Bolan smiled. "Likewise. Your people speak highly of you."

"Well, it's kind of you to say so, but I've gotten pretty used to them giving anybody a hand job only to score a few points with the man." Nasenko laughed. "Of course, anytime they want to throw a little more money my way, I'll welcome anything they have to say about me, good or bad."

Bolan sent him an easy smile. "Still mushroom city?"

As Nasenko directed him toward a car parked at the curb outside the terminal, he replied, "Don't you know it."

Once they were headed for the city limits, Bolan said, "You go by a cover?"

"Most everybody just calls me Grigs."

"Grigs it is, then," Bolan said. "How much have you been told about my mission here?"

Nasenko shrugged. "Not much. Not entirely sure I *want* to know, either. I was told that you were interested in the whereabouts and activities of Yuri Godunov."

"That's right."

"Well, then, it's an early Merry Christmas for you, because I know just about everything there is to know concerning that bastard. We know he has ties to the Russian syndicate, at least that's who we think it is, although we really don't have any proof of direct connections. He takes his orders from a high-ranking diplomat headquartered here in Saint Petersburg. We worked for a long time to try to determine the man's identity, but so far we've come up with squat."

"Well, if Godunov does have that kind of political affiliation, then it's no wonder his activities have gone unchecked."

"That's an understatement," Nasenko said with a snort. "Godunov's a rat bastard who surrounds himself with rat bastards."

Bolan smiled. "So you like the guy."

"If you ask me, Cooper, that guy's nothing but a terrorist. I don't care if he's with the Russian *mafiya* or some other organization. At the end of the day he's a menace, and it wouldn't break my heart one moment to see him get his comeuppance."

Bolan tried not to laugh at the last. His comeuppance? The Executioner hadn't heard talk like that in a good twenty years. He knew there was something different about Nasenko, but he couldn't put his finger on it. Bolan had always possessed an intuition about people, an ability to determine very quickly the volition of most men in Nasenko's line of work. Yeah, this guy happened to be one of those rare finds, and he could understand why the NSA considered him such a valuable asset. He seemed tough, smart and unwilling to bend his beliefs—a rare trait in most covert operatives.

"Our intelligence indicates Godunov operates from some type of underground network of passages beneath the city," Bolan said. "You have any knowledge of that?"

Nasenko nodded. "You bet your ass. I knew where it was the moment the case chief briefed me. It's an old access to the sewer system, which is now used to service the subway line. We'll be able to get through to it from an abandoned opera house."

"Were you able to get your hands on the equipment I asked for?"

"Yeah. I got everything except the FNC. Best I could snatch with the short notice was an MP-5. I'm partial to 5.56 mm myself, and I know it certainly makes for a better first hit probability, but we still have a few limitations here in the Red Zone and I'm afraid that's one of them. I had to beg, borrow and steal just to get that."

"Don't worry about it," Bolan replied. "I'm sure what you got will do well enough. As long as you were able to meet the ammunition requests."

"Ammo you've got plenty of, and I managed to scrape up some of those Diehl DM51 grenades. Man, I was shocked when I found out we even had any of those things. I'd never heard of them until I got the call."

His statement was no surprise to Bolan. The Diehl DM51, manufactured in Austria, served in both offensive and defensive capacities. Bolan had grown rather fond of the DM51 for its versatility. In offensive mode, it was packed with a combination of PETN and RDX explosives, and had demonstrated a repeated ability to do the job when the situation called for more aggressive measures. The grenade boasted equally impressive defensive capabilities. It worked by the mounting of a sleeve on the outside that contained thousands of 2 mm steel balls. When it blew, the pineapple-shaped external sleeve fragmented and directed the superheated fragments with the intent of dissuading clustering of personnel.

It took Nasenko about fifteen minutes to reach the abandoned opera house. To Bolan's surprise, he didn't bother to make a recon pass of the building; he merely parked the vehicle at the curb and shifted in his seat. "I'll go ahead and pop the trunk. You can get your equipment from it. The MP-5 and ammo is in the long bag, the remainder of the ordnance you'll find in the satchel. I was able to get you a total of four grenades. I hope that'll be enough."

Bolan nodded and then looked at the darkened front of the ornate building. No light emanated from the windows, and dried weeds had all but taken over the foundation. Some part of the soldier considered the possibility that Nasenko may have been setting him up. Still, he had to trust people now and again. Nasenko hadn't given him any reason to be suspicious. His not offering to accompany Bolan didn't mean anything other than the fact that he was a professional, and a professional followed orders.

"How do I get in?" Bolan asked, nodding in the direction of the opera house.

"There's been talk of them opening the place back up to tourism. I happen to know the former proprietors, who still had the key. Here it is." Nasenko reached into his breast pocket and held it up for Bolan's inspection. "The front doors are padlocked, but the key will fit into the side door. The entrance to the underground passages is on the far side of the building. You'll find it hidden behind an old, massive upright freezer."

"Thanks," Bolan replied as he took the key.

"Hey, Cooper, send my special regards to Godunov. I don't know exactly what you have planned, and I don't want to know. But I hope it includes sending that bastard straight to hell."

"Yeah, will do," the Executioner replied.

THINGS WERE EXACTLY as the Nasenko had described. Somewhere in the distance, the sound of dripping water echoed through the dark, dank passages of the underground complex. Since the floor in the opera house had been dusty with disuse, Bolan assumed Godunov made his entrance to the complex from some other point.

After seeing the advancements in luxury of Godunov's estate in the Hamptons, the warrior found it a little difficult to believe the Russian was willing to live in such a place. Bolan could faintly smell the former purpose served by this subterranean hellhole, and it clung to him like slime. It seemed almost fitting to a degree that Godunov would surround himself in such filth.

Bolan moved slowly, carefully, stopping every

ten or fifteen yards to listen for any sound of human occupation. He knew it wouldn't be difficult to get lost in the catacombs; he could spend the next several hours in search of Godunov and not find him. But the Executioner was also a tracker at heart, a hunter who had followed prey time and again into the worst places on Earth. Godunov had managed to escape him twice. There wouldn't be a third time.

Bolan had traveled approximately ten minutes when he paused at a faint sound ahead.

He froze, the MP-5 held tight and low. He'd traded out his blacksuit aboard the plane for a fresh pair of slacks and a new polo shirt. He wore the leather jacket over that, and had stuffed Diehl DM51 grenades into the pockets. Fortunately, they were deep and would mask any sound of the grenades touching each other.

There it was again: voices.

Bolan crouched and waited to see if he could determine the numbers ahead of him. Try as he might, his efforts proved futile, since the maze of passages tended to distort sound the farther they traveled. Bolan knew his only option to gain some understanding of the odds against him would be to move closer. That would pose its own dangers, but he would have to deal with that as it came. This wasn't a time to be picky.

He rose and continued forward, his MP-5 positioned and ready for action. He managed to get about twenty yards closer to the light that emanated from a side hall, but then realized his mistake. He felt the tightness of the object at shin level at first, causing him to pause a mere heartbeat before the pressure suddenly dissipated.

Only the twang of the trip wire alerted Bolan to the fact that things were about to go hard.

The Executioner wheeled and threw himself as far as he could from the site of the booby trap. He got a scraped chin for his trouble, but it was better than having his head taken off by the explosive charges that blew out the walls on either side of where he had stood moments before. Cinder block, dust and chunks of concrete rained onto his back. Some of the pieces were large and would leave bruises in their wake, but that only meant Bolan was still alive.

As the echoes of the blast died out, the soldier heard the shouts of men who had been stationed around the corner.

He flipped onto his back and pointed the muzzle of the MP-5 in the direction of the corridor that ran perpendicular to his. As he surmised, the sentries expected to enter the blast area and find his dead body, so they weren't prepared for his survival.

There were three men, and Bolan waited until they had exposed their flanks, searching for him in the immediate rubble rather than clearing both ends of the passageway first. It was like shooting ducks in a barrel. He held back the trigger of the MP-5 as he swept the muzzle in a figure eight. A sustained salvo of 9 mm stingers cut through the trio in an instant. The men danced like marionettes under the impact of the rounds, slamming into one another as Bolan reaped them with a flurry of destruction.

He climbed to his feet even as the soldiers were still falling. He did a quick inspection of his body, determined that nothing had been broken or punctured, then quickly moved to the corpses. He patted them down for any forms of identity, but didn't find any. It didn't surprise him, although it frustrated him a bit since he wanted to gather as much intelligence as possible. He'd already convinced himself that eliminating Godunov wouldn't eliminate the threat of the Russian Business Network.

This war had only just begun, and even if Lutrova agreed to cooperate with Stony Man's efforts to shut down the crime syndicate, Bolan held no illusions that that would put an end to their activities. Maybe they would go into hiding, regroup their forces as best they could, with the lines of communication cut off indefinitely. But just like al Qaeda, the RBN had managed to gain a foothold in nearly every country. If they could set up shop in New York City among diligent Americans, Bolan had little doubt they could maintain their operations in every other place where they weren't opposed.

For now, however, the best he could do was get whatever information became available to him, and exterminate Godunov's personal security force. Thus far, Bolan's blitz had paid off. The strategy to keep Godunov on the run, to push the man as far as he could push him until he had nowhere else to go, had worked.

Bolan entered the corridor and discovered the source of the voice he'd heard. A small radio sat on a wooden crate, and there were other empty crates along with some metal trays coated with what remained of the sentries' dinners. Bolan realized the guards being here, eating like this in a lit antechamber, could only mean one thing: Godunov was somehow expecting him.

As he moved down this new passage in search of the ultimate target, the Executioner couldn't help but wonder what sort of surprises lay ahead.

CHAPTER TWENTY-SEVEN

Based on his initial encounter with the enemy, the Executioner determined that a new strategy was in order.

That strategy involved hitting the enemy hard and fast while looking out for any additional pitfalls like the one from which he'd just barely escaped. The tunnel system of Godunov's underground base didn't help matters much on that count, especially given the poor lighting and cramped quarters. This combination of parameters could be deadly to Bolan, and one mistake would not only mean the end of his life, it would spell certain doom for future victims of the Russian Business Network.

Bolan meant to see it ended now.

He made that message very clear to the four armed RBN thugs who rounded a corner on the run. Traveling through the passageways at that speed had proved to be their downfall, since Bolan heard them coming well before he saw them, and prepared. The four were surprised to see him, and had slung their weapons, so there was little time to get to them in the confines of the narrow corridor.

Bolan took the first one with a 3-round burst to the chest, 9 mm Parabellum slugs punching holes in his breastbone and lungs. The impact spun him into his comrade and knocked the SMG from his grasp. The guy managed to recover his weapon while disentangling himself from the teetering corpse of his associate, but it proved too little too late. Bolan got him with a second 3-round burst. Two of the rounds smashed through the soft tissue of his throat and a third struck just below his nose. The man's head exploded and doused the remaining pair with blood and brain matter.

One of the survivors finally got his SMG clear and in position, but Bolan had already moved. The RBN gunman looked surprised even as he opened up with abandon, only to realize his target was no longer there. Bolan came out of his roll and snap-aimed the MP-5 from the hip, holding low and tight as he triggered a pair of tribursts. The Executioner's rounds nearly cut the man's legs out from under him, bullets smashing his hips and pelvis, and puncturing the major artery in his left thigh.

The remaining gunner realized the odds had been narrowed considerably, and apparently determined self-preservation to be the course of the day. His only mistake was to shout to reinforcements that were apparently coming up the same corridor.

The Executioner saw his opportunity to seize advantage of the precious seconds afforded him. He reached into his pocket, withdrew one of the Diehl DM51s— sleeve in place for defensive mode—yanked the pin and lobbed the grenade into the adjoining hall.

It then became a matter of stepping back and waiting out the show. Bolan heard someone scream a panicked warning, but the man was too late, and when the grenade blew Bolan could clearly see the effects firsthand.

A fireball erupted and he heard ricochets of some of the shrapnel off the walls.

For a moment, he felt as if his heart froze in his chest as the aftershock of the blast rumbled down the corridors. It sounded as if the entire roof was on the verge of collapse, and the Executioner wondered just how stable this underground network of tunnels actually was. Nasenko hadn't given him any information on that count, but Bolan knew chances were good given this present evidence. The other scenario he hadn't considered related to the tunnels having once been part of the sewer system. It was entirely possible pockets of sewer gas existed in pipes he couldn't see, and if a weak part of the wall gave way to a grenade blast, it could spell curtains for Bolan as well as his enemies.

When the rumbles had died, Bolan rose with weapon held at the ready, and advanced on the position.

Wall-to-wall bodies filled the narrow passage. Most guards had been killed instantly, but Bolan could hear a couple moaning for help. He located them quickly and ended their suffering, unwilling to let another man die an agonizing and undignified death. He was a soldier, not a psychopath, and he had always worked to maintain that standard for the sake of his own sanity.

Once he'd accomplished his grisly task, Bolan set off down the passage in search of the prize target.

Yuri Godunov burned with hatred as he listened to the report coming from sentries inside the base.

Thus far, he estimated they had lost at least eight men and possibly more. Godunov didn't know how the American had managed to find him, but there wasn't anything he could do about it now. The most sensible thing for him would be to escape to the government building in Saint Petersburg. His master would protect him there, be able to move him to a secure location until the danger had passed. Godunov knew he had earned at least that much respect for the sacrifices. While he couldn't be sure, it made his heart ache to learn that Stepan was likely dead. Somehow, this devil Lambretta had managed to whittle their forces down to scant numbers. These were highly trained men, and it bothered Godunov that their training hadn't proved more effective when tested under real conditions.

Part of Godunov didn't want to run—even the thought was something he considered an act of cowardice. But he also knew that if his men had been unable to defeat the American up to this point, their chances of bringing him down now were slim. As much as Godunov didn't want to admit it, the facts were what they were, and he planned to take issue with whoever had contracted the former Spetsnaz.

Maybe he'd been responsible for all of this himself; maybe he couldn't put the blame on anyone else. He'd allowed the men to become soft and apathetic, instead of instilling more discipline into them. Either way, it didn't make much difference now, because regardless of the outcome this day, Godunov had successfully retrieved the funds so desperately needed by the Brotherhood of Social Justice. No matter the defeats they experienced, they would have only lost a battle and would still emerge the victors in the war.

Godunov gathered papers off a gray metal table he'd used as a makeshift desk, and headed for the emergency exit. The two men assigned by his nephew as bodyguards followed him wordlessly. There were enough men remaining to form a resistance against the American and buy Yuri enough time to escape. He'd never liked these primitive accommodations. Next time he would ensure his assignment was a bit more pleasing, as had been his rather unusually long stay in America.

Yes, perhaps Germany or the Greek Isles would do nicely.

FIVE MINUTES ELAPSED, then six and eventually ten, and still Bolan hadn't encountered further resistance.

That bothered the Executioner because it meant Godunov might have escaped again. Bolan counseled himself to be careful what he wished for when a fresh cluster of enemy gunners appeared at the far end of the passageway as it widened and eventually ended in a T intersection. Bolan estimated their number to be a dozen or so.

The Executioner dropped to his belly, propped his weapon in his fists with elbows planted, and opened up full-auto burn. Three of his opponents fell immediately under the vicious onslaught as he raked their position with a metal storm of gunfire. One man took two rounds to the belly and toppled forward, the second lost the better part of his chin and the final one danced like a barefoot islander over hot coals. A few more of the RBN gunmen had the discipline to find whatever cover available, and Bolan knew his action would falter before too long. They had him outnumbered by at least four to one in the small-arms department, not to mention the fact he'd been able to bring only a limited supply of ammunition.

Bolan rolled from the position, settled again and delivered another sustained volley that took down two more of the enemy gunners. Even as the men fell with rounds in their stomachs and chests, the half dozen or so remaining opened fire on Bolan's position. The initial rounds came too close, some chewing up bits of concrete, while those coming in on more shallow angles ricocheted in myriad directions.

The soldier scrambled to his feet and found the comparative safety of an outcropping, some kind of wall-to-ceiling barrier jutting into the corridor. Using the temporary cover as a reprieve, he reached into his coat pocket and withdrew two more of the Diehl DM51 grenades. This time, he would use them in combination fashion. Removing the sleeves from each of them did away with the fragmentation, and they became pure bombs meant to wreak as much explosive force and destruction as possible. Bolan armed the first one and lobbed it one-handed, then pulled the pin from the second, letting it cook off a moment before tossing it to join its twin.

The blasts erupted simultaneously as Bolan had planned, blowing rock dust and cinder block in every direction while the concussion once more threatened to collapse the ceiling. Before the enemy could recover, and in the brightening flames of the blasts, Bolan spotted the reason for this massive rock. He noted a metal door in it, invisible in the dim light up to that point. Bolan stepped into view of the gunners, still unable to see them with the acrid smoke and dust left in the wake of the grenade explosions. He tapped the door, heard a hollow clang and immediately threw his shoulder into it. It moved on rusted hinges, creaking and groaning as he pushed harder. It moved a little more. A few shots sounded and bullets passed by his head. Bolan increased his efforts until the door opened enough so that he could squeeze inside. He found himself in a vertical pipe of metal lined with concrete. Running the length of the pipe was an iron ladder that stretched upward into the darkness.

Bolan didn't know where it led but figured beggars couldn't be choosers, and he immediately began to climb after testing it with his weight. Obviously he'd missed a couple of stragglers and it wouldn't be long before they were behind him. He hoped that he'd entered a manhole and that he'd be able to open it when he reached the top. There was no other escape.

Fate was on his side.

Bolan reached the top of the ladder and found a manhole cover. He gave a shove and it popped up and aside quite easily. As he began to climb out, he had to duck, narrowly avoiding having his head crushed by the bumper of a large truck. A blast of cold air brushed past him, and he risked a look downward to see silhouettes in the passage squeezing through the open door.

The soldier reached into his pocket and withdrew the final grenade. Leaving the sleeve in place, he yanked the pin and leisurely dropped it down the center of the pipe, followed by the MP-5. He quickly cleared the street above this time, then climbed out of the manhole and kicked the cover back into place. The grenade blew at about the same moment, but only a close observer would have noticed the slight rattling of the manhole cover.

Bolan got out of sight from the street, which fortunately was almost deserted this time of morning. Once he was clear and had found the cover of some trees in a small park nearby, he took the time to assess his surroundings. The area didn't look familiar, but that came as no big surprise—he'd covered a considerable distance beneath the city and estimated he was at least five or six blocks from the opera house, possibly more.

Bolan figured if there were any survivors below, they weren't many. He'd eliminated a good number of Godunov's men at the mansion, and doubted they had been able to carry more than a dozen in the private jet. Even if there had been men waiting here, they were now leaderless without Stepan, and Godunov couldn't very well travel with a group of armed men without drawing attention. In fact, Bolan wondered for a moment if Godunov had any of his men with him. What was it Nasenko had said?

Bolan's memory went back to that moment: *He takes his orders from a high-ranking diplomat headquartered here in Saint Petersburg.*

Bolan remembered them passing the Constantine Shlev, the federal building that housed all diplomats. The Executioner set off in search of the phone book, but then remembered he wouldn't be able to read it, for all intents and purposes. His next best step would be to find a hotel, a decent size one that would be open all night and would most likely have at least one clerk who could speak English. He'd look like just another tourist who'd managed to get lost.

WHEN BOLAN REACHED the Constantine Shlev, he paid the cab driver and then got out and headed in the opposite direction. The last thing he needed was the cabbie giving authorities information on what he looked like. At least if the cab driver was questioned, he'd be able to say he had only one fare and that individual didn't go anywhere near the federal building.

Bolan walked two blocks in the opposite direction, turned on the street running parallel to the building and continued another two blocks. After making sure he hadn't picked up a tail, he headed for the Constantine Shlev. It would be well guarded; there would be electronic security and a tactical unit ready to respond in a moment. He considered his options as he drew closer, and not many were coming to him. They wouldn't just let him walk in without an invitation.

The big American had nearly given up hope when the answer suddenly pulled up in a familiar looking sedan. The power window on the passenger side came down and a familiar face peered through it. Gregori Nasenko grinned from ear to ear.

"I thought you might just try this next."

Bolan looked in both directions, saw that the street was deserted and stepped quickly to the car. "What are you doing here?"

"Well, golly gee, I missed you, too, Cooper," Nasenko said. He rapped his palm on the window frame and said, "Hop in, I know exactly how to get you inside."

Bolan considered it and then got in the car. "Get inside of where?"

"Oh, come on, give me a little bit of credit," Nasenko

replied. "It's obvious that you're going to find Godunov, and you figure he'll head to the Constantine Shlev. I didn't just step off the turnip truck, Cooper. I've been doing this a pretty long time, and I get a few ideas of my own now and again."

"How did you know I'd go there?"

"Don't get all paranoid and suspicious on me. I know because it's exactly what I would've done. I shot off my big mouth and told you we thought Godunov was working for somebody inside the government. I just figured you'd remember the information and act on it if Godunov managed to slip away."

"Fair enough," Bolan said. "So how do you figure we're going to get inside the Constantine Shlev at this time of the morning?"

Nasenko chuckled. "The exact same way that Godunov would get in there at this time of morning. I mean, you don't actually think the guy could get away with it if he didn't know a few people, right?"

"You're not Godunov," Bolan said.

"No, I'm not. But I do know a few people."

True to his word, Nasenko not only got them through the gate without a bit of trouble, but he managed to get them into the building. The guards didn't ask any questions, nobody searched them and other than a brief conversation between Nasenko and one of the security officers that seemed more casual than official, they didn't encounter a bit of trouble.

Nasenko suggested they take the stairs rather than the elevator, and Bolan agreed. They exited the stairwell on the fifth floor and walked down a gloomy hallway, their footfalls silent on the expensive carpeting. They arrived at an office door and Nasenko turned and held a finger to his lips as he put his ear close to the door. While Nasenko listened—or appeared to do so—Bolan checked his flank and then decided to make his move as soon as Nasenko turned his back.

Predictably, Nasenko opened the door as he gestured for Bolan to follow. When Nasenko's attention was diverted, Bolan reached beneath his jacket and retrieved the Beretta 92-SB Nasenko had managed to acquire for him. He immediately placed the small of his hand against the other man's back and shoved him into the room, which actually turned out to be a posh, spacious office. The move took Nasenko completely off guard, and the big man tumbled into the room and hit the floor on hands and knees.

The CIA agent recovered with admirable speed and reached beneath his jacket for his pistol, but Bolan was prepared for such a maneuver. Even as the gun came out, the Executioner stepped in and kicked it from his hand, following through with a heel to Nasenko's jaw. The kick snapped the man's head to the right with enough force to drive his shoulder into the ground and neutralize him temporarily.

Yuri Godunov had been seated behind a massive desk with his back to the broad, floor-to-ceiling window that looked onto the glittering lights of Saint Petersburg. Fury rolled across his expression like angry, blue-white thunder across a purplish sky. He leaped to his feet and turned to leave, but Bolan tracked on him immediately with the Beretta.

"That's far enough, Godunov," he said.

The Russian turned. His eyes fell to Bolan's pistol

and a look of resignation crossed his normally smug, superior expression.

But what surprised the Executioner most was that Nasenko didn't act appalled that his betrayal had been detected. He didn't even plead for his life or launch into a tirade of righteous indignation. Probably because he knew it wouldn't do any good; Bolan wouldn't have made his move this way and in this place without having thought it through.

"I won't insult your intelligence by playing the role," Nasenko said.

"I'd appreciate it if you didn't," Bolan replied.

"How did you know?" Godunov asked.

"Nasenko played his hand too soon. He did a little too much talking and not enough acting."

"Was it in the car?" Nasenko asked.

Bolan nodded. "I never said anything about Godunov getting away from me. That meant you had either made a very astute observation or you already knew he was gone when I arrived. Guessing just didn't seem likely. Did you set me up?"

"No, I only found out just a few minutes before I started driving around and searching for you."

"You're a fucking idiot, Nasenko!" Godunov shouted.

Bolan ignored Godunov's tirade and asked Nasenko, "How did you find out Godunov got away?"

"A call from the people I work for."

"I thought you worked for us."

"I used to." Nasenko spared a glance at Godunov. "It seems that Yuri didn't do what we told him to do, and let himself be duped by you and every other American agent from here to New York City. Not only did he lose millions of dollars and cause the deaths of many good men, he didn't even accomplish the mission assigned to him."

"It's a lie!" Godunov said. "I did as I was told, and all would have been fine if Lutrova had not betrayed us. They cannot blame me for this! And no matter what happens to me, they will go on!"

"Who's they?" Bolan asked. He knew, but he wanted to keep Godunov talking.

"Shut your fucking mouth, Yuri!" Nasenko said. "Don't say a word—!"

Nasenko never finished the sentence. He tried to use the outcry as a distraction while he reached for a second pistol concealed in an ankle holster on his right side—a holster Bolan had spotted when Nasenko first picked him up at the airport. The Executioner took him quickly with a single shot that entered below his left eye, cracking the cheekbone before it tore through the inferior brain lobe and exited behind the base of his right ear. Nasenko's body stiffened a moment and then went still.

Bolan immediately acquired Godunov in his gun sights when the Russian tried to make his escape. It only served to hasten his departure from this life, for the Executioner wouldn't let Godunov evade him again. Bolan triggered three rounds. The first two 9 mm Parabellum slugs entered into Godunov's right flank and perforated his kidney and liver. The impact of those spun him in an odd direction so he ended facing Bolan. The final slug caught him in the chest and drove him back with enough force that his body smashed through the window. He plummeted five stories to the cobblestone square.

No question, the security teams would notice.

Bolan left the office, retreated down the steps and made his way unobserved off the Constantine Shlev property amid the bustle and chaos. From there, he walked a few blocks to the river, dumped the pistol and then set off in search of a cab to the airport.

Bolan didn't doubt what the late Yuri Godunov had blurted relative to "they"—he could only have meant his masters in the Russian Business Network. With Godunov out of the way, Bolan had completed his mission objectives. There were so many dignitaries within the Constantine Shlev it was unlikely he could ascertain the real power behind the RBN. But that didn't mean it was over—not by a long shot.

Mack Bolan's war against the Russian Business Network had just begun.

* * * * *

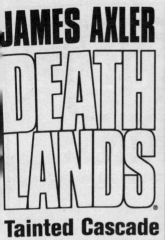
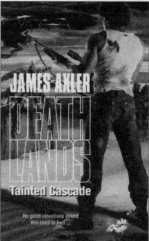

AleX Archer
THE OTHER CROWD

Fabled folk seek a terrible revenge....

Instructed to travel to Ireland and return with faerie footage, archaeologist Annja Creed figures it's a joke assignment. But people have vanished and she soon realizes there's more in play than mythical wee folk. Feeling that something otherworldly is in the air, Annja is torn between her roles as an archaeologist and a warrior. Can her powerful sword protect her from the threat of violence?

Available May wherever books are sold.

www.readgoldeagle.blogspot.com

GRA30